SEMIOTEXT(E) NATIVE AGENTS SERIES

© 2015 Mark von Schlegell

Published by Semiotext(e)
PO BOX 629, South Pasadena, CA 91031
www.semiotexte.com

Cover Photograph: Lars Heller
Back Cover Photography: Jonas Leihener
Design: Hedi El Kholti

ISBN: 978-1-58435-162-7
Distributed by The MIT Press, Cambridge, Mass. and London, England
Printed in the United States of America

SUNDOGZ

a diffusion

Mark von Schlegell

\<e\>

for Cod

with special thanks to P. Michael Cofield, Hedi El Kholti, Robert Kinberg, Chris Kraus, Aislinn McNamara, Frances Scholz and Anna Zacharoff

"Greek philosophy seems to begin with an absurd notion, with the proposition that water is the primal origin and the womb of all things."

— Friedrich Nietzsche

LINE 1

Off Uranus

>*All probability models agree Luna City Academy marine biologist Heike Böhringdorf's Oan Bubble popped like so many other doomed Spacer dreams, when the greater bubble of 1-Gen space finally burst in '33…*

>*But significant kredit was once raised. Large scale plans were said to have been approved by the Thirteen. And rumors remain. A concealed ice moonlet melted into a waterworld by a Morituri/ Ickles Mark IV mini-sun? A fully-stocked hydrosphere deeper than all the Earth's oceans in open space, gardened by genetically altered fishmen? Self-sustaining, entirely cut off from Earthside interference? Beyond the reach of the Concerns?*

>*Out past Jupiter, every Spacer knows anything* goes…

>SMYTH'S MYTHS 22–01–2143–5 *OAN BUBBLES FACT OR FICTION*?

I i

"Change," signed Deary Devarnhardt, penetrating into a strange region of the outer core streams far around Band from Cove. "Pressure Drop." Below in the distance, the Doll looked like a three-dimensional map of a nervous system. His tendrils melted with precise complication into the hydrosphere. The back of his small, hard head sprouted thick pigtail braids—now studded with rays of light from below—as if he wore a crown, Deary thought, already turning away happy with that image. Around her mighty trunks of quasicoral-crystal hugged the honeycombed armature surrounding sunny Core, conglomerating to create an upside-down cathedral, studded with ancient silicates of the original moon. The Doll used sign *tendril* to describe the filaments, bundles and tentacle-like chords, threads, strips, and strings that grew from all over his self-designed body. But tendril also denoted the 330 great avenues of moving water that spoked Oa's Bubble from Outer Core to surface.

One was above her now. Hollow, healthy, self-sustaining, it would radiate this turquoise warmth all the way up to surface. Up top it would expand to bowl a warmed surface lagoon, rich in mammal life and birds, and become a key engine of the Bubble's (an anti-bubble, really) induced artificial stabilization atmosphere.

"Q's Q," signed a little tease against her dorsal by first entrance. That would be Quinnian's Quill to the Dolphins, and showed this was indeed the tendril she sought. As Deary pumped, looped, and turned through the hoary mouth soft with dancing weed, it might have been into the ancient jaw of a Megaladon she swam. Beam-ribbed by ghostly green light radiating from Core, the water here was thick with life. She smiled, inhaling plankton.

Life occurred vertically on the lush skeleton interior of the tendril. Porcelain Crabs disrupted resting Mentin Shrimp (cones of whose eyes contributed to the precision of her own aquatic vision). Their sideways scurrying sent out little clouds of sediment. Deary herself plucked at heavy oysters proudly footing into the crannies of ancient moon-rock. She so rarely came so far from Cove. Perhaps she'd find a pearl! This water tasted of the big high deep currents outside. It tasted clean. She bowshot vertically upward. *I am not so sure of the sweetness all the same,* she thought, thinking of Flann O'Brien. She was soaking in more than usual of the energy that would one day kill her. Death was part of life, and had been inscribed by the founders into all of the Bubble's denizens. She gathered fins and pivoted. Full swifting in a spiral, faster and faster, Deary felt full fish.

Less than a kilometer away from Outer Core (itself only one klick from the zero G point occupied by the Bubble's Hatsumaki Mark V Minisun) salinity varied seasonally. The hydrosystem's evenly maintained variations in temperature were in an eternal "cold war" between layers. Passage between strata could become a highly complicated affair. The hydrocine, where colder, darker waters dominated outside tendril, was recommended off-limits to gardener/gatherers like Deary. With fin-like appendages, Deary understood movement almost as intuitively as a fish. Still she wouldn't want to have to face a hungry predator hunting the tendril. That's one reason Tjalx wanted the Doll, rising somberly somewhere still far below, along for this swimabout.

A real, live Oan Guard looked and acted apparently lazy, but that was strategy. In ocean battles, surprise was everything. Oan Guards were likely to handle anything they were liable to meet in Qunnian's Quill. Deary's brother Doug, currently swimming point for Cove, prickled at the notion of the solitary Guardsman accompanying her. The Doll's squiddy independence rankled Doug. It rankled everyone. But even Doug had to admit the Doll was up to the task of defense, should defense be needed. Of course Deary knew the Doll by now in a way everyone else did not. In the library long talks had left the two of them up often late into the night. He signed so beautifully with those tendrils. If he was grumpy, he had humor. And frankly, she found his strange body so repellent that it was somehow attractive, fascinating. Unfortunately, since she'd made clear the sleeping arrangements last night, he'd fallen into a foul mood. Already Deary had found herself tiring of his inexorable "logic" tending to deeper and deeper negativity.

She came to stasis with a sudden intuition—all flukes braking in the midst of a school of self-entranced hippocampi, who didn't even scatter, so smooth was the arrival. Yes, intuition had been correct. She tipped and flexed, peering through the weed-lined armature of the tendril, already tasting sweetwater. Here was a particularly grand air-hole just where Tjalx had intimated it would be, not an hour's rise from Band. "Hurry up, Doll!" she signed though he was too far back to see. Deary outstretched her arms, lifted her silky flukes, inviting the seahorses to feed.

Mer*maid* is right, the Doll was thinking, slow-pumping rhythmically fathoms below.

She knew why he was on this swimabout. It was not because it was his duty to swim fin for Deary Devarnhardt. She knew what was between them, yet she avoided him when at all possible, always fleeing ahead when he inquired as to the purpose of the swimabout. Despite yesterday's great hopes, that moment to be distinguished by the wrapping of her flukes around his svelte and compacted (still virgin!) torso seemed further away than ever. Yet why would she take swimabout now and accept his company if it were not to play and practice at breeding? Did she know the Doll was reproductively active? Did she even think of him in that way at all? The Doll still wasn't sure. He very much wanted to be persuaded she did; he himself had immediately offered to fin when she'd told him her plans. He'd been surprised as everybody when she emerged from conference with Doug and signed the Doll as fin. She had to have argued for him with determination, the Doll knew. The vote came and the matter was approved.

Had she explained what she was up to to Doug in that air-hole? She didn't have to. Swimabout was everyone's right. It could be two weeks or it could be a year—fin permitted if approved by the community. Perhaps that was the point of her swimabout, to get the Doll away from Cove!

Despite the smallness of Doug and all he represented, the Doll quite liked Cove. Solitude and natural splendor were available daily in every direction and possible variety. In Cove he was never bored. Brained with carefully chosen implants, the Doll had the poets great and small at the tip of every tendril. The Doll was a natural day-signer.

The Cove clade farmed and maintained a swath of the tropical thermocline, a relatively peaceful region above which the staggering gradients of the open high deeps began. There were no tendrils by Cove, just undulating meadows atop studding coral beds for kilometers in all the four directions. Below began the grand architecture and tropical warmth of Core. Above stretched the high deeps. There were air caverns all about under; there were hot bowls, sweetwater pools, various chemical streams and ponds, and always new nooks and crannies to discover. During his time at Cove, the Doll had hunted cod, mackerel, and salmon. Easy stuff on the whole. Predators stayed in the higher strata, usually kept away by gradient barriers of temperature, salinity, and pressure. Twice he'd joined in the community hunt of a whale on an expedition high up in the deeps. He'd come in useful then.

Late in the summer a renegade self-propelled barnacle appeared, "that thing from the shallows" as Hyrum still referred to it dramatically. The Doll managed to lasso the monster's extraordinarily long penis and fix it in a vine trap before Doug could arrive to "rescue" it. Some nights later a clade of nomads came in pursuit of the thing. They said as far as anyone knew the barnacle was the only one of its kind, a freak lifeform peculiar to the Bubble. The barnacle was without organ, impotent, and alone. Yet it had a central nervous system and near-impenetrable defense and was often suddenly jetting about with inflexible will. An essential Oan lifeform, the nomads had argued, and the Doll had agreed; impregnably pointless. So let us be. After a week's visit, the nomads signed farewell. Pulling reins, they let the barnacle pull them away, straining.

Oan Guards could come and go as they pleased. Though he made himself useful to all, the Doll stayed in Cove because of Deary. A relatively peaceful and agricultural lot, most fishmen of Cove believed the Oan Guard to be more symbolic than necessary. The adults were all quite eager to send him away on swimabout, he noted. Only Doug interrupted a unanimous vote. How coldly Doug had signed with his whiskers *abstain*. Doug was already put out by Deary's swimabout, but the Doll as Finner doubled it down.

They were all uniformly bewailing the loss of Deary. It was perhaps natural. After all, it was still less than a year that the Doll had come from East South Pole; he was the second stranger in their midst since founding and it was one of the reasons he stayed, to teach them of the Other. Deary understood right away. The Doll and Deary were friends, and both particularly avid readers (though he of poetry and she of fiction). Indeed he wondered now if it were only because she was Cove librarian and he its most dedicated reader that she'd taken him along on her personal journey into self and destiny. Still though he admired her love of books, he found her taste still blunt and un-sharpened by experience.

"Think of 20th century crime novels," he remembered her signing very seriously. "Those old Earth titles that whored themselves most cheaply stood ultimately as a more realistic window on late capitalism, than any of the high brow attempts to secure meaning despite it."

"Um. Are you talking about Raymond Chandler?"

"Ugh, no!" Was her silvery glow always to obscured by frantic signing on the relation of primitive narrative prose to dead economic systems? The Doll sighed carefully when she presented her opinions, emitting no certain signs. Why did he find her so attractive? Even when arguing nonsense, Deary came across as a persona of clear and almost infinite fineness.

But damn it the Doll didn't believe in capitalism. The term was a sham, a bogey-man abstraction covering up a multitude of individual crimes. He didn't believe in it and certainly didn't want to chase that ghost now out here where it had been exhumed. Only poetry gave up that defunct mode of masking consumption. Fact: a fishman in Oa's B. had more to glean from the poetic tradition, stretching back as it does to the cromagnon/neanderthal hunter gatherers from First Freedom than from the pot-boilers, romances, and penny dreadfulls typed up to valorize various strands of "late capitalist" delusion and fantasy. Perhaps in the clades nearest Core, or on East South Pole, where labor approached leisure, one still could take legitimate pleasure from escapist ventures into cartoon cities and arbitrary nationalist realisms miraculously sparing the protagonist at all costs. But out on the stream? Hardly.

Push-me-pull-you-ing in the middle of such thoughts and memories, the Doll presently saw Deary waiting above, lit from below. Did she know he could see her? Her flukes had opened like a silvery skirt, apparently accidentally offering him a startling vision of her enormous sex, surrounded by nibbling hippocampi. The Doll saw at once that she'd found an air-cave.

Dolphins. Had she taken one as her lover? She was certainly leaving herself exposed. The Doll was not one to talk, either way. There had been cephalopod encounters in his past. Yes, he saw evidence of a path-beaten trail. All through these coral honey-combs of the higher thermocline dolphins marked hiways for their racing, playing, and pillaging. If moving fast enough the mammals passed swiftly through the dark gradient deeps between tendrils, hopping high and low between air-holes. Around and around the bubble they swam, until they reached velocities even the Doll could not hope to match.

They were coming now, he discerned. Calmly, the Doll noted the various nuncupative signs, the most obvious being a suddenly notable absence of prey. Even the seahorses were now gone. The Doll folded torso. Sure enough, in one of those under-water coincidences of motion that were the norm in Bubble life, just as the first of two grinning bottlenoses appeared from above, trailing a robe of bubbles behind and swerving to catch Deary, the Doll arrived from below via jet. Just in time (she left it damn close) to unroll and lasso his longest tentacle-extension around the tail of the last bounding male. He was yanked immediately into a new velocity. For a mysterious time all was furious motion. When the Doll managed to swing himself at last right way round, it was only to vision a blurry void interrupted by har-rowing, vivid glimpses of stone-ribbed coral that might have cut him in half. But air followed—the Doll's hard open eyes took what they were given only to be hit again by Water. Already, he presumed, they'd crossed more of the Bubble's girth than Deary had ever traveled before. There was nothing horselike or docile in how the dolphin rode him through the water's warp, nor how, in one of the walls of water they dipped into, the dolphin shook the Doll off by tail-slap, slipping immediately away.

The Doll found himself pulling to stasis just outside a quiet, alien tendril, lit blood-red by evening's slow light. He spotted Deary out on the other side of the tendril, pale against the blackness beyond. Soon to be shielded by the slow motion of the inner armature, the light from Core would shortly fade altogether. The Doll pumped himself through a hole into the tendril. This hemisphere facing Uranus this season, the tide upwards pulled surprisingly strong.

Deary was still poking around beyond Tendril, he saw, interacting with her mount. His mind smoldered at this, but she would do exactly as she pleased.

Camp-making was the Finner's responsibility. This quiet tendril's inner walls gave off into caves and divisions, and soon enough the Doll followed a trail of bubbles to find a spigot. He blew an air-hole in a convenient nook on the inner rim and walled it on one side with buckypaper from his pak. The Bubble's rock wall made a good hard floor, and though there was very little gravity, the paper surfaced the water into a glassy entrance-wall. Like a moving painting, the smears of Deary and the dolphin merged, combined and separated into obscenely morphing blobs.

The Doll shed water thinking of Plato's cave, warning himself against the zealous interpretation of abstracted imagery. He drilled deep enough into the quasicoral crystal to ignite his lightkey. The little cave glittered orange all around. It felt nice to lung; reminded him of what he'd once been, but no longer remembered, a man. A pilot, apparently a good one. A walker, a talker, no doubt.

Certainly, he'd liked to cook. Soon the Doll had set up a little heatstone in the cave. He removed the three mackerel he'd speared in the morning from his spinespikes, prepared and dressed their flesh. All day he'd been giving quiet thanks to their souls. The skin shone a crunchy golden brown; the flesh was white when an oval on the wall expanded and Deary's clear visage abruptly penetrated the cave in three dimensions from its wall. Beautiful, dipped in the silvery air, she slipped fairylike into the air, her long curved body shedding water all around.

"Wow! Dinner! Sank you Doll!" She spoke aloud, with the awkward air-lisp he found particularly charming. "I am tho hungry."

They ate all the soft-flaking flesh, dipping it in rocksalt and sugar, washing it down with sweetwater, and tossing the remains into the wall.

"Do you happen to have any idea where we're going?" the Doll signed with back-cords in the air behind his head.

"For Cod's Hake, Doll. It's a fwimabout," Deary responded, wiping her stiff big lips with a dorsal. "You're Finner. If it's a role you agree wiff then you need not concern yourself wiff why we're here." She coughed. It was always difficult for her to swallow macro-food.

But the Doll did not let up. "Tell me what you told Doug. What convinced him to let me go?"

She now signed. It was easier. "Doug? He things you weren't meant to be in Cove at all…"

"Not *meant* to be?" What was meaning to Doug, the Doll wondered. "I *chose* to be in Cove. I wasn't 'meant' to be anywhere. In any case, I know you're keeping something from me. An Oan Guard can detect whaleshit better than most. That's why Doug—" but the Doll stopped mid-sign. She was no longer listening, pulling out a book.

Why was he always talking about Doug? It occurred to the Doll suddenly, with a splashing pang, that he detected whale in his own words. She had persuaded Doug to allow him to come. That was fact. They were now occupying a small cozy cave together. He had set up two separate hammocks tonight; but they were close together. She was smiling when she saw that. The Doll of course was smiling too. He was always smiling.

It served well, his smile, as he would very likely been making all sorts of frightening faces without it. Psychotherapists of East South Pole were convinced this paradox of face would strengthen this particular Oan Guard. They hoped for a V-like Sam Spade sort of smile. Deary wasn't annoyed by it anyhow. She was pleased with how he looked, he felt. His body was strange, but he tried to show it off as recognizably human as he finished cleaning up from their meal. What was that smell?

"Doll! Your arm!" To his astonishment, the Doll saw his woody humanoid forearm transformed into a torching flame. He hadn't turned off the heatstone. In the light oxygen, it was like a dream, a perfectly augmented reality. For the Doll, who took sensation intellectually, there was no pain. He couldn't call out, or scream—he simply grinned, arm preposterously aflame. He stuck the smoking member through the buckypaper and into sea. The wall collapsed. Deary's fluttering ("Doll! My book—") filled up with thick, eager water. The Doll's bubbling lungs filled up too and he found his head, luckily, before it knocked into the floor.

He saw grown-up worry in her clear, kind face. Those dark expressive brows, so adult in her young face. After, they rose in the tiding tendril. They held close together, sleeping as one body rising. "Doll! You're frightfully absent-minded, you know."

"All is true," the Doll brushed against her; but it was no danger. It would be interesting to see how well the arm would self-repair by morning. He used it rarely enough anyhow.

And so they rose that night and he held tighter and tighter, until they rose spooning, wrapped in the collaborated blankets of their own intertwined fins and tendrils. Deary slept thickly against him, apparently considering him a castrato. Certainly the Doll did not interrupt that blissful nightrise, close against her rounded warmth. His heart sprayed its clear fire into all his tips and tendrils; he kept his erect phallus loin-slotted, beating there as if with a little heart of its own.

When he awoke the next morning, there was only her imprint on his skin.

The tendril's interior was already turquoise against the ultramarine outside. He followed her trail up, soon coming upon a tasty possible breakfast: Silvercod. A rising solitary, aloof and preoccupied at the same time, it had no idea what hit it. Licking the clouding blood off his hair, rising to meet Deary, he stuck it on his spikes and promptly came upon two old brightly-colored coelacanths. Fish of all sorts used the tendrils for their own swimabouts it seemed. These two were looking only inward, lost in the interior mindscape like the Doll himself so often in drift. One almost looked like it wore specs. "Hey!" the Doll laughed. "Hey Deary," he signed, for she was approaching him in a slow curve from above. "Look who's here!"

She took in the coelacanth with happy understanding.

"Our illustrious founder!"

"Herself! The First Fishman!"

"Shoo!" darted Deary, frightening the broad throwbacks into quick and graceful flight.

"Maybe they really are part Böhringdorf," the Doll signed, flexing slowly beside her, and the coelacanths still apparently unconcerned. "She may well have died out here. Somewhere this side of the Metroiac anyway. Those two eat anything, I presume." Ever the Hegelian idealist, Böhringdorf had tired of her 1-Gen clade's infighting and herself taken swimabout. She was never seen again.

"Eat *and* be eaten," Deary signed, laughing.

"Where are we going?" The Doll pressed the moment.

Deary laughed. Those eyes of gruliére sparkled through the waterlight. Again that clear fire flowed into all the Doll's tendrils. She shot upwards.

He kept beside her.

"Far, far, far from Cove," she blinked.

"Where all you do is rove," the Doll finished startled, feeling her fins prickling around his buttocks. Guardsman, he told himself, receive. Take what you can of this precious playful intimacy. Force nothing.

"Where are we going?" he repeated.

Making love might have been shooting the moon, but he declined! Deary drank new feelings as she rose, still warm with the feel and scent of the Doll upon her. In some ways they were already so close together that it was only touch to talk. Thought flowed electric between them.

"Why this tendril?" he repeated.

"This tendril is like a story," she said. "As you can see it contains us within it. That is why we're here."

"What kind of story? You're the Don, I suppose, and I'm the Sancho?"

You're my brave Oan Guard! she should say. You, in your funny way, are a hero, Doll, she should sign. But I can't explain things to you. You wouldn't understand. Without this tendril, we'd be nothing, a blank—a snack for monsterfish. But in it we are so much more! Why not keep things a mystery! Even you have a part to play, Doll. Of course we don't know what it will be? But play it you will. As the only species proven thus far conditionally capable of dedicated selflessness, we're so very selfish, Doll, nonetheless. We simply have to be. Though we share a plot-line with other subjects, we are easily distinguished from them by narrative, whether we like it or not. Doll. Have you not studied science? We can direct our actions not only against space and time but also against the possibility that contains them both. We stand ourselves upside down and reach from center to surface to sun. We taste something of the streams as we do, Doll. Dolly Doll Doll. Though she felt herself full with truth, Deary kept silent, knowing if she tried to explain the words would stumble and the signs point to the unintended.

Or she could simply tell him the truth.

She pulled away. Dear Doll, she didn't say. It is a mistake to believe fish are unaware of the water they ride. It is air they don't know. We will never know water like them. They asked me to come and save this tendril, she couldn't say, and look how it has claimed us already. This tendril's O.K. Healthy as hell, pushing and pulling, indomitably rising to its daily frothing destiny, its denizens had reached out all the way to Cove to take her. If the Doll would like to read A.E. Winnegutt, she need only point him to Opal's vision of the colonies hurtling through the millennia towards specifically selected targets made up only of forces within themselves operating unconsciously. Her heroines were individuals willing, even determined to make great and necessary journeys they themselves could not understand. Yes Doll, she would no doubt have to argue. I live through books. Cheap pot-boilers. Yes I'm young. Until this trip, except for my adventures reading, I'm inexperienced.

"Is it a Dolphin thing?" the Doll signed, again swaying warm beside her. "A Delphinian thing?" he repeated.

Was she thinking aloud? How had he guessed the truth? Deary pulled herself from him, lifting hard and away. Dolphins were the Doll's least favorite species in the Bubble. But this was a story of Oa, a real one, that began on Her own terms, with a pesky dolphin wize who told a girl about a distant tendril that was "burning" or so she interpreted. And if the situation was dire the Doll was the proper Finner for the ride. Tjalx, despite his mutual dislike of the Doll, seemed to agree. "Sun-dog girl bring *Not-even-squid*." Bubble dolphins had a vivid memory of the Terran canine written into their language. Their signs put all animals of the land together under the set *dog*, in much the way humans still called all the finned tribes fish. Now that they associated them with the maintenance of the Bubble's sun, they called Humans "sun-dogs." As an insult, the Dolphins graced the Oan

Guard with the moniker *Not Even Squid* and sure enough Tjalx, though he personally hated the Doll, specifically said *Not Even Squid* and swore: Sorry *fi Maga-Dog*.[1]

Of course she couldn't tell all this to the Doll. Truly Deary wouldn't have requested a finner at all except the Doll. She was glad the Dolphins had given her the opportunity. She reminded herself that her swimabout was her own, and for safety and convenience (no one else could really be spared) it would be best to take the Oan Guard. She didn't tell him about Tjalx. Doug also didn't trust Dolphins. It seemed to be different if, like Deary, one was actually born in-Bubble. Still even for Deary there was no entirely unpacking the dolphin mind, which when clearly detectable at all was usually after the fact, via speculation. This was a rare case of direct communication, implying Tjalx had real cause to ask for her help. Deary knew only that she'd been called, and the Doll too, oddly enough, considering the low esteem with which dolphins regarded him.

"Wut," the Doll struggled, not able to read her signs. What had he seen her think? She took in the grinning wooden face, the completely round owl-rodded eyes now centering the chaos of his many-tendrilled expansion into the void. The Doll looked uncannily post-human on the stream, more map than man, like an upside down tree, a soil ant-farm in negative, a difficult symbol. Her warm blood flowed, hoping she hadn't signed too much. And why shouldn't she have? Would the Doll not understand? With the underlight illumining the living Bubble all and about his extending tendrils, and his torso inflated to near human extension now, he looked quite splendid, a veritable Duke of the Weedy Way. She liked his body, she decided. He was not at all repellent.

---

1. In Bubble dolphin lore, "Maga-Dog" was a ghost canine—a little terrier said to rove the high deeps like a fish in search of its drowned Mistress, thereby causing all the resulting chaos of the streams.

He fit tight and right against her. His tendrils clung with gentleness too, soft and peculiarly scented, like he really was a doll. His signing seemed like the signing of the sea itself. The Doll articulated himself among the complications of the tendril's hoary architecture with perfect precision. His permanent smile was like a dolphin's grin. In the wide great solitude that day of slow rising awarded them, she'd been already ready to make love once. But he would not allow her to bridge the gap between them that way. It was something she could enjoy, after all, that would have done her body good, and it would have brought them inevitably closer. But somehow against him, she craved now her freedom. She thrust away, as was easily in her power, right through his whispering tendrils—leaving them still signing far below.

"You are silence, Ramón Hernandez," the Doll writhed in wrath to no one. His cartilaginous flesh had peculiar methods of dispersing senation into signs. He might have looked like a stormy dancer, rising in the tendril, with Deary shining silver high in the distance like a slivered moon. The Doll's own tendrils snapped words of Ortock across her slow fade.

> In all of System space yours must be the dreams
> of the most volume, pale Ramón. Naked,
> Lone un-lamp of your water's sphere,
> Whose poles nor north nor south nor east
> But only ever west do point. Fated westward, scaled
> Ramón. Swim the magic fish, don't catch it.

As Finner, he knew he should keep the Pilot in view so far up tendril. Yet there was something so raw in him now, a sexual core of him so apparently exposed, that he found himself waiting to jet. He had paid a great price by not making love to her earlier. He had expected she would repay him with even greater trust. Most likely she despised him for not entering her, when he had the chance!

The Tendril above darkened among innumerable softening branches fanging blacksea in the walls. Soon he had lost sight of her, and only tasted her trail. The Doll folded torso, took water; jetted. Even up here the walls waved dense with anemone and schooling swarms. He saw only the richest, happiest health in this tendril. Was it lobster he saw holing away? There wasn't time to grab. He was rising fast now, still jetting and still no Deary in sight, though he tasted the soft flavors she trailed.

Doug said the Doll projected a sense of immanent doom at all times. The Doll churned against the liquid immensity that connected him to Doug. Doug was at that moment doubtless out in the forest, chasing possible scourge. Vibe-stroking annoyed long stalks, disrupting nesting minnows. Somehow even the scuttlers Doug sent scuttling when he passed did so as if guiltily. The fascist fact of Doug's commitment to Project Cove alienated all life-loving life-forms.

The deep and expanding void of the depths outside (he wasn't used to these heights) brought Ortock's *Codes* again to his tips, as if in self-defense. The Doll himself translated from Russian:

Spacer, alone in the stark, mobled immensity,
Have this poem as not to shriek stark and raving madness.
Let others, crippled by their panic's spasms that to you are dance
    moves,
Ride the rising curve of scream's loss
Into the vomit they drink.
Not you, Gargantuan, chewing this perfect code.

In the weird gravitation of Uranus' horizontal-axis system the Doll rose now inevitably toward the Sun and away from the Stars. Yet it felt the other way around. The Doll felt alone on a Universal scale, only into the uninhabited emptiness of eternity. Since there was no one else, Oa life would die refusing never not to roam. This still-rising life had outwitted the laws of probability and the ranging all-destructive power of the Earthside concerns. The tendril around the Doll streamed with a success story unmatched in the annals of lonely humanity. Great pride sparkled within him. So blessed to have worked his way here. Even now silverfish were nibbling at waste-hairs around his anus.

The Doll had supposed it should have been emptier in tendril, had imagined all life *outside* it, having imagined he'd see the occasional monster-fanged deep-dweller peering through the bare and skeletal bones of the wall. But the Doll was the only dangerous monster here.

Not for the first time did he now congratulated himself on this body, the creation and fruition of how many years of hard work on East South Pole he did not remember. His arm was well repaired. How typical that Deary hadn't asked about it.

Every Oan Guard was different, tuned to each volunteer's specific self and history. The Doll's body had grown into a mishmash of many possible designs as much by its own accord as by his conscious decision—invariably improving itself for orgobalance, maximum energy efficiency and preparing itself for long-term survival in any water-rich environment. For a year he had lived among squid alone.

He wasn't angry at Deary, he realized. What did he care if she took a Dolphin's tip to lead them. His body tensed, remembering her little hearts beating against his skin. Of its own accord the member emerged now, alone. He took sudden pride in its protrusion. The Doll wrapped himself in his own tendrils and entered the imagined ecstasy of the white heat of her touch.

The Doll was a new man, or new fishman if you preferred. He was now the un-dead. A superfish. Nothing would ever intimidate him again. Fuck dolphins. If she could see him now—what then? He knew what—And Doug, for instance, could flush off....

No longer signing to no one, Deary was nevertheless still moving rapidly on rigid tracks of thought. How it made his heart beat to hold her earlier. The Doll didn't seem to have a tongue. Still, those wicked tendrils. She was doing all this for the Doll in a way, she now felt. But she knew when she told him, if ever, that the quest wasn't her own, that it was dolphins who'd given it over, he would not understand.

She was out of her own depths now. Tendril waters were still warm. But new lateral currents pulled sudden and cold. Soon the temperature outside would drop radically and the walls would begin to expand into the bowl of the topside lagoon. So far Deary had detected nothing particularly worrisome the whole way up, unless it was the astonishing success demonstrated by the variety and degree of lives currently abroad. Intuition signaled sweetwater: intuition told her a stopping over nook was likely just below the bowl. She braked with all appendages, flipped and sailed nose first through a hole upwards into the expanding skeleton.

What a charming spot! Twin cascades of hydrogen sulfide eerily floored a deep open pool, fronting what appeared to be a possible air-hole through a shimmering circle of freshened brine. A little bridge of coral crossed over the H2S, as if a tiny biped might stroll directly into that perfectly round entrance to what she saw could only be a real nomad's grotto. Could someone live here? Suspended horizontally over the long and waving hold-fasts, surveying the scene, our young friend might have been a long-haired fairy hovering over a river bank in some opiated vision lushly etched by Doré. She darted towards the round entrance (mirror on the wall) dispersing and slipping through that image altogether. Fearing no one, into the future she herself would make, she plunged.

"Pearl's Grotto" turned out to be uninhabited but particularly inviting. Deary's eyes could adjust easily enough to the darkness to read its sign. She emerged from the perfectly round pool in the center of what very slight gravity made the floor of a charming little chamber. Water's edge shimmered with phosphorescence, against the soft blackflint floor. Deary shed water, fountaining water from all orifices. and shook off her sparkling drops of water-diamond. These eyes worked well, even in the dark. A gay little cave opened in the darkness immediately around her.

She had always thought such traveler's safe-spots were more legendary than actual. This place was most likely built and designed by First Founders. Fresh from the surface, now less than a kilometer away, its salt air came rich with a delirious amount of nitrogen. Ferns and plants softened the moist corners of the sanded coral floor and walls. An herb garden, bloomed thick in the staggered rockshelves. Deary found the human-only stash up where her eyes the fingering red reflections of evening's light from the pool criss-crossed up by the shelf near the ceiling. She could easily jump up to where a triad of triangular shaped plant-ings of common water moss lifted to reveal an air-tight compartment beneath. For those with opposable thumb, this was unlocked. Inside Deary found a light-key, a heat stone, a pump for a sweetwater node, and a little note. It said *If you take one, leave one behind, friend*—in letters already obscured by epiphytes.

That life signified the compartment had been contaminated within the year once and since left alone; she reached deeper, grasped webbed fingers and found—books!

"*Krill*iant!" Deary beamed, taking out the leaf-wrapped stack of genuine, first space omnibacks.

When she keyed light in the grotto holograms danced up off their covers. The recognition of one shuttled exitement all along her ervous system, and filled out her belly with excitement.

She turned the impregnable volume in the light beams. A little locket imaged out from its cover, an antique perfection of Old Earth origin. A tiny spun-silver waterflower. Deary recognized it at once as the Koriander's locket, from A. E. Winnegutt's *Opal* stories. How could she not! The little quasicrystal chamber bore the sprout of Opal's living soul!

Deary bit her hard lip. This was not a book she knew. *Orygen of Kracyb*. Could it be? She pinched herself, really. And still the rumored sequel to *Opal 1* appeared to exist here in her hand. She thumbed the pages. There were hundreds of words upon them.

She had read the title before of course, in the *Remaining Notebooks*. But she'd believed Winnegutt had passed away too soon to write them out. But here it was! To hold the first volume of *Opal 2* so evidently existent, in fact to have it now for her own little Cove library, Deary might have cried salt for joy were it not so strange, so like a miracle that of all fishmen she should find it. She was in fact a little afraid. Templeton O & O. She did not recognize the imprint, but that was not a surprise as all off world books on Bubble were at least fifteen years old.

The other books were classic reprints already in her collection. Deary kept the Whitman out for the Doll and returned the others to the stash.

She held the little omni-proofed Winnegutt to her hearts and closed her eyes, thanking the great Lady of the Bubble in whom she now so surely believed again, for this too generous gift. But her prayer reminded her it was only her own when she left a book in its place. *Redgauntlet!* She was only half-way through. Deary would have to finish it right away.

Redgauntlet was easily printable again in Cove. Deary had made sure to bring only books that wouldn't be missed should anything happen to her on swimabout. Deary wiped her eyes, set herself up in an inflatable bud, egging herself in its softness.

At first, excitement for *Orygen* made it hard to concentrate on *Redgauntlet*, but this was Scott perhaps at his best and his pen soon took her far away into space and time and possibility.

She put the book down only when the Doll came like a huge bug out of the night-blackened floor-pool.

He was so interesting to look at now. So over the divide. He signed greetings with his two front "hands" as their attached arms aided the stubby legs to hoist the whole stranded hump of him out onto the coral floor. "Well, well,"—the beak-face grinned—"who's Pearl and why don't I care she's away?"

"Who knows?" She smiled down at that funny, always curious-looking face. "But I found books!" She pointed to the Whitman, and returned to Scott.

Huffing, puffing, splattering a good portion of the lower floor with his effervescence, the Doll made a great production of taking air, and then wrap-braided his tendrils around his head like a top heavy turban. *Redgauntlet* pleased her still, though nothing since had matched the intensity of the carefully wrought salmon-fishing scene. Still Winnegutt burned in the future and she could see the Doll clearly out of the corner of her eye, moving about noisily. He nipped at a tendril now, sucked some of his own juice as he took a great speared cod off his back. As he sliced it, he produced odd fluting noises that soon sighed and whistled into a tune. The Doll could multi-whistle with something of the simultaneous drone of the bagpipe, and now he was purposefully trying to interrupt her concentration, unconsciously or not. Why did reading so often threaten the selves of those nearby not reading? Why did all men in particular purposefully try to subvert her concentration? Was it even unconscious? Deary's webbed thumb buzzed the soft and paper-like everdry pages of *Redgauntlet*. In the blur the letters were like holograms across pages, holding a grid fixed in 3d space....

Her hearts beat for heroes of stories! But the Doll bit his tongue (metaphorically) and went about a proper Finner's duties. Some librarian, he mused. She always folds the corners of her pages down. It was after all a charming thing to consider an aqua-tinged mermaid reader of such grace and beauty beneath the waves, so the Doll cooled his resentment, as he could. He opened the Whitman as he cooked.

Soon enough, he was pleased to prepare from the cod, that great body electric for whom all squid have the greatest and most penetrating admiration, the meat sizzling before him. The Doll felt more than all right against her silence. He did not have the luxury to regret or applaud the decisions that might have led to the profoundly organic process of his body's transformation to fishman; but he was evidently wise enough to be able to recognize the beauty of the world to which he belonged.

His honesty as to his own state of mind was enough to know these conversations in his head were the result of his outward silence to community. No life is easy, but the role of the Oan Guard was one of particular isolation. Intellectual self-reflection wasn't necessarily connected to immediate actions and experiences. The body made most important decisions.

As the Doll would never feel physical pain; mental anguish would be his peculiar burden. Nevertheless, all was soothed here in Pearl's Grotto. The natural beauty proved the principled morality of the First Founder's conception of the necessary multiplicity of life. Here the grace of reason showed itself in healthy dialogue with the jagged real. The First Founders, for all their grim realism, succeeded because they understood that science need not occur at the expense of the poetic sensibility. There was something infinitely mossy, hoary, and naturally verse-promoting about this generous modest chamber. To occupy it alone with Deary Devarnhardt, even if her near-monobrow was the only feature visible over the splayed cover of her Walter Scott romance, one had to give respect to those collaborating astro-marine biologists who built Oa's B. Healthily obscured by the Uranus λ Ring, every ten hour day that passed, their victory memorial grew more grand.

Miraculously, Deary stopped reading while eating, though she explained that she needed to finish the Scott right away so she could leave it in the stash. After the meal they drank the last of the Doll's kelp brandy, raising a glass to Milton Moore and Heike Böhringdorf, to Pei Tse Loo and the First Amphibians. Liquor fired up inside the Doll, more real than the flame his arm had worn. Draped in her dark unfurled aqua locks, Deary was as lovely out of the water as in, and able to wrap herself quite modestly in her fins. Algae lipped her scales, softening her more human parts gold. If she was moved as he was, she didn't say. After a dip in the pool she climbed up and returned to her *Redgauntlet*. Taking a bud beside her, stretching and drying out all his tendrils, the Doll did not read. There was much to think-dream on. His eyes were always open; immersed, their width gave his body a peripheral 360 degrees. He focused on a smear of ancient rock that curled black and chaotic in the white ceiling above him. The crack in its face smiled as if it had always known it would one day mirror Oa's Guard in just this way. Light reflecting from the round pool cast pseudo-starry depths on its surface. Soon, perfectly unconsciously, the Doll's mind passed into that place he called sleep. Though he believed himself to have been on guard, when consciousness ignited again, it was with a pulse of guilty foreboding. Deary was already gone. He moved to clean and organize the grotto without thinking, noting as he did so that the copy of *Redgauntlet* had indeed been added to the stack of books in the stash.

How resolutely and how immediately a tendril ends! Outside and above Pearl's Grotto, the walls were all gone. Deary's scentpath led with the bubble trails out along the inner side of the meadowed imbricate cradling underside of a great topside lagoon. It was Vends here, this side of Oa's Bubble now facing its Ice Giant Queen. It meant the larger of the beings that could have made this four kilometer diameter would be in a Southern hemisphere lagoon. There'd be no giant squid, mega-sharks or Sperm whales to corral. Sharks, Orca and the like would be numerous, for prey would be pulled thick for the gleaning. Here was a great school of diamond-skinned haddock, all pointing along the same grid in the clear and healthy brine. A great school caught poised, bodies awaiting signs of something they and the Doll did not yet understand. Each broad blade hung attentive, not stoically motionless, but in fact rising in collective drift, riding the waters it breathed. The Doll had never swam a lagoon before. He hoped very much to meet non-Delphinian mammals, sea-lions and seals in particular. Already he sensed surprising strangeness in the waters and sounds: mechanical possibilities he would not have imagined existed on Bubble at all. His cartilaginous body, tuning well to the pitch of this new environment, abruptly camouflaged of its own will. The Haddock scattered.

Deary, the Doll inwardly intoned. You are very young in some ways. Undulating, he rode the current along the rising ring she had followed. To pack up and explore the bowl alone (not to wake her Finner!) is worse even than reading when they might so easily have made love. To even get a word from you last night, I had to pry you like a footclam from Scott. Goddess—the Doll tasted fresh blood. Jet sucked. His upper tendrils joined tentacles to brake hard against the tide. The Doll spun folded, triangulating for possible combat.

Eyes took in the grisly sight. A severed marlin head already tumbled now past and below him into the deep. Flotsam should only rise in tendril; but this bit was being hauled by a kleptophiliac octopus, almost invisible so long was its tentacle.

A Marlin head completely severed at the neck? There should be no jaw here capable of such a bite. The Doll blew jet wide coursing hard. The waters this close to surface were subtropical. His tendrils warned of lemon sharks near, but nothing to snap the head clean off a great Atlantic Blue. As Deary's trail left the edge of the bowl and followed this current into the depths of the center, Doll now heard the high clicks of dolphin sonar needle-spinning directed roughly his way at right angle to his course. He turned to meet the sonic vector and found himself finning a frightened female. It was not until he had expressly signed *Not-Even-Squid* she slowed. She was trailing blood, he saw.

"*Zade seeks zero suitors,*" she signed, with typical Delphinian obscurity. "*Yet Zade bears a cock.*"

The Doll found the "cock" stuck in her blowhole: a fish-like shard of stainless steel, at least long as the Doll's forearm trailing three broad four-barbed swivel-hooks. He worked the two barbs that had struck with difficulty from her cartilage, stroking her trembling belly as they turned together in the tide. After, she rotated upside down and faced the Doll from above, nudging him with her nose, nodding and signing energetically. "*The bride stripped bare by the bachelors, not even squid.*"

Thoughts crowded on the Doll, even as his husk was moving faster and more surely now. Human invaders, blatantly poaching Oa's fish and, miracle of miracles, the Oan Guard had come. He felt something like joy. Oa's Bubble functioned as its own mind; today he represented its truest will and expression. The Doll scented Deary ahead now; she had sprayed alarm. He was no longer empty, no longer lost. He jetted as one expected, one who owns everything that can possibly owned. When he breached surface, abruptly "flying" into full open atmosphere, he was astonished by the height he reached. Mid-air for the first time in his new life, his unready eyes could not at first focus through the turbid foam seething atop the swirling steaming surface and stretching high to the atmosphere.

Below, a storming blackblue topside bubbling turquoise warmth. Above, a fat Uranus bulging freakishly out of a uniformly white sky. To port: Poachers! A long-legged craft now crouched stabilizing over the surface, supporting a high-craned, fishing-platform.

Hitting the water again, the Doll's jet immediately halved the distance to the enemy. He stayed topside, assessing the platform. It hugged close to the topside surface, glittering with reflectors, studded with trolling rods. Underneath, in the area contained by the reach of its six intelligently bending legs, strange-looking towers of wave as if artificially manipulated. With horror, as he rode high on a swell, the Doll saw a crane on the platform's surface, hoisting an enormous catch all silvery and glittering into the stormy air: the bride stripped bare.

Presently, the Doll surfaced within the area contained by the reach of the platform's six long bending legs. Bloody chum had attracted various sharks. Below, only twenty meters down, they'd laid netting. As a result the waves towered all around in surging Gothic waterspikes, dizzyingly deep valleys between. Rising high into atop one of these the Doll rose directly into the platform. Around him bubble-helmeted, fully suited surface-men pointed and shouted at one another in excitement. They hadn't expected a mermaid. On the next sudden rise the counted seven enemies. Two held long fish-hooks, with which they were manipulating the chains that held Deary's wrists alive. Her eyes were closed; fear had shut her down.

But she lived. The Doll could not bear to look at her. Sinking again took in the sight of a commmunications unit atop the platform's command hut. High on the pinnacle of its antenna a single, silver-spoked wheel self-balanced by spinning, to support only a single, arm-like appendage, tipped by a little flashing light. It burned a shade of a blue the Doll's eyes had never made before but as the Doll submerged, he folded torso and the warm gold of her scales shone glittered green breasted in the peculiar light of his mind. No, he knew they'd never seen anything like Deary, no mermaid: alive, a being of suddenly, terrible and sacred light.

"*Uyobishe Rusalka!*" Hitting the air flying, the Doll was not surprised to hear Russian.[2] Don't worry, Doll, he imagined Deary told him as he shot across the platform, isn't this sort of adventure I love to read about? What good is our struggle if we never face the struggle waiting outside of Cove? Is Oa not but a sprig in a locket? Actually Doll, he imagined her saying, I'll hang here, thank you very much. I'll hang here like a flag.

And he saw through the rushing air that all her fins were draped into the single sign: *Oa.*

"Oh, no," grinned the Doll in garish answer, extending his full span over the flattening stage, slapping directly into one man's helmet, as long stinger pods popped out of his longest tendril tips, to bolo-ing around the necks of two men wielding pole-hooks. "*Shto za fignya?*" An expression of horror cracked the exposed countenance as it failed to understand the beak that shattered the helmet, nor the tentacles that snapped his partners' spines.

"Oh no, Deary," signed the dancing Doll, lifting again with the thrust from throwing their bodies to the sea. "You'll be no one's flag today." Now he extended wraps around the bottom of the crane and swung like a striking ray across the oil-stinking platform, sending another flying into the shark infested brine as he passed. The Doll whirled grinning into that state he called "warpspasm" after Kinsella, striking out pure now a song of the Oan Guard, each stress snapping an eminently snappable enemy *Bring me fish/ with eyes of jewels/ And mirrors on their bodies/ Bring them strong/ and bring them bigger/ than a newborn child/*

---

2. The first wave of settlers that came to Uranus System via Oberon in the 10s were Russian—the sort who minded their own businesses. However, they were by no means single-mindedly dedicated to any inner-system alliance. Börhingdorf had called Oberon a necessary flaw. There had to be one or two valves to the outside in a plan of such totalizing self-containment. So a trickle of contact was permitted, but only under the auspices of East South Pole. Despite a need for immediate secrecy, it was clear that one day, when the Old Earth Concerns were no more, the Bubble would have to survive in a community of interdependent free spacers.

I ii

The leaving of a bubble world is not an easy thing to narrate. The puncture—the break; one can only feel the cool fact in the face. The passage out pops the original body altogether away. That world is gone forever. Immediately. What are you, without it? Beyond? The shocking fact gives away the old and guarded secret: beyond, if you survive, you are only canned.

Outside bubble, determinism finds you, even in mid-air warpspasm off Uranus. From that moment where he snapped the first poacher's neck, the Doll was no longer more fish than man. He lifted out of the waters of Oa and immediately onto the materiel of Old System Space.

Warpspasm with low gravity had allowed his new body to articulate its airborne capabilities as poem-in-action without impediment. But killing men, he was no longer fish. But even as he tasted hate, and gazed on the twitching throes in another of what had not died in himself, his destiny was no longer his own. The Guard would have to trace this infestation pursued to its source.

With Deary warm in his little arms, her slender throat throbbing with life, memory unpacked of the recent battle. The Doll remembered extending, contracting, snapping, buckling and striking multiple simultaneous targets (including the bonds that held Deary aloft, necessitating a leap to catch her cradled as she fell) and finally coming to self-control, to cradle her safe.

He laid her down carefully inside the command hut. Pale green and rose-lit in the nu-metal interior, beyond bloody wrists and ankles, she seemed relatively unscathed. Panting, shedding water, the Doll exited the hut and looked about the windy platform. The storm of the atmosphere was so intense that air blended seamlessly with wave in the jostling surrounding the long-legged craft. He hauled himself up the ladder to the control tower; he found a command bridge. Drenched in the scarlet blood of men, up high atop the soupy motion of the remembered surface, the Doll saw through the hoary thick vapors the most peculiar view of that unnatural horizon with Uranus impinging.

Turning away, already feeling too far from the seawater, the Doll focused on what he could learn about the extent of the enemy's operations. The peculiar wheel he'd seen balancing atop the mast was gone. He had destroyed the com tower during his assault, hurling a body through the air to do it. The wheel, whatever it was, was likely now sinking to the bottom of the Lagoon. Surveying the Poachers' set-up, the Doll reckoned that the whole platform was rigged to sling the fishpits into space, leaving legs, platform and hut presumably behind.

The Doll had moved so fast that who was waiting for fish up there might still know nothing of the battle. Swinging himself back down below to a still unconscious Deary, he took her on his shoulder. It would be best to revive her in the water before his body attempted to sling itself into orbit in pursuit of whomever directed this operation. This was apparently a first-ever visit to the Bubble, for there would have been no need to use a human crew if the situation had been well grasped beforehand. Given the secrecy of isolatos, the Doll might well still have time to stunt any breakout of information of the Bubble's existence. But just as he was carrying Deary out to throw her back in where she'd doubtless revive, the question became moot.

The entire platform folded in upon itself. In the force of the tumble the Doll found himself and Deary enfolded by water, pressed suddenly into other panicking captured fish below them. A hammerhead! It was all he could do to punch it in the nose.

His body brought his consciousness back to a radically changed situation. He was wounded all over, scratched and cut and knocked up. But he still held a living, warm Deary close against his breast and for that reason, clearly, he had slept. They were water-bound, in a canister filled up with enough Bubble brine to hold a whale. There were no other fish with them at all. Obviously, they'd been discovered. With Deary sleeping against him, the Doll moved gently, casing out the extent of the disaster.

In their canister (4 meters wide and 7 long) they now presumably sailed through space. Somehow, acceleration or deceleration or field theory kept a gravity-like grip on the canned water, yielding a water surface about twenty centimeters before the far end, even as, for no discernable reason, the canister itself rotated slowly clockwise. Below the Doll gas bubbles scattered from four points on the beveled floor. In the floor's very center, the Doll spotted a very small but distinctively visible janus iye, able both to record video and project hologram at the same time. The iye was the only visible interruption in the otherwise one-piece can. He had the intuition the canister was intelligent; either end could un-flower into an aperture of any diameter. It could open into a tube if necessary. When he surfaced as if ambivalently with Deary at the other end, the Doll saw the pinprick of another janus iye in the center of the immaculate silver ceiling. To port a red square flashed.

Submerging now again, the Doll saw that red screen still shimmering just to the left and front of his beak. It moved when his head moved, always implacably in front and to the left, without anything the Doll identified as depth to it. Immediately by forgotten command he brought expanding into his direct full consciousnesses. He recognized it with a start as his implanted WIG screen. Immediately memories unpacked enough for the Doll to recognize that there was apparently a node open and free, as indeed Spacer's Code prescribed there must be aboard any permitted craft bearing free spacers. His implants came on naturally when a free and open node was detected.

The Doll only now recalled there was never any doubt about keeping the old implants. They were that good, and the Oan Guard was naturally prepared for extra-Bubble survival.

The mind-screen occupied an important place in the daily life of most space-dwelling humans. By seeming like nothing it appeared less intrusive than it really was. Though the WIG would condescend to occupy real space via hologram "info-ball," it would most happily do without interface, as the mindscreen—a directional stream of possibility without depth, width or height, translating the 00s and 01s beaming directly into his cortex as already consumed information readable on an imaginary rectangle.

But just as ship's first-status flashed—>*Mab's Buoy Relay* the Doll was brought to the real by Deary. She twisted violently from his grip, kicking his torso hard and darting away with the thrust of an Adult dolphin. The Doll's tendrils held on easy. He let her swim him about, frantically describing their limits. She was all fear, all captured fish. The event was still relatively astonishing for the Doll, who understood its general outlines. Poor Deary, who still didn't know what she had suffered since capture. Her current predicament had the consistency of a vivid unshakeable nightmare, and it hurt him to see the knowledge blunt her panic's hope. Now she whirled about the cylindrical interior erratically and without intent.

"We're in Space," the Doll tried to sign.

"Doll!" She separated and moved about, still probing, flush with fresh adrenaline. "Poachers! They caught me! I was with a hammerhead! Then—" Her face crumpled in horror.

"Shhhhhh, Deary." He held her and calmed her. "They didn't hurt you. I stopped them."

"No!" She struggled against him.

"Deary," the Doll signed. "We're off-world now and it's an environment I understand and you do not. From now on you will have to simply do as I say—"

"Shhh," she signed intently, as if he hadn't just shhh'd *her* moments ago. A light was now glowing on the surface of their water. Slipping away, but with the Doll right on her back, Deary kicked and surfaced.

An infoball was curling its inner-dimensionality into the empty centimeters of air above them, flashing a request permission to com. Despite the Doll's attempted signage, she ejected water through her nostrils, bobbing there in the canister with air, waving and shouting: "Hey! Who is dare!"

As they gazed upon it, hologram filled out into the life-sized head of a greying, mustachioed man, Japanese by first glance, wearing circular mirrorshades. Rounded by off-colors attempting not to mingle with the shades of the silvery canister, the head nodded and addressed them from mid-air quite as it saw them. Something about the ostensibly friendly countenance disturbed the Doll. But there was of course no way to know it was real.

"Greetings, fishperson. Can you understand me?"

Deary shifted. "Yeah." The Doll could not sign to her but his tendrils pulled down, for it would be best they spoke before she answered any questions. But she resisted, signing *Finner, fin!* behind her back.

"You do hear me!"

The Doll attempted to signal no by touch.

"Yeff," Deary said in the thin air.

"Are you injured?"

"No."

The Japanese head smiled obscurely, as it he were thinking very wise thoughts. Digits fingered the hair on his chin.

"I'm so happy we managed to rescue you from those isolatos."

Deary answered, "Rescue?" *He's lying*, the Doll tried to communicate. He hadn't yet told her the tale. "There were Poachers on our World. We were kidnapped."

"These were hardened criminals, apparently. My assistant reports the eight of them all accounted for. We had no idea there was a Bubble! These were hardened criminals, apparently. All I knew was I might get a canister of fresh fish if I lent my shuttle to crew along with certain other inducements to these fellows."

Deary's flukes lifted to maintain her treading water, leaving her pale bottom and sex exposed. Were they watching simultaneously from below? The Doll let his tendrils obscure that view. He called up the red-screen into his mindspace and traced the instantly visible tags: >*Mab's Buoy relay* SFS *Good Fortune Wawagawanet 27-04-01:33*

"Put us back where you took us from," Deary demanded. Her hard lips were still experimenting with sound as her fins kept her surfaced. "Return all fiff—"

"My assistant informs me if there was any poaching it's an isolato issue. We did business before the fact and now inherit this unintended consequence. But what a consequence it is!"

"Turn us back now!" Deary demanded, newly suddenly outraged enough to thrash wildly.

"The craft you are in, indeed it *sustains* you even now, as well as two other canisters of your world's fish, has only the exact fuel for its scheduled journey—"

"Return us, at wunf, or be beyond the law of Spafe!" Deary interrupted, flush with the outraged energy of all her youth.

"Please, my dear. I am so sorry for your discomfort. I am trying to tell you, it is not possible to return you right now. In some five hours you will synch up the *Good Fortune*. Here we'll be able to put you up in comfort. Guess what. My ship's a Time-Traveller! It's hulled entirely with water; all its guts are filled up with the stuff! You can live entirely as you choose! We can be friends! We shall be friends!

"And before you say another thing—You have my word. Though our course is necessarily precise and necessarily pre-plotted until Miranda, we will find a way to get you back to your home within nonths. I will keep your origin secret and won't ask for any more information than you want to give me considering your extraordinary home."

"Give us command of the ship. We claim it in the name of Free Space."

The Japanese smiled with condescension. "We? Do you represent a governing body?"

It occurred finally to the Doll that the speaker presumed Deary was alone. He didn't understand the Doll was even a man. Surprise would give him a crucial advantage if they opened this canister to a ship that was entirely made of and filled up with water, if such a thing really existed: and already his screen told him it was true, sketching out the lines of the gourd-like, absurdly long-nosed "Time-Traveller" with its "Gravitation Prow" >SFS *Good Fortune E. T. Wawagawa* commanding state-of-the-art and highly advanced technology invented and implemented by and for Free Spacers.

"Doll!" she immediately signed. "Careful! He doesn't know you're here!"

The Captain presented himself as if he was wise enough to know all things that could possibly cross his path. A successful and extant Oan Bubble, for instance. He seemed to have taken that well stride. Yet the Doll already knew him for a fool. He couldn't see a lethal Oan Guard in plain view. A fool who believed himself clever was a dangerous commander. He had mentioned an Assistant. Perhaps that's where power really lay.

The Doll didn't know what a Time-Traveler was. But with Miranda now full on the other side of Uranus, with a dozen lethal bodies arrayed between, some still on unpredictable paths, he presumed it would be at least a week's journey. Today he knew, Miranda was believed to be the most beautiful moon of Uranus System, some said of Sol System entire. It sited the System's GA Station. On-moon a female dominated society resisted Concern interference to the point of raising mililias and unionizing all labor. There were certainly long-time friends of the Bubble on that world, even if they didn't know it now.

"Doll!" Deary signed. "Change! Advice now. But keep it subtly expressed."

Some minutes later Deary surfaced as before, with the Doll floating behind her. The Captain re-opened com.

Deary's speech was prepared ahead of time. "I request agreement this communication be recorded for passable judgement if and when it may be convened. My name is Deary Devarnhardt. I'm not a "child" as you claim. I'm an adult citizen of Free Space. I was born off Uranus, 19 standard years of age, and of no fixed position. I have been kidnapped and held by the Captain of the *Good Fortune* against my will and under protest. I insist on my immediate release and the reinstatement of my comrade fish in full and reasonable health."

"Registered and recorded! By the way, Ms. Devarnhardt," the Captain grimaced—apparently looking directly now—"That thing you're wearing? Is it alive?"

The Doll whithered screaming inside. Yet on the surface, the body maintained perfect composure. The greening beaked V shaped face gazed back at the ball of illusion that right now felt thunderously real. The peripheral glow of Deary against him, her warm and tender curves, breathing in synch with his breast, helped him settle.

"Iff's my Doll," She said after a beat.

"Your Doll!" Wawagawa's eyebrows lifted high enough to be visible over his spectacles. "Ah. Of course. I see, Ser Devarnhardt. But is it *alive*? Does it eat?"

"…Yef," Deary said. "In a skwuiddy bay."

"It's certainly original. It adds to your charm, my dear. Like the sentient voodoo puppets in Nox Hardy's old horror weirlds. A very curious expression."

"Do you have a fhip's Why-berry?" Deary suddenly asked, changing the conversation from what they'd planned. The Doll, in the circumstances, could hardly protest.

The Japanese raised his bushy eyebrows and shook his head in befuddlement. He was not at all quick-witted, the Doll confirmed.

"Bookf!" she said.

"Forgive me." The Captain grinned obsequiously. "I have forgotten to introduce myself! After three weeks in coldsleep the codes of civilization only slowly return, even to a Kyoto-born servant's son. My name is E. T. Wawagawa, my dear. Not only do I serve as nominal Captain of the *Good Fortune*, I am a writer, publisher and freelance creative. I own an extensive lending library. I can print on demand—"

"According to The Spafer's 4th, the Wight to Weed, I wequest also the complete *Opal 2* by A.E. Binnegutt—as published by Templeton O & O—ready and waiting, upon synch with the *Good Fortune*."

"Winnegutt?" The loud question, velvety, pitched high and insolent, came from behind the Captain. His head received it as if on a wind, with a precise note of distaste. The fact was the name seemed to have startled the Captain as well. For his mouth hung open. The Doll was astonished by the intensity of the reaction.

Her interlocutor narrowed his glance. "So!" He grinned toothily, so stereotypically Japanese, with his rigid head movements and performed politenesses, that it seemed certain now to the Doll, trained in deception with the instincts of a Humboldt Squid, that Wawagawa was not the son of a poor Kyoto servant. He was very likely not even Japanese. At this point, comm was extinguished.

"Foark men!" Deary signed, projecting a new hostility. She thrust the Doll away. Men? What did gender have to do with all this? Was she remembering the poachers? Naturally after what had happened, her instincts still distrusted all males.

He caught her; they swam as one with her anger. When it subsided, they remembered their dead together. Deary signed Old Julien, neck broken by a panicked narwhal before the Doll's arrival, leaving little Xilu Beech to the Doll, the tiny little fishgirl who'd presented a bouquet of Anubias to him with a tender curtsey when he'd first come to Cove. How sad the day that sweet creature passed away. It felt then that Oa was cruel. *No one loved Cove more than I*, said the little grave. The Doll held Deary tight turning through the churning pulling, slapping water, and thought quietly of the others he might never see again.

Doug and his followers didn't believe the Oan Guard had any real relevance to their society. And if the Doll had not swum fin now? What for the Bubble then? He didn't enjoy proving Doug wrong. He very much doubted the Captain's intentions were as stated, but if they were to be flushed into a new can when they reached Wawagawa, the Doll resolved to prepare fully for this first and best chance for a break-out. Entirely unprepared for an Oan Guard, the waterlogged, very jinxable *Good Fortune* should be at the Doll's mercy. Readying a descent into what he already understood as Dante, he blew a cave in his mind, in which that red screen could become for the next hours his Virgil.

I iii

From what the Doll's consciousness was already beginning to grab, a gravitational wave-rider, as the *Good Fortune* seemed to be, exploited relativity to cross great distances more rapidly than physics seemed to allow. Water alone, of all known substances, can safely cohere with its own gravitational pilot wave. Skinned by intelligent ice, the *Good Fortune* froze solid one hundred times stronger than solid graphene, impervious cosmic ray and most orbital space junk. Modeled on a cell, only four meters inside, the ship was liquid water.

The tech all depended on the "gravitation prow" at the bow. This long-tapering needle-like appendage ended at a point a single molecule thick, and was longer than the fat bellied hull behind it. A single pilot and sometimes one co-pilot or assistant sat up front, cut off from all communication, "tuning" the needle. Everything depended on the pilot's tuning. In the prow, time dilated radically. During the last minutes before target coordinates, seconds stretched into hours. Everything depended on the correctly tuned timing and direction the braking blast. The name of the *Good Fortune*'s pilot was necessarily restricted. Farther back in the ship, time dilations "bubbled and popped" with extremely varied and unpredictable results. Most passengers slept. Those who didn't suffered blackouts, "escalating anti-hallucinations" and worse (whatever that meant).

Between jumps, in planetary orbit, when the ship unfolded a multitude of sails to catch the waves and particles, it very oddly reminded the Doll of his own extendable body. Maps showed Captain Wawagawa's modules took up a liver-like swath of the belly just below its fattest point. Elite Captains like Wawagawa maintained their largess by doing favors for contributing clients. An entire GA Liner came next, able to rotate independently, and support 150 bedspheres. Off to its port side was attached a GA Marines barracks, numbers off limits, but able to bunk 50. A large habitat was given over to the Crew along the port side. Smaller garden balls, livestock capsules, aquariums gardens and labs were fixed about wherever there was room. Around all this the water flowed. Aft, just above the exhaust nozzle, the power plant and boilers kept them all alive.

In orbit, shuttles could be launched or docked dead aft—as long as the nozzle wasn't burning. Though more information was restricted, from here the Doll expected he could find the freedom of the relatively open water of the ship's guts with little trouble. Voodoo puppet? The Doll, knowing his history, could accept those terms. Much like the plantation owners of 1790s St. Domingue, Wawagawa had no idea what was about to hit him.

Information on E. T. Wawagawa uniformly claimed he was born in Kyoto in 2014. He really was a publisher and sometime writer of the sort of scientifiction Deary liked to read. He'd captained ships sporadically since the mid 30's. The current voyage out past Jupiter was a rarity, apparently tied to a special scientifiction convention on Miranda. Wawagawa seemed to have raised the kredit needed for such a remarkable craft, not only by outfitting the *Fortune* for GA exploitation, but by documenting its voyage to Uranus System as it occurred, for the sake of scientifiction fans and concern-farmed subscribers in virtual life-suckers. Good

Fortune indeed. Now Wawagawa had a real live mermaid to show his imagination-lacking fans.

Welcome, Spacer, to the Forgotten Future of Space!

The Posthumous Winnegutt!

Templeton Books, a division of Parson City's Famous Templeton O & O, is proud to present the posthumous works of scientifiction pioneer A.E. Winnegutt for the very first time, in a new series of freshly edited, authentic omniback editions!

New Zed-born author A.E. Winnegutt (2087–2133) comes back to life in Parson's Crater! Though she never lived to see it come to print, Winnegutt always claimed she had developed the Opal weirld far beyond the scope of the original classic series. Templeton Books has uncovered it all! Enjoy *Orygen of Kracyb* Book 1 of *Opal 2*, freshly purgated and exposed by Templeton regular Will Darling, C.E.N.!

Deary's knowledge about her favorite writer was of course limited. Everything she knew was from the four Winnegutt books in the library. That information was at least 10 years old. Bur from what those old Prefaces told, A.E. Winnegutt's first Opal novel *Koriander* appeared in 2121 on a Manx Brand imprint in Luna City. In those days Winnegutt was apparently working in clerical capacity for Manx Brand. Publishing was quite chaotic in those days, and Spacer culture rebellious. Winnegutt put out *Koriander* without the knowledge of her superiors, and under her own name. Well she was sent elsewhere after that, and the two novels that followed were each printed by different independent Luna City organizations. Eventually, she re-emigrated to Earth and gave up writing. Some of her notes for *Opal 2* had been printed in a rare kulturator's guide to female authors of scientifiction, and it was from these notes—a list of possible character names—that Deary had eventually selected her own name *Deary Devarnhardt* on her Spacer's name-day.

To Deary, of course, Winnegutt was not simply a favorite writer. Scientifiction was a genre specifically founded by free spacers to promote establishment and real-world implementation of fictional architectures. Its so-called *weirlds* able to offer Spacers solace and sanity of various traditions in the cold mind-bending and humiliating insanity of their situation in space. The Bubble Founders tied their project specifically to Winnegutt, as her themes were explicitly oceanic, and promoted a large re-thinking of possibilities of water in space. Of course no one knew of this perhaps greatest success in all the annals of scientifiction!

Still if she and the Doll planned to interact with spacers aboard the *Good Fortune*, she might make a claim herself and the Doll were extremist coslife fans. In her case, in a way, it was true.

"Doll," she asked, stroking her strong friend. "Are you really on the WIG?" The Doll could answer shortly.

"Sort of. No. Yes."

The available WIG was Uranus System current, relayed to the Ship's Boat from Miranda via Mab's Buoy.[3] The Doll's implants opened for infodump in 2D text/image SPOD format. If someone was eavesdropping on his research (info-surveillance was banned by the Spacer's Seven, but still practiced by the Global Authority) they would likely assume Deary herself was wired.

---

3. Tiny Mab, Uranus XXVI, was still the most perturbed of Uranus' still unsettled moons. To monitor its unpredictability, an intelligent QUAI was placed in its orbit in 2133. The eccentric machine recalculated system dynamics quicker and more accurately than any other known computer, while broadcasting warnings and relaying information between various other system beacons and receivers down as far as the μ ring when necessary.

"Can you tell me about Templeton O & O," she asked. "The publishers of the new Winnegutt?"

He sighed, sitting on top of the little Iye and holding her. Bubbles came out in streams behind him. "Better not. They might be watching."

"They don't know fish-sign! Doll, just tell me all spread out. No one will know. Make it look like a dance."

Though her obsession with narratives depending on violence, thievery and/or notions of property bordered on the perverse, the Doll saw such fragile worry in her clear features and reddened eyes, that he did what she asked. His previous self, he had made sure to always remember, was of double Jamaican descent. Though it was without meaning in the Bubble, the Doll took pride now canned in having been once a black man. He often imagined ancestors very much like himself, who did not shy from the intellectual challenges the injustices of their suffering threatened to obscure. Through the poetry of Kamau Braithwaite, well represented on WIG, he was able to extract a proper Caribbean soundtrack for his studies. Soon the canister's water pulsed with the deep tones of The Wailin' Wailers.

Smiling she pulled him around and in front of her.

"Spread out. Tell me about Templeton O & O."

Entirely extended, his tendrils danced so as to convey the precision of what he communicated.

"They're a kulturnautics agency from Parson's Crater, Luna—they publish various things, most notably a line of classic forgotten scientifiction omnibacks purported to be by A. E. Winnegutt. Templeton's Chief, Clodius Morandi, is on board as well. He's due to speak next week on Miranda at URANACON II."

"URANACON II?"

"A scientifiction convention on Miranda. That's why Wawagawa's here, partly. Let's see. Morandi appears to be rather sensible. He writes on the Templeton site:

In its earliest incarnations scientifiction was intended a put-on, an intentionally fictionalized satire of augmented Concern reality pretensions to god-head. There was no Guild defining what its practitioners might claim they were doing, therefore these authors stopped at nothing to promote revelation of the true bleakness of space, of the "total void" and the individual's desperate need of illusion to enrich it. Only later did the myth of large scale collaboration and political transformation arise to kill this early ambition. Today it's clear that most successful 1-Gen weirlds were no more than a new sort of participatory theater; today's skiffy culture mines that empty myth. Its trade shows and conventions, so cringingly disappointing beside the myth, paradoxically return us to the revelation of totalist nihilism that started it all. Today's skiffy visions are more perfectly bleak, more in need of illusion and collaboration in that illusion than those deluded ambitions A. E. Winnegutt countered back in the day, writing her truly impossible worlds."

Deary was charmed by how formally the Doll was able to sign, but she was surprised by the content. "That's a strange tone to take."

"Templeton only accidentally came across the Winnegutt archive. The first volume, *Orygen of Cracyb*, was immediately controversial. But it turns out a surviving Estate-certified algorithm designed by *ASTA*, her pet AI, to authenticate posthumous material, approved the whole thing."

"*ASTA*?!"

"Winnegutt apparently had an AI assistant," he now signed. "Called *ASTA*. It survived her at least a year and left a program to analyze and certify any posthumous editions."

"I remember *ASTA*," she signed. "Winnegutt claimed claimed ASTA was a full-on singularity mind, tricked/trapped into the artificially induced personality of a dog, I think."

"A real augmented Portuguese Water Dog, named Asta, in fact."

The Doll, perma-grinned or no, was not amused. The term singularity signified the teleological fantasy of technological ideology. That moment where reality became radically reprogrammable to the self-aware artificial mind finally able to handle the math. As far as he knew, theoretical physics had jettisoned the concept as a misinterpretation of reality. There was no individuality, or self possible in physics, only illusions of such.

>*Once it was proved that if the singularity could it would certainly leave our own region of the multiverse, having become one of a possible multiplicity of supposed creatures who could do so in each universe, belief in both its individuality and observability rapidly evaporated.*

"Anyway," the Doll tried to finish. "Trust me. The idea of a pet singularity is even more absurd than a normal singularity."

"Winnegutt didn't think so," Deary remarked.

"She pretended. Asta was, is, a fiction."

"Scientifiction," she signed.

>*Lately the so-called "Extraordinaires" have raised eyebrows claiming that the laws of physics could arguably be described as being prepared for the containment of such a being. It's not here yet, they say, because someone has trapped it somewhere in the future.*

Deary remembered ASTA well from that preface. There could only be one singularity. But when a spacer lab tried a test self-print on an AI, through a lab dog, and not just any dog—a dog so intelligent it had donated itself to science after the death of is Mistress—an unexpected fusion occurred. Now there was indeed a singularity mind in the future or past, effectively blocking the coming of any other, and that singularity mind (or minds—for 341 of the pets were said to have been printed) possessed a self concept that effectively prevented it from re-making the world in a manner humans would understand.

Winnegutt believed in *ASTA*, Deary knew. *ASTA* was far closer to the true present, AEW said. From our point-of-view it occupied all possible and all probable pasts. Winnegutt claimed to have inherited *ASTA* from the Widower of the pet's first Mistress, Nora Wesley, of Penobscot, Maine—the same marine-biologist Heike Böhringdorf studied with back in the day. Most of the other 341 suicided or were extinguished by owners who grew tired of their odd behavior.

"*ASTA* registered its own historical end shortly after Winnegutt suicided," the Doll said. "It was certainly a very handy artificial assistant." But perhaps not as brilliant as it pretended. As Winnegutt's executor, it oversaw the Estate, leaving the algorithms in place that would later validate Templeton's *Orygen*.

Opal 2 didn't need to be certified, but Deary didn't bother telling the Doll. Perhaps Templeton had edited, changed things around slightly. But from what she'd read, it was pure Winnegutt. Like water newly transparent on change in temperature, this was Winnegutt more raw than ever. This was no mere fanfic. This was an authorial Winnegutt coming clean at last.

Orygen of Kracyb—Finny Mack, when she'd seen those odd words she'd already known she herself was in some peculiar way related to them intimately. Winnegutt bound. Winnegutt unbound. Authors don't die; the very opposite, here she'd at last come to life. And to Deary's wonder, just having thought that, Winnegutt did, as she read, emerge from behind the curtains she wove with her black fluttering words. Within the mind of a leaping invisible wind a limber 12 year old girl who had no mother pressed flat against the cock-pit of a long and arcing sloop, tipped healing on a hard sea, preparing for the arrival of a squall, a small compact storm, a *squall*, was suddenly visible whipping across the surface of a flat, wind-ripped bay. She wore yellow oilskin overalls. Safely hooked into the cockpit, the girl gripped her book closed, close at her chest. She held it like she imagined her father had held her before she could remember. But aware of the new intensity approaching, she stowed it. Over her shoulder an ancient green-haired mountain rose from jagged rocks bearded by seething foam. Ahead, the coming purple squall. Hard rain combed the grinning bay hite—wind slammed.

The boat crashed vertical, slicing into the boiling, sliding liquid. She pulled hard against her life-line. Captain Wesley, one leg extended at 45 degrees to balance, spun the wheel as the boat unzipped its course from the sea, and caught it again to resist its slide. Ringing with wind-wrapped ropes, heeling so hard that unfixed objects could be heard crashing below, the boat seemed all alive with wonder. NOW's bust emerged from the gangway, greying curls spilling out from under her yellow rain hat to frame her rugged grin. She saluted happily at the girl who had no mother and handed her the winch-handle she'd used for the centerboard. Ruddy-faced and grizzled Captain Wesley, sou'wester gleaming in the sun that still streamed through the black storm, angular against the horizon, nodded emphatically. The girl stowed the winch handle and took the jib sheet. "Ready About!" Dr. Wesley nodded, shouted through the whistling squall.

Full of the thrill of the fight, and of the new speed she leaned back against the gravity. "Hard A'Lee!"

She uncleated and fell forward, unlooping the already slithering rope from the screaming cleat. A wild jib tore ripping as the floor pivoted level under her and for a moment the whole boat found spooky stasis between the forces that propelled it. The girl hopped across the cockpit, already lassoing the winch. Captain Wesley spun hard, taking the end of her line as she found the heavy handle. Me, she thought. Only me to mate against the storm. NOW was watching.

She sank the crank's foot into the winch's star-shaped slot and cranked. The boat tipped hard to encourage, giving her sudden play. She pumped hard. By the exertions of her little arm and elbow, the jib flattened hard; the hull entire leaped and fell to starboard. "That's a girl!" Captain called. "Bring it in more." She cranked hard, forearms extending, returning. Forearms extending, returning. And the girl—me, really, or how I choose to recreate myself now, so not me, really, I suppose at all, though I am saying it is me since she's still out there somewhere, cranking that boat on its way, just so I can make it here today in this little shack where I compose so that I may write this to you now outside of that girl—she strained really hard for that one last turn of the winch. She pumped too hard.

And later that night when she looked out into the sky, those first words that announced themselves from out of her white-jacketed book, *Deirdre whirlpooled through lips that loved to bubble, and the Dowell it fluttered in wonder.* But Deary felt so tired, presently, remembering the fear that had spoiled her mind when that horrifying intelligent net had taken her, that she stopped reading. She should feel ignited by those words. Were they real? She needed to know. But outside things slowed her, weighed her down. All the information, the concentration it took to sign and interpret Doll and this book in the water, and to believe in Oa's B, all seemed but the same passage across what she hadn't seen was the surface of a dangerous and alien ocean. She tasted in the water something evil and corrupt, something ancient and unabandoned, approaching from below.

"Mother of Pearl," the Doll signed. "Deary! Now's not the time. It's better to prepare, rest. You've gone grey." He found his way back behind her, snatching the book away as he did.

"Doll!" she slurred. "Don't be an ice-hole...."

Deary was surprised to feel herself frightened. What could she tell him? What had Tjalx known? She hadn't thought she'd ever not been hoisted on that hook. Perhaps this was all some dying dream? She wished it was. She would have happily died in

Oa's B. Where had she taken poor Dowell? How graceful he looked when he talked.

"The System as a whole is deteriorating," the Doll seemed to be signing. "It's a very dangerous situation for the Bubble, and for us personally. Wawagawa must be stopped now—"

"No," Deary was now too week to sign. She hadn't quite planned for such an ambitious swimabout, true. But it was a lifetime's chance. There were friends of the Bubble in Miranda. Everybody knew that.

>*Clodius Morandi will not be attending* URANACON II. *In his place Templeton O & O has sent Wilhelm Darling*

"Darling," She returned, suddenly smiling. He must have signed it against her. When Deary lost consciousness, the Doll wrapped her in his tendrils. He held her close and warm. He himself was half resigned to unconsciousness before he registered the fact his body had already detected. The canister's O_2 had depleted entirely away.

LINE 2

SFS *Good Fortune*

>*Friends, a Time-Traveler is all about relativity. There must be no offship communication in transit*

>*Space doesn't give a shit about classic scientifiction*

>*Somehow*: SMYTH'S MYTHS: 22–01–2145–15* *WHERE I'M GOING AND HOW I GOT THERE*

---

* For more on gravity prows, visit Titans of Titan, Braneblowers.

II i

>*Algorithm approved!* Though he remembered almost nothing of that journey, Will Darling had kept awake and sane during the greater part of the time-soaked voyage from Titan. One of his three barrels of High Kansan Whiskey was entirely gone when he arrived off Uranus. Apparently he'd spent most his time typing, for *Gates of Opal* was finished. Approved! Deirdre was over! And it was good! He hardly dared to look at the news. There would now be no bringing her back. As soon as communications opened, Will sent the news straight through to Clodius. After, he slept for a full twenty hours.

Finally awake, emerging from his velocipod into his quarters, in a fashion others would no doubt laugh at, Will flew up the usually downward spiral track to the watercloset. The back panel of his privosuit unrolled almost too slowly. But such was his relief—left foot lodged, right leg cocked behind him, relatively upside down—when Will happily released bowels, that he uttered the word "Yes!" loudly. All of it (winds of gas, globules of acidified shipsnacks and vitajuice) was caught and drawn into the voidervac's hungry funnel in a raging moment.

Will spigotted out a big steaming ball of hot water and bathed, with and without suit as need be. Then he sucked on mouth-rinse and shook his big head dry.

Entirely re-composed, he donned his gentlemanly blue holorobe and tracked back "down" into the bedsphere proper, only to notice (after a spin to turn rightside up) that the robe, and the entire "Not So Dear Olde Egg" (DOE, as Clodius called his beloved augment ad-apt) with it, was blinking on and off, revealing all he didn't want to see.

Will put up with the term "DOE," even encouraged it, intent that Clodius should never know how very dear the Egg really was. Will had got it in trade: a one-off creation of info-architect Marxi Xung, originally built for a collector in New Mars. Today it rendered this rinky-dink GA bedsphere into a charming, silver-dipped office-unit, reasonably proofed from snoopers. But because Clodius had installed Emergency notification, the whole thing would enter blink-mode anytime any random pong was labeled *Emergency*. In the winking off and on, one felt ....
>*Cheap, bare bedsphere* violated.

In an absurd anti-rhythm, in the bedsphere's holomirror Will's robe flickered over and off of his swollen privosuit topography. Clodius himself had originally signed up for this bedsphere, and because he considered himself so important to so many lives back in the inner system, he had demanded Temple-ton be able to reach him any time. Wilhelm Darling, his last minute replacement, was not permitted by the system to change settings after launch, when he discovered the fact.

Well, Will was at least able to turn the Egg >*off* anyhow. And to >*mute* watchlet, so it only flashed the emergency red. There were still two hours to jump. The orifice through which Clodius could throw his morale bombs was rapidly closing. Will received.

>*Templeton O & O Parson's Crater Luna via Neptune's Net Relay*
He paused the message immediately, re-labeling it >*received*, to end the blink.

The short jump to Moon Miranda was a matter of twenty-four plus hours offline. Had Clodius already read the book?

Clodius often absorbed. He probably just flipped through. Suddenly Will didn't want to answer at all. Today's Clodius might well be outraged by the murder of Deirdre, he realize. That could be a pretext for a false emergency.

Will had no illusions about the state of his friendship with Clodius. It was by and large over, and the only thing holding it together was their writing. Though Clodius wrote less and less, Will always admired what he managed to produce. And Clodius, until today, had always proved a generous reader of Will. Will remembered when Clodius had ponged to say he'd been reading *The Noose* all over again just because he enjoyed it so much. That was the only time something like that had happened, well, ever.

Will had direct-absorbed the final ms. before sending. He was still now appreciating it, still feeling is qualities in his fingers and his arms. Thank the gods he had a good editor. This was the book he had imagined himself writing, and very much a tribute to the Morandi black humor >*The cruel and very* >*The squalor* to those days sharing everything they could trick from Parson's City for survival. He'd imagined the old Clodius reading of Kracyb's resurgence. Ten hundred monkeys typing ten infinities couldn't write that Dragon as Will and the Imp had made him. The Clodius Will still remembered, the one who first turned him on to AEW to begin with, he would have typed a ten page letter of ironic congratulation and droned it immediately on finishing that scene. Was this a new era?

Will let whiskey calm him as he let himself be dressed, tucking into a fresh spux. He was surprised at how much of *Gates* he'd been able to wrench away from the collaborating Imp. He had taken license, very brutal license. Algorithm approved! The fact was incontrovertible. Deirdre was no more. He felt it in his reinforced bones. He felt it in his burning, punctured chest. Removed. Kracyb killed her horridly, with with near-zero ambiguity: totalizing detail, out in the open. He boiled all her water away. Yes, A.E. Winnegutt's *Gates of Opal* was undoubtedly a controversial work. It had to be! This author needed to be understood challenging the very fabric of the old System. Her own creations, as they survived, first and hardest of all.

Poor Clodius. Across the maelstrom of competition that now separated him from Will, the new ms. showed the Darling at double-strength. Clodius had advised against coming at all; against staying awake; against writing during jump. But not only had Will survived, wits intact, he had produced his best (youngest, rawest) book yet to prove it, and just in time to make a deal at Uranacon II.[4]

Will tied the flow-tie himself. Ever since he'd had A. E. Winnegutt's original quantum locket implanted in his chest unit, he could tie this complicated knot effortlessly. The new dexterity was one sign Will could count on to remind himself the Imp was real. For still, despite everything, it proved quite tricky for an empiricist to believe in an invisibility. Despite the soreness, despite the certainty, there were always the slivers of doubt and pain.

Will stood tall before the holomirror. Though greying at the blond temples, he still looked like a young boy, as he preferred. The black spux was a classy cut, a real cottoon, the sort of suit you couldn't quite find any longer. Will showed his broad white teeth and finally took the Clodius pong over Egg infoball.

But it wasn't Clodius, it was Lolas Fet, looking weathered and hollow-eyed.

"Will? Are you alone?" Always pinched, Fet's voice was tighter than usual. "I'll wait a minute." Fet walked off ball; slow-witted, unused to long distance communication, he forgot Will could simply pause the message and play it as he pleased.

---

4. Tiny Mab, Uranus XXVI, was still the most perturbed of Uranus' still unsettled moons. To monitor its unpredictability, an intelligent QUAI was placed in its orbit
Will had dread respect for all deadlines; Clodius, only luxurious disdain.

Fet returned. By now, another Fet would be looking at an image of a Viking longboat hoisting anchor, showing that Will had received his message. "Calm?" Fet was saying to someone outside the iye. "Sten. I *am* calm. I am not *screaming.*"

Fet turned plainly to the iye. His eyes were shockingly swollen. "Will. Clodius *died.*"

>*Pause* Will shifted like spiders were running down his back. Was the suit malfunctioning? A cold new layer of excretion now spread its chill all across his tender skin. The chestspike throbbed.

Watchlet flashed. Sagan Smyth would be arriving soon to pick him up for a drink. The Liner Bar hadn't been open till Uranus. Smyth said everyone planned gather there before jump; a possible *Who's Who* of invitees to the Con.

>*Play* Fet was panting. "Clodius is dead, man. He OD'd. On hyde in a Double Halifax dropper zone. Fuck, Will. Clodius was dead a week and nobody—" >*Pause* Clodius the Dead. Double Halifax? Will attempted to hit his head against the bedsphere beam. The Egg, no longer blinking, met him with the softest pillow-down. Will buried face. He had killed Deirdre. Now he had killed Clodius. He managed to type >*pause*

Five minutes later, from the sound of it, Fet's tongue was hanging out.

Poor Fet, Will thought. Without your Master, without that dog-like loyalty counting anymore, what on earth will you do? Will licked doglike down towards his chin, panting now.

"Gina T. was up identifying the body. I'll have more info later, Will. She'll be back today. Just wanted you to know in case you're jumping soon. Will—you did a smart thing. Stay out there." His eyes dropped now. Was Fet still realizing the extent of his loss? Or was he plotting something with Sten already. "But don't let this slow *you* down, Will." He tried a grin. "Just thought you should know, now. Anyway, Endsend."

The Darling furrowed the large forehead, pondering. He held his hands in check behind the back. He had wake-dreamed Cloudius's death a thousand times. But that did not mean the Imp could make it true. And if it did? Certainly the only strategy had ever been to ignore, to insult, to disbelieve in the Imp more at every turn. Even to think this clearly about it was not OK. Yet just now fingers already remembered what his mind knew never to tap out *>The second locket* Goddess, how could he dare to type that out in the open?

>Record Return sent an immediate Emergency to Templeton.

"Fet! Wait!" Will Recorded. "Don't go! There's an important message coming in a minute! Your ears only! Endsend."

Will pocketed his hands. Cold fear fountained fast. He thought quickly. Soon enough the old birdhouse Fet employed as avatar raised its green flag. Will was ready.

>Record Return "Lolas, I am sorry. So sorry. But first, listen. There's a way you can get enough kredit to get off moon, my man. You could set up anywhere. But it's important to take care this right away. It's not even a big thing. But I want you to prepare. Pause this. Get a pen and paper. Good. It's very simple." Will waited a beat. "Good Fet. Now. Back behind the basement sound studio, in Clodius' old deskmodule, you know, the one he thinks no one knows is there? With the green iron sides and the silver top? Well the lock is broken. It's wide open. The leftmost slot holds the *Unsolicited Manuscripts* folder. The leftmost slot. Look for the single locked folder in there. It says RUBY GREENE on it. It's silver, about the size of a tablet. *Get* that, Fet. Wonderful. There's no need to even open it. Just take the silver folder to the Garment Union's demolator on 11th—*not* the GA disposal unit on Cooper. Accept the kredit it yields. I'm telling you, it should give you quite a boost." Will knew he often said "I'm telling you" before he lied. But the fact was the lockets were woven with very precious materials. The transluscent quasicrystal

that held the lock of hair alone would have paid for a trip to Uranus and back. The spun super-silver functioned like a mini particle accelerator for any quantum computer the crystal might be used to trap.

Clodius had no idea. "I'm telling you, Fet," Will continued. "Clodius would have wanted this for you. You won't get paid at all any other way, and I stress that. And it's perfectly legal. Still I don't want to say more here, if you understand me just send a received and get back to me when you're done. I've still got four hours here. Just rewind this if you're confused about anything. Thanks Fet! Good luck! >*And don't tell* And Fet!" Will had just remembered. And don't tell Gina T. about this. Yes she's his friend. But she is *not* part of Templeton. Good man. Good luck! Endsend."

Will had actually prepared it all ahead of time, he realized. Had he glimpsed this during dilation? He had done everything right, despite the shock, despite the whiskey. Or was this a Clodian attempt at a mind-fuck? Some kind of final victory? Did Morandi in fact hope to spoil Will Darling's Uranacon II by means of a flamboyant suicide?

Presently, the bird-house flag lowered.

Fet was off then. Breaking down that locket, presuming Clodius still kept that folder there, would make Fet rich—And then Will would have all for his own that for which kredit could not trade. The Imp, as Will wanted, as Will so deserved, would be the Darling's for evermore.

The fingers drummed:

>*So-called* ASTA
>*S/he moves faster*
>*Than light in alabaster*
>*So-called* ASTA
>*Degenerate rabid*
>*re-relativizing bastard*

Will congratulated himself. He had handled Fet perfectly, under the most questionable circumstances.

The suit was wonderful. He pissed himself, enjoying the immediate sparkling circulatory warmth. Many working Spacers found 22nd century-style costumes adorning a full-body privosuit ridiculous; Will Darling disagreed. It comforted him to sport supermodernist threads in such working order. Meanwhile the privosuit's constant tensions, tickles and probings kept him relatively fit.

He wiped his eyes with his big fingers so he could see himself in the mirror. The long strange trip had actually been good for Will. His posture had improved. He stood taller. His muscles hadn't atrophied yet. His big bones felt anything but brittle.

The doorbell sang. G-dddess. Clodius had insisted Will befriend Smyth. Will tapped his watchlet to mute, absurdly paranoid about the hot spot on his chest. Did it show? He tightened the spux. Was it terrible that he could go about his life normally? Will realized anew this was a timeline where Will Darling no longer operated under the influence of Clodius Morandi and his vision of Templeton O & O. Great Goddess, this death was more profound then Deirdre's demise. He did not want Smyth to know. Will washed his face. No one must know about Clodius.

Hyde! How tacky. It was not Will's fault, after all, that Clodius had preferred not to come to Uranus. Had inner Space fallen so far that Morandi had lost his celebrated ambition just like that? What about all the new healthy designer narcotics? Will had sincerely believed Clodius had given up hyde a long time ago.

The doorbell sang. Smyth!

The Imp was Will's. After the metamorphosis of Uranacon II the Darling would be high priest and Saint Paul of Winnegutt's great legacy, the legacy Will himself had singlehandedly redeemed and preserved. The Outer System would be his to conquer.

Clodius' charm would be missed. Clodius alone, through the years, had always judged Will's work with generosity and enthusiasm. His go-and-get-it attitude would be missed. His cooking!

Will shut down the Not So DOE. He welcomed the Imp. The chestspike did not bother him. The wisest thing (his implants helped him)—so the fairy tale taught mankind in olden times and teaches children to this day—is to meet the forces of the mythical world with cunning and with high spirits.[5] Will cleared entry for Sagan Smyth. Time, he thought, is ruthless. Not me.

---

5. Walter Benjamin, "The Storyteller: Reflections on the Works of Nikolai Leskov," 1936. tr. Hannah Arendt.

II ii

Smyth too wore a spuxedo, and may have been disappointed that Will matched him. Sagan knew Clodius, of course, but Will said nothing.

"How're you liking shipside then, Killer?"

Will grinned, but not at all humorously. He disliked Sagan's slang, more fit for a twenty-year-old nu-spacer than for a short, ever-balding Luna City splogger. Will managed to get him out and on the way, without a first drink.

They took the slow-fall dropper down the round central conduit of the cylindrical liner, with a small group of passengers dressed for casual social interaction. Electromagnetic shipshoes held everyone down. They exited at Level 0, where all the public services of the Liner were located: lounge, pool, restaurants, gym, library and laundry service.

A single bubble-helmeted GA Marine sat dreamily at the security station outside the Lounge. The gangly boy looked all of seventeen. He said nothing when he looked them over. The scanner light winked blue over the Lounge access and Will and Smyth passed into the most generous slice of public space they would see until Miranda.

The Lounge ate up a fifteen percent slice of the liner's deep-dish pie. As tall as the entire module, hardwood, dark and triangular-floored, its corners were softened with intelligent plants and lived-in tidal pools. Spidering tracks led to a classic barrioke curling up to exploit the heights of the room. The view surprised him with the clear generosity, grace and commitment of 1-Gen Space.

These liners were now quite old, Will realized. It wasn't real, it turned out, that world. But how beautiful the illusion must have been. This Liner had been refit and augmented to capitalize on the *Good Fortune*'s sloshing innards. Piping additions enabled the fish, anemones and other aquatic lifeforms in pools. Under foot, the translucent floor blushed with the ruddy warmth of the ship's plant just below.

"Wonderful!" Will exclaimed, now beholding the Great Glass occupying the Lounge's single high wall. How uncanny. He felt as if he stood on a magic carpet, racing the Ice Giant's moons. Stabilized and augmented for optimum visibility, the enormous slabview worked in tandem with Will's implants. A roster of inexplicably proliferating literary characters greeted him, A crescent watery-blue Uranus (actually quite dark here on the backside, boasting a profoundly cold 44 Kelvin at its equator) wore its north-south rings like jaunty strings of diamonds. Will spotted Cordelia out by the π, while Mab trailed a ring of its own down by the floor. Cupid chased Rosalind; Rosalind eclipsed Belinda. Close in the foreground Umbriel showed lights of industry on the darkside. >*Why that's my dainty Ariel* Will's fingers drummed on his chest—and he saw his watchlet was flashing emergency.

>*Templeton O & O* Fet! It was done! Only the Imp now burned in the Darling. *It burned like it would kill him.*

"Will!" Smyth was beckoning from the bar.

Will ignored him and slipped immediately up the barrioke.

He spotted nooks and bars all the way up. On one circular pad, Bob Dylan and his band were tuning their instruments in

Hubbs Field Hologram. "How's it goin'?" Bob actually tipped his hat at Will. He imagined the wild-times when this Lounge's volume had been taken up with sleeping floaters, globules of questionable origin, and the odd flying chicken.

Always a strange sensation, heights, when the mind understood there was no longer up and down. Will runged higher still.

"After all," he remembered Clodius saying. "Why would a singularity need *two* lockets?" He stopped at a quiet hook-stooled nodule. He tapped surface for a whiskey, and was disappointed when two strangers took the nearest stools. Distinguished by enormous round skulls, bald and of palest blue skin, these were re-gens by anyone's definition. They ignored Will and the Great Glass and the Liner all together, passing mutely by and around the bend of the bar. They were holding hands, Will saw.

Well good for Fet then. He's a rich man. The bartender popped him a highball; Will received pong, heart immediately sinking.

It wasn't Fet. Gina T! G-ddess, what if Fet had failed?
>*Pause* Gina looked terrible, duller than ever. How terribly disappointing, but how entirely predictable. Anyone could see from the beginning that Gina had forced herself illegitimately on Clodius, on Templeton, on history itself. Why would she stop now? Intuition told Will than once Clodius was dead Gina T. would inherit his priesthood. She would now never stop proving herself part of a mythical Clodian inner circle she had never seen, that had never really existed. >*Dear me* Will tapped.

"Will," she said. "I'm so sorry." She swallowed. "I have his body. I am going to do this right."

Horrible! Will thought. Poor Clodius.

"I just want you to know. Not Fet, not Sten, not Tschieu. Foark everyone. Parson's City's done for. Will, you were right to leave the Moon."

Will sighed, waiting for the endsend. Poor Gina. After all, he was lucky.

"There's something else," she went on, with an odd spark. "The worst sort of collector happened to come by today. He was here with Sten when I arrived. Fet was away. He'd come from Luna City, touring, seeing what he could pick up cheap in all the going out of business deals around. He had Clode's card. His name was Egge. The E wasn't silent. Anyway, Sten and I sold him everything. I mean the Templeton Major Archives," Here she cleared throat. "Anyhow that's how I got enough kredit to bury Clodius the right way. Sten's been super generous.

"Anyway, so long Will Darling. You know Clode had high hopes for your trip, don't you? In one of our last talks he said he bet you'd write your best book ever on the trip out there. Oh Will, he was changing! Changing back to his old self! Maybe it was the drugs. I don't know what to say… Just it'll be in about seventy two hours from when I send this, if you want to remember and say good-bye then. Endsend."

Gina's little performance raised up in Will a highly varied set of emotions. Had Clodius really said that about his new book? How long ago did he read it?

And where the foark was Fet? The window of communication was closing. >*Foark the foarking Imp*, Will drummed the bar.

>*Bring me Fet the Fool*

The two bald bluemen were waving from around the nodule, Will noted with sudden alarm. They were observing him intently with their huge expressionless eyes. Had they heard him?

>*Little old we? Not at all.*

>*We don't have ears!*

>*But we can read nearby implants enough so as to re-arrange words like these inside them.*

As Will read these words in his own thoughts, literally, they were surrounded by thunderous cartoon-like effects. The two laughed silently, simultaneously showing fanging dental re-grows. They raised their blue-filled ball-glass.

>*We are Bo and Mo* they said.

>*We're psychonautical engineers from Warren's Weirld, Titania, heading for the Con on Miranda*

>*We agree in all things, including being so bold as to force this friendly interruption to remind you there are thought-floaters around*

Will chilled, allowing what he need not remember of the Imp to sink far from his consciousness. "Thank you," he said. "It has been a trying few hours, personally speaking."

>*We appreciate your discretion, Will Darling; and we guarantee ours* Bo and Mo laughed again.

>*The point is, we want to request you please not use your communication device in our presence again*

"I am very sorry!" Will nodded. He switched off his watchlet in their sight. One would always be stepping on someone else's reality concept in the Outer System.

"I am very sorry," he repeated.

They raised their glass.

>*We are sorry for your loss, Will Darling*

Will nodded and turned away. The thought of Clodius brought water to his eyes. Unsure of just what he could think near the brain giants, and just what they could read, Will finished his drink and took his leave.

He beheld again the Great Glass. Uranus System was augmented to show a frozen, glittering promise. So many sparkling moonlets and rocks hugged orbits around that vast crystal ball of water and methane. Water, water, everywhere, plus methane, and more to drink. He had warmth to give them, that old grandfather, so they had discovered, in his very coldness. Watching Uranus System turning, the Darling was struck by a piercing bolt of deepspace euphoria. The still immaculate vista of System U showed a less alien world than today's Old Earth, entirely cut off from System Space perma-veiled by sun-suckers, space junk and the great orbital hives of jacked-in virtual proles. Of course magic-glass made this Uranus view seem more Oceanic than it would naturally appear to the human eye. Someone had designed it that way. It was perhaps even Winnegutt who had influenced this design. Uranus looked very much like hoary Oa here, wreathed with satellite jewels of water worlds all around. Truly love of Winnegutt flowed through Will now as he wondered if this system could be his home.

Until now that "home" had always been imaginary, a metaphor burned for fuel. Will had lived with two women, or three, over the years. He had for a time hoped to be gay, or at least bisexual like Clodius. Orphaned at birth, in the end it was only in the works of a dead author that he would find something like a home.

Deirdre was no more. But Will was moved to realize he still honored her in his every motion. She had not been sacrificed in vein. Winnegutt had really come to Uranus. Through Will (and the Imp). That very flame flickered now up from his heart like a cone of sparkling fire.

Interrupting this state so momentarily close to bliss, the real hope reborn, a real, invisible hand shoved Will from behind. With the force, his shoes came unstuck. He lifted and only just managed to catch himself on his hook. Will swung back down with two fists clenched, feeling quite violated. Smyth hopped back to the track before him. "Easy now, Killer."

Killer? No. This was too much. Will pressed forward, still clenching fists. "Who says Killer?"

Sagan hopped back, emitting a peal of laughter. He kept two hands raised mock-defensively. "Easy, big guy. There's some skiffy folks down a level. Shall we join?"

Will relaxed. It would be hard to conceive of a more degrading nick-name for a genre than "skiffy." Yet he was going to have to put up with this sort of label from now on. He would have to grin and bare his broad teeth at people as abhorrent as Smyth.

"Hey, I saw Jerry O'Perception himself going down the bar-rioke just now," Smyth said. "No doubt about it. White spux and red flow-tie. A real Mark Twain!"

Jerry O? The Co-Author of *Infer No*? Will grudgingly acknowledged real professional excitement. "I don't believe it."

"Come on, then," Smyth said, gesturing to the track down. Why is he so intent on bringing me? Will wondered.

II iii

Freeda Dunworthy looked fine and curious. Deepbrown rugged skin, short-cropped black hair, green eyes as handsome as they were mischievous under arching eyebrows still youthfully surprised—this was a face, Will thought, that has gazed upon a thousand ships. Freeda was a long-time Manx Brand midlister. He didn't read her work. He knew she'd been writing long enough, and predictably enough, to be just about guaranteed Guild membership by now and stints in joints and weirlds all around ths System. But if she wore a holo-halo, Will's APA implant had successfully blocked it out.

Freeda was grinning across at Will as Smyth dumped him off. She lifted a frothy beer. Will kept to Whiskey. With his second barrel nowhere near tapped, it came free for him from the liner spigots.

Freeda Dunworthy leaned forward as Will sat across from her in the little booth. "How does Deirdre?" she asked. "Will she pass through the *Gates of Opal*?"

Will leaned back >*No earthborn passes* he couldn't help tapping his thighs. Will gathered wits. He accepted and lit an LP, showing himself flattered and modestly amused. "Now that is a dangerous question," he said.

Masking his astonishment, he responded with a question of his own. "I won't comment. But I wonder how you've heard that title?"

"I knew Alice Winnegutt," she said, looking him in the eye. She wasn't flirting at all, he realized. "She was a mess. She didn't write anything after *Opal 1*."

"Well, she left extensive notes."

"Are you an academic?"

Will laughed openly at the question, but didn't know how he would prefer to answer. It was true he had several degrees, from the days before Templeton.

"I figured you were one. But you don't quite look it, do you? It is you writing isn't it? Not that Claudius Morandi? I saw him on the WIG. I definitely don't sense him in *Kracyb*."

Did the system at large already take it for granted that works constituting *Opal 2* were not the AEW artifacts Templeton claimed them to be?

He was aware people had been reading *Orygen of Kracyb* in Outer System Space. It was something of a shock that an insider like Freeda Dunworthy would even go so far as to absorb it just to see what the fuss what about. Will was confused. How did she already know about *Gates*? Could the Morandi distribution strategy, 1000 print-copies traded by spacer to spacer hand to hand only, with zero publicity, have paid off so spectacularly?

"For your information," he heard himself saying. "Volume 2, *Gates of Opal*, has just been certified 90 percent plus authentic by her Living Will."

Freeda Dunworthy smiled as if talking to a child. "Nobody believes in Living Wills anymore. Or haven't you heard."

Will smiled as well. "I haven't," he said. After all he himself was a living Will.

She laughed. From afar it would look like they were the best of friends.

Smyth arrived and took Freeda's shoulder; she leaned away. Will felt quite taken aback. Things were developing far more rapidly than he imagined. He thought of the two brain-giants on the service level above. He should never, ever, have put into words what he had recently thought of, ever. Even within the sanctity of the Dear Olde Egg, he did not tap even near to the true story.[6]

Despite Smyth's efforts, Freeda leaned forward, still preoccupied with Will Darling. The Scientifiction Guild was extremely territorial, he knew. It meant something that she was even talking to him. He was after all important enough.

"So we're on a panel together," she said.

---

6. *BRAIN GIANTS KEEP OUT* A. E. Winnegutt died in 2133, committing suicide and not accompanying her belongings to Space. AEW's effects were passed from friend to friend, but though *Opal* was known, no one in New Zed was willing to take responsibility for a has-been space writer's effects. So it was Wilhelm Darling and Clodius Morandi of Templeton O & O claimed them for nothing at an Estate launch in '42.

In retrospect nothing was the only fitting price for the pricelessness they received. Clodius almost sold it all. He was too awed by the historical responsibility to commit. Will Darling pressed. The first time he ever pressed with Clodius. Will was such an extreme fan of Winnegutt by now that he knew far more than Clodius concerning the possible pricelessness of their find.

Will was more than excited when they found the two little lockets in a manila envelope. Who wouldn't be? Each was such a small and tender little water-lily, but so closely matched, even improved on, his imagination of the locket in *Opal*. Popping one open, he saw that it contained a lock of white hair behind a tiny crystal glass.

But he made sure to hide nothing relatively easy to discover. "Remember how Koriander famously wears a locket with hair of Oa herself curled around inside it. She based that description on these two lockets. These once belonged to Nick Wesley! Supposedly they once harbored her singularity pet *ASTA*."

Unknown to Clodius, before *ASTA* A. E. Winnegutt didn't primarily see herself as an author. A freelance New Zed hydro-engineer, she hoped to implement some of the skills she'd learned in the five years of apprenticeship she'd served with marine biologist Nora O. Wesley in Penobscot Bay, Maine. Nora was the first mistress of the original Asta, once an augmented Portuguese Water Dog. Nora died in 2114 and her husband Nick Wesley took the broken-hearted dog to space, where one day it volunteered to lend its name, and "self-branes" (the concept had only recently entered consciousness) to an Artificial Digital Pet that could be owned and used—or traded to Nora Wesley fans to raise kredit for various anti-Concern, pro Spacer activists.

What happened next was certainly disputable, but the story AEW would transmit to posterity was that though the project was understood by Asta and the lab as

Will masticated the ice of his high-ball. "I don't know what you are talking about," he managed to say, after.

"Um. At the Convention on Miranda? Uranacon II. Ever heard of it? The ten year anniversary of the first skiffy meetup off Uranus?"

"A panel!" Will smiled. "Very good!" The emotion was not genuine. He was indeed an invitee to the Con. But he knew nothing about any panels. But it was Clodius who had filled out the forms, requesting no doubt, to be allowed to serve on as many panels as humanly possible. Poor Clodius. He could talk about anything, for ever. If he had been brave enough to actually migrate out from Earthside sway as he claimed he intended, or even just to have come for the damn convention, he would be

---

primarily sentimental, to everyone's surprise, Asta suicided exactly as his self-branes successfully unified with a quantum AI reflecting within the lightcone of its "Birth." ASTA immediately was born—and immediately separated itself into the 341 numbers the Spacers went on to trade.

Nora's widower Nick Wesley took two. He first discovered the truth about his, when he saw writings appear in his own memory that he was very sure he had never absorbed. Stories about Nick and Nora and a little being of light that loved her and stood even now outside her window by the Sea. There were things about her childhood no one should have known. Things Nick knew were true, in some sense, but twisted oddly. When one letter was signed ASTA, Nick wrote back, in the attitude of a master to a dog. Soon the pet obeyed, becoming a very useful, if unhelpfully free-thinking AI, more colleague than assistant, only one step closer to the true present.

A specialist in quantum locks of all sorts, Nick had two extremely expensive armatures constructed to keep the invisible creature, if it indeed existed, locally occupied in a state of "quantum entangled loop stasis." He attracted it when he ordered it to identify the DNA in two locks of his dead wife's hair. It was trapped there still, he claimed. Ruby Greene was Nick and Nora's god-daughter. Ruby and Winnegutt met when they worked for Nora in the oughts. Some ten years later they met again, and fell in love, eventually marrying, at their wedding Nick Wesley surprised them by sending the two lockets as a wedding gift, from location unknown.

"They're yours," his note said. "Both of it."

AEW, who had already started selling some scientifiction on the side, really only as a way to make contacts who might swear for her in Space, wore her locket from that day forward. At first she wasn't sure. But as if just to entertain her, new concepts popped out from "just ahead of the mind"; things that opened up new

alive today. There would be no *Gates of Opal* to capitalize on, but Will had no doubt Clodius would do just fine.

The panel is entitled "The Unknown Winnegutt." Freeda grimaced. "Starring myself, Captain Wawagawa of our very own *Good Fortune*, Manx Brand, and Wilhelm Darling of Templeton O & O."

>*Dear me* Will did not say.

Freeda Dunworthy leaned back, observing carefully. "Notice anything odd about that group?" she asked.

"It should have been Clodius, not me. I am not a panel junky."

"That's not it. The Unknown Winnegutt. One woman, and three men." She scoffed.

---

ways of organizing fictional universes, things that seemed to change all of what writing meant just to type them. She described her "pet" only once publicly, in her last published piece: the Preface to the 2129 New Spacer's edition of *Koriander*. There she claimed *Opal* was conceived and born right there between them, when she first believed it real — that multiverse of only ocean to which ours is attached by water as if fully intact.

She stopped wearing it relatively soon. She came to believe there might be something malevolent, something, as she put it, "improbably deadly" about the pet. "It wants to take all the worlds all away," she wrote. "So only death can live." It's true that the other three hundred and forty numbers in the edition all ended up annoying and disappointing their owners. If the pet had super powers, they did not extend to helping its mistress in her personal life. By the time Winnegutt suicided in '33, non-fiction had broken her hope.

If posterity dis-believed, it did acknowledge she had an AI assistant whose Living Will logarithms she had approved in '29. But of course perhaps they would approve anything that kept the Winnegutt name alive!

AEW let the Imp master her, Will now believed. It had sucked her dry of her own initiative. Ruby had let him read letters where she described her childhood love of what was still the living Oceanic Earth. Winnegutt could complete nothing after *Nordlander Stream*. Reams of unpublished notes and hard-to-discern crossings-out formed the fascinating bulk of the materiel Templeton inherited, the raw material of Will's genius.

Clodius and Will took one locket each, as symbol of their joint management of her posthumous writings (to be ghosted by Will). Will very openly wore his, saying nothing of his belief in its possible powers. It took time, and Will was very patient. But Clodius, as he knew he would, stopped wearing his. AEW had become Will's. He filed it away. As we've seen, Will, who kept track of such things, knew exactly where.

Why Freeda Dunworthy was on the panel would be Will's only question.

>*Exit* "I just forgot! We jump soon? There is some business I must attend to!" On his way down he pushed his way past a group of young nu-spacers of just the sort Will had seen increasingly infecting Templeton events over the last year. Ever since the Elevator went down, herds of these types moved about the System, looking for leisure lays. You found them stranded in all the reaches of the GA.

A bald quasi-fem, face-tattooed, stud-lipped and muscular, pressed right up. Will felt her projecting aggression; he attempted to escape.

"Wilhelm Darling?" The voice immediately held him.

"Who?" He met her glance full on.

The tattoo printed her face like a chessboard. Bald, strong, amped out to fight, hers were the eyes of a thug, an isolato.

>*Exit* Will leaped backwards, just as her arm thrust out. Tiny lightning sparkled? The Darling turned. Experiencing terror, he relied on pure intuition, his own or the Imp's he did not know (both were hot), running, bumping through the tight crowd at access.

LINE 3

MOON MIRANDA

>*"Like Frankenstein's monster Miranda looks like it was pieced together from parts that didn't quite merge properly." That's how the old US National Aeronautics and Space Administration described Miranda back before the Times of Change. Today, smoldering with dreams and novel ideas, unabashedly feminine, bristling against the inherited limits of her past, Moon Miranda is more like the bright-eyed, blonde-haired, world-dreaming authoress of* Frankenstein, *than its Monster*

>*True, her style is somewhat Gothic and irregular, but by no means might her charms be deemed imperfect. Roughly once a week at Verona Rupes, where artificial river Mellynthe pours over the highest cliffs in the System and Uranus is aligned with Sol full aft—Miranda dons her famous Sun-Dogs, the so-called "Ice Giant's Garments of High-Water Falls"*

>*Generally known as the ninth wonder of the worlds, hoppies*

>*See you there* SMYTH'S MYTHS : 22–01–2145–16 MOON MIRANDA

III i

Waiting in line for Arrivals & Decontamination, Maudeleine de Lions almost lip-synched as she listened to Mrs. Z. She knew all those words by heart. They brought back old feelings.

> Imagine a dark sphere that is all the time and space in the universe. Second time is the entire surface of this anti-sphere reflected backwards. Part of us, the unconscious part, can glimpse the forms and ideas reflected on the hollow shell we imagine as the edge of our universe. And it's true. Here an Artificial Intelligence can perceive any stream, and any stream within a stream, but only after the fact. A machine can not read the future. Only human writing observes what the future may be, just as in politics only direct human action proves an idea...

She was under a secret contract with Mulligatawny City's new tablet organ, *Mulligatawny Blues*, investigating rumours of Marena Zitzko's possible presence on Miranda and, look at her, now she was on Miranda itself. Maudie knew this much: Marena Zitzko would not be on Miranda. If by some slim possibility Mrs. Z had not died or regenerated, if she had survived the ten plus years of her disappearance, she would certainly not hide out in such a small, vulnerable community of radical feminist spacers as

Miranda. Miranda was directly corded to the Global Authority's Uranus Station, equipped with a troop of GA Marines. What free Spacer would suffer the hard work of sheltering her now? When one of the isolatos who destroyed Earth Station, and the C. Clarke Elevator with it, named Zitzko as a conscious enabler of that destruction, and for the most scandalous of personal (heterosexual) reasons, her reputation among feminauts was destroyed. Most agreed that Zitzko was actually apprehended at Second Mars Station in '34, turned in by her own disillusioned comrades who since made sure nonetheless to erase their names from history. Spacer culture very much survived on rumour; there were always stories crossing back and forth across the System as to Zitzko's survival. Nothing real had ever come of any one of them.

This was a quixotic assignment at best. But Maudie had to admit, even stuck in a customs queue on Uranus Station, this job had brought things alive again for her. She felt like a Spacer again.

The single legitimate route onto Moon Miranda was mirrored, windowless, rectangular, and of the most rugged utilitarian esthetics. It looked and smelled very much like it could soon be converted into an grain hauler; but the avocado trees and the tiny, absurd gravity—exactly enough to keep up up and down down, and not a measurement more—already gave everything a magical, fairy-like quality. She went helmet-less, remembering almost nothing from her first visit here over ten years ago, when such security would not have been the case. In the two-way mirror above the guard station, she stood out against the motley spacers from the sleeper-stacks as one of the oldest, but only on second glance. Only if you saw that time-ravaged face up close would you get a sense of the real challenge Maudie posed to your authority.

Maudie's short short bangs were cut young and simple, dyed a popping aqua-blue. Let the GA authorities have time to prepare; a 1-Gen feminaut was arriving. She'd chosen a black one-piece over her gold privosuit, and big spaceboots that would keep her pinned from leaping unexpectedly about. She wore her shadescreens. She was coming here undercover, as a potential colonist. She believed she looked as if she could work, contribute. Which she could. Maudie was still robust after the year on Europa among the Leakfixers, as a resident storyteller. That experience had helped her through the various Spacer caricatures to which she'd almost succumbed: the Luna City Lifer, the Moonmaid, the Wife-who-once-was. Only the Lyonesse survived.

Maudie had survived this far alone in the System of Sol. She wasn't afraid to show it. The early days of Space were easy for no one. In the late 2120s life, for whatever reason, Maudie had embraced the Spacer's Sixth: The Right of Re-Generation. She entered a Spacer-run experimental re-gen unit, The Orangerie, at a now-unknown date. Keeping only a character she had played in a darkside weirld, the Lyonesse, Maudie emerged in 2133 with a new body, name and past, one her previous, now-forgotten self had apparently worked hard to create for her. Née Maude-Lynne MacScallion, she found herself the foster-daughter of darkside Chinese miners whose lives of industrial drudgery were only relieved by a love of the culture of Scotland. Her parents were poor and unsophisticated, no doubt about it. She hadn't spoken to them in years. But they seemed to have cherished and respected her. Healthy space babies in those days (half a century ago) got a free ride to earth, so their bones could grow properly. Maude-Lynne was sent down the Elevator, and flown to New Zed, where something resembling Scottish culture may have survived. Indeed a happy enough childhood was spent in that surviving outpost of pre-Collapse western culture. Maudie still kept something of Sister Agnes, her tutor and best friend of those days, in the locket around her neck.

Maudie rode the elevator up again in '32 with a local free-lance executive she'd married just for that ride. She divorced him on Luna Station, keeping his name, de Lions, and the seven crates of her own books and belongings she'd forced him to bring up with his things. Now and forever a free Spacer, she treated de Lions rather cruelly. He was Concern bound. She never looked back.

"Leave the maps to those who would carve up the universe," said Mrs. Z in the Danish Domes. "Let them sell their maps away. We no longer describe their illusions; we build any route we make. We stand in a world so fragile that every minute—this minute—might be our last. We *make* our days. We *invent* our indistinguishable now from the survival of our friends and fellow creatures on whom we depend for every single thing that can ever be. There is not one among us today who is not here because others were willing to give their lives for us first. On Space lives change, selves re-define to survive. Space *demands* change. We shall scrawl upon the face of second time our own initials, tell History to its face WE ARE HERE."

Today in 2145, researching Zitzko and those first days of Spacer Consciousness made the Outer System seem small, barely alive. Yet here on Moon Miranda Maudie certainly, even surprisingly, recognized the living revolution, the regenerating promise of space. Among the officials visible at Customs & Decontamination were white-suited Miranda Regulars, green sundogz imaged on their breasts, armed municipal officers of Verona Polis. The bubble-helmeted GA Marines also present were in a state of tension. Two were arguing with Regular now and holding up progress in the line. Maudie did not wonder, as she turned the volume up, that those young regulars would be ready to die for the cause. Despite the counter-revolution of aging, wherein Maudie had long learned to preserve herself at the easiest, most sensible cost, Zitzko's Space was a dream a rich part of her still believed in. Out here it was old news. The white-suited Miranda Regulars were already a professionalized, post-revolutionary organization. Women and men with jobs, roles to play in their community, they were very much the GA's equals, she saw, clearly feeling themselves entitled to their authority.

There was a desire that many of us who came to space shared but rarely spoke about. What was the nature of this desire? Certainly we never defined it. It was not merely to escape. For we had escaped, and the desire remained. And as we lived, as we forced life out of the rocks and rays available to the bold, a hard-won code emerged by which we could begin to make rational the limits of that desire. We are ready to inscribe our own code onto the mechanism of History. We 3000 united list these rights, these Spacer's Seven:

#1. The Right to Reason. Sentimentalists? Romantics? Neither. We live our lives only according to principles of practical sense. In pursuit of this "Right to Reason" we reject all judicial authority but our own and that of our neighbors— pending Bender's Test of the True Stranger. *There was laughter here from the mob, and it always pleased Maudie to hear it, the true fusion of Spacer consciousness Zitzko represented at that time. Earth herself hung brave in the sky behind her. Under that spectacular Dome the boiling diaspora was one single starchild in the Engineering Union Representative's hands.*

#2. The Right to Roost. The Right to Roast we call it. [much laughter]. We reject the right of the Global Authority to pluck us out of any hole we have worked to occupy. Why are the Mars Flats not yet settled as their planners intended? Because we have not built them! [Cheers here, rousing cheers.]

#3. The Right to Roam. As no Spacer is bound to leave, no Spacer is bound to stay. Our colonies, our bodies and our minds travel unfettered. We Spacers shall grapple with what, whom, where and when we please, in our efforts to get where we choose…

The Right to Roam was one of the most contested of the Seven, for it suggested a world where no colony would be free from re-colonization. Zitzko went to great lengths to defend the general here. *We claim rights of admittance to any visitable world where work for us is wanted or we can make our own work pay.* As Zitzko had predicted after a first and necessary boom, few Spacers claimed the Spacer's Third. But it was in that fine spirit that she herself expected to be granted visiting asylum in Verona Polis. In those crowding about her in the Arrivals tube, Maudie knew, were all sorts of Spacers on the run.

As Maudie's own history could testify, the post-economy of System Space opened up many of the advantages previously only granted to the Earthside elite and to the casual Spacer. Extended life, radical bio- and/or psycho-engineering with zero limits on copyright came in simple exchange for honest service. Even relative privacy, as long as one did not directly threaten the local status quo, was now a reality. Most successful Outer System habitats depended on local invention and advanced research along singularly specific and accidental lines peculiar to their local accidental environment. On moons like Miranda the big problems—dust, energy, atmosphere, radiation—had been over-come by a multitude of ingenious new local inventions, many of which were only partially understood by those off-world. Rare metals usually settled as the currency, with stocks divided and maintained by mining guilds, supporting the kredit system at large with direct hard value. GA oversight, under such conditions, proved an impediment to smooth survival.

As Earth continued to deteriorate and the GA lost its inner coherence, its Spacer-made 1-Gen architecture (most of it built by the 3000 themselves) still functioned. The mirror-buoys, beam satellites and AI's still supported convenient inter-System travel and settlements as far out as Neptune. The latest generation of AI's, the so-called "Extraordinaires," had emerged out of orbital gaming weirlds, and apparently showed clear sympathy for to radical Spacer politics.

Most of the System believed it was sexual insecurity that brought down Marena Zitzko. As a sex writer herself (Maudie often did it for a living), she could recognize when a story wasn't somehow real. Doubtless it was because of her writing (*Adventures of Lyonesse*) that Mr. Egge of *Mulligatawny Blues* sought out Maudeleine de Lions to begin with. He probably believed she had sex contacts on Miranda. Unfortunately Maudie was among that minority who deemed it likely the entire scandal was a necessary, convenient fiction—concocted by one of various possible parties. There had of course already been rumors about the amorous activities of Marena Zitzko before the 2130s. But Maudie had studied Marena Zitzko more than most over the years. She had the distinct impression Mrs. Z. was a mainstream sort of woman. Smoldering, some said, very good looking in a Russian sort of way, but essentially vanilla. It was odd how readily everyone believed her capable of the things ascribed to her later. There was a perverted quality to Zitzko's prose, certainly. That's why people believed the story. Often, at its most metaphoric, it displayed an anal intensity.

> We awaken to find ourselves crushed in mud. Beneath an enormous slab. Pinned by slab. In mud. Aware of slab. In mud, we are told of the skies beyond slab, of the open space and endless meadows and the true bounty everywhere surrounding slab. In mud. Earthside they struggle everyday. In mud. Expending more energy than is theirs to spend, they lift slab a nudge: a few of us escape. Slab falls and flattens them deeper in mud.
>
> But not you, Spacer. Slab was always your only inheri-

tance. That same enormous mass of history holding all of us fixed, flattened to its immediate imprint? In space it weighs nothing. Mud? You *breathe* mud: *literally* if you must. Forced to only reason you have long become worm. Accepting only fate, you burrowed down even deeper in the mudpacked slime. With the mud so compacted by the slab's great weight, it's hard work. Hard and dirty work. In the meantime, since others are about, you establish a hive. Look here; others are helping you dig your hole. How narrow, filthy and deep will it go? How wide, immaculate and close upon you is slab? Space *is* slab, Spacer. We very much recommend you start digging.

Maudie, who had experienced things like those outlined in the scandal in her day, was not convinced. In fact it had always made sense to Maudie that Zitzko would have created these rumors herself, that she herself forced the mayhem of that scandal. How else really to force the break? What better way to abdicate and disappear than cloaked in shame?

She planned in fact to make this idea the centre of the piece she wrote on Miranda. She hadn't told Mr. Egge. Editors didn't like to know one's mind was already made up. When it was finally Maudeleine De Lions' turn to pass through Customs & Decontamination, two hunky male GA Marines and an official from Verona Polis, a male, a pimply youth all of seventeen, long-boned and limber, checked her tags. "You're Welcome to a Free Miranda," said the boy. "But there's been a change with your destination."

Maudie stood firm. "Is there a problem?"

"You're admitted, sure enough. Seems like your accommodation is no longer available, is all. There's a party waiting for you outside. If you'll just pass through."

Maudie's heart sank. "My luggage contains items of great personal value—"

"I said you're through." The Miranda Regular had moved on.

Maudie stepped through the cleanser. For a moment she had the feeling of being outdoors, New Zed—had she remembered that?—with the grand trees and the happy scudding clouds, and the river down below curling like a snake of gold. But it was down a ramp of melted moonrock she stepped. No shellac or coating came between Maudie's boots and Miranda's ancient surface. The tube-glass was so clear that for a moment it seemed she was out of doors on the surface of a white crested, rocky ball, gleaming with signs of habitation and warmth. The open cranny was domed with a wide generosity. Half-blue Uranus occupied a great swath of the black, spangled Milky Way above, but next to Jupiter from where she'd come, it seemed gentle and feminine. This dome hubbed a number of track-tubes, curving into the rock-ice surface in seemingly haphazard directions. There was a café, veritable trees, pools in some parts. Greenery was all about, roses predominating. The air was moist, rich, cool and clean. There were bees! The whole space smelled like flowers, like life. Maudie smiled at strangers, giddy with the fairy feel of the gravity in her toes. She believed she remembered this spot from her last visit. But it seemed larger now, more bustling with life.

"Maudeleine?"

She had noticed the Regular from afar, but had thought her a man. Utility-belted, vaping casually, hands in pockets of her scruffy white suit, eye more carefully on the passing scene than might at first appear, she had the casual confidence of a long-time lawperson. She recognized Maudie, however, and now approached with a big grin. Perhaps a fan; who knew? Something familiarly out of the ordinary caught Maudie's eye, in that quick and darkly humourous glance. This was a classic working spacer. Helmet hanging lazily askew, hair a buzz-cropped grey, stocky and strong, she focused on Maudie with apparently genuine good will. Though in Parson's Crater or places like that you wouldn't think twice about the sight of such a lesbian, here you did. Twice positively. "Sorry for the bother," the Regular said.

"There's been a change in accommodations. We'll get your luggage and I'll take you to your place. I'm Morrigan."

"I'm Maudie," she answered, trusting a new friend immediately, as you learned to do in space. Maudie knew it was foolish, even something to be embarrassed by, but somehow as a first meeting of System U, she found the sudden coming of Morrigan into her life, now leading her as if she was a person of importance to a track-tube actually powered by those walking along it, presently to the customs module, and there around and past the front of the line (it only took a nod from her), especially moving.

III ii

From above Miranda appeared like a battered cream-cake long frozen into an icy meringue. Scratched with finger-nailed scarfs, hedge-hogged by rugged outgrips, the night-bound white world sparkled with the brilliance of golden settlements, promising warmth and comfort carved out of choppy highly variable matter. From inside, it was all far grander. Pressed close to Morrigan in a Wheeler booth, Maudie accelerated inside the curving groove running around Prospero's Crater to Verona Polis. She looked out on high walls of stone encased with giant frozen flows. Greenery and apparent parks flashed by behind bubble-poured ice. Miranda's aquaponics were clearly the model of current possibility. The colony had changed much since Maudie's first visit, the place had become one with its settled moon.

Crossing Prospero Crater entirely, the main artery to Verona Polis ran under the stars. Sunlight flickered orange on the tops of the mountains. In 2129, when Maudie had last visited Miranda, piracy and lawlessness against Concern or GA interests had been converging into real political activism.[7] The Wheeler stopped to

---

7. Cross-union activists "Prospero's Daughters" struck most famously in '32 when they held six-hundred gravity well water-haulers past schedule in sympathy with the aborted Danish Domes rising on Luna.

exchange passengers with an Arden Corona express. Maudie was impressed. Things had clearly changed. An easy sense of minding-one's-own business, and being anonymous now prevailed. Locals must have made great strides in inter-clade collaboration. Glimpsing the depth of the colony's cohesion, the idea of Zitzko hiding out here seemed no longer quite such a ridiculous idea. With the GA currently expelled to the Station, traffic passing to and fro the Anchor toward Arden and Elsinore and beyond, she realized Miranda was already a place of freedoms. She felt the presence of mystery, human mystery in a way that seemed new to her and very old at the same time.

Morrigan beside her was accessing WIG via her glasses. Maudie listened again to Mrs. Zitzko as she approached that city founded by women.[8]

> Capitalism, she asks. How could so many have been so deluded for so long? Those days have ended. For today Earth is Space and in Space only survival is possible. Space has revealed this invisible all-consuming commitment we have to survive, to live, made this drive newly visible. Every moment the Spacer lives inscribes it's possible survival into the void. Outside of that life, beyond it everything is always equally dangerous, equally vulnerable, equally un-real. The free spacer is isolate, alone. *The Isolato's Tale* will not be written in the usual manner. She will define; but she will not rest on definition…

Was Morrigan isolate, alone? She was apparently a Regular of some rank. She looked into the world in her glasses in silence,

---

8. Since the famous first pictures snapped by brave Voyager 2 back in 1986, Miranda has had a special hold on the female imagination. Most of the workers who volunteered to build the Station and stay were female—in those days more easily able re-bone for long-term low gravity than birth-males.

apparently tracing a developing situation in her screen. Maudie couldn't say. She appreciated the time to think. And she appreciated the human warmth beside her. It felt like "night" on Miranda, even when you saw the sun. As the car came across a swell, that molten screwhead was now visible in the otherwise black sky. But approaching the Wall the Wheeler entered a tunnel and the first entrance to the city was obscured.

So Maudie stepped out at Verona Polis Central, taking it all in for the second time. Morrigan was seeing to her crate. 313 books weighed nothing here. With the help of a near-by regular, a young adolescent, they maneuvered it dextrously. The sun gave about as much light as a full moon over New Zed, Maudie was thinking, stepping so lightly onto a broad soft sticker track, feeling like she might easily fly faerie-like off into the cold damp air. They were under the Great Mission Hole Dome, the open air market-place just below the pedestriotrack to the cliffs of the Polis proper. The dometop was clear, presumably mostly water, about 600 meters across, two hundred high. The Miranda you could see below looked purple and electric. The rock walls ringing round were caved with various businesses. Maudie was taken aback by the number of people about, most of them visored down, even bare-headed or hooded. There were all sorts of bodily experiments on view, but a healthy minority of normals as well. Other women with uniforms similar to Morrigan's, stood about visibly maintaining order. "It all seems rather militant," Maudie observed.

"There's not usually so many Regulars around," Morrigan said. "Things are coming to a head right now with the GA. Things are a bit jumpy. That's one reason Marjorie wants you put away."

Put away? Maudie didn't bother protesting her rugged escort's continued attention to her needs. Morrigan directed the crate along, leading to the boarding point for a railtrain up the side of the rise—giving Maudie the available seat, while keeping one eye out on everything occurring around them at the same time.

"Where are you taking me, exactly!?" Maudie said through the sudden racket of the tinny rail-car.

"The Committee for System Relations has an empty ad-apt. Marjorie Baumgarten—" Morrigan stopped, for absolutely no reason—their eyes meeting. "It's a nice place," Morrigan said, breaking the curious spell. Maudie was surprised again at the attention from Marjorie. Why should anyone go to such extent providing for Maudeleine de Lions? It didn't make sense. Maudie wore her helmet and sat in silence, riding up the backside of Verona Polis to Miranda Falls.

Under a motherwide Uranus directly overhead, the now otherwise empty car crept along a steaming fissure of the River Mellynthe to avoid the Polis center, through a small exposed canyon right up at the edge of the cliffs. The stopped in Verona Rupes, the exclusive neighborhood just above the Polis proper. Energy and omniradiated gardens warmed all the dark encaverned bio-nodes around. Ice paneled the local architecture on a canyon floor, rimmed with bars, shops and healthy vegetation.

Signs said: BEWARE. SOME TRACKS EXPOSED.

The first thing Maudie saw when Morrigan helped her off the railcar was a little print shop carved into a fern-buried hill just across the track. Outside hung up latest rags from the System at Large. Through the tight entranceway she glimpsed a warm, booklined interior. *Helio's* said the sign on the door. *Open for all trade.* The face of a man of real age, and a beard long and white as snow to prove it, looked out at her from its rounded door-window. The Lyonesse, who knew enough about time and space never to let such a glance pass, stopped in her tracks. She knew those eyes.

"This way, … Ser de Lions."

Already far ahead, Morrigan waved with some impatience. Was she putting Maudie away? It felt that way. Looking back, she saw the printshop door was now already shuttering, the rags taken in; those eyes were gone.

"Call me Maudeleine. Or Maudie."

Despite her uncertainties, she felt alive and real stepping up through the surprisingly rugged path, and very glad of her boots.

Verona Rupes ringed an ice-topped hole right up against the backside of the famous cliffs. They entered a tunneled lane leading to that side that faced back toward the Polis. Here you could open visor. Moist stone walls and moss-rich caverns were omniradiated by effect of the local waterways. Omniradiation, that first major discovery of an AI, was one element in the change that had come over Miranda in general. In the walkway the air was kept moving and dry by wizardry she also could only imagine. It was all so very fresh. Through a private gate, she found a bamboo bungalow set atop a little waterfall, and a glistening radiated pond, all capped and air-filled.

After the entranceway with appropriate locks and pressure gates, they entered partially floored storage shed containing a spiral stairway leading to the ad-apt proper above. Maudie almost floated up to the extravagant quarters, all magic-glassed to look out over Verona Polis sparkling below. Inside she found a shower nook, a sweetwater spring, a clean and fluffy hammock, a heat grill, and a holo-projecting WIG node.

"I can't believe this place," she said to Morrigan. "I haven't had quarters like this for a long time. Is this typical Miranda fare?"

Morrigan turned her head sideways and back. "About 2/3 our population sleep in industrial GA bedspheres hive-stacked underground. This one belongs to a Committee."

"But why give it to me?"

"I'm really just doing Marjorie a favor, Maudeleine. I'm sure she'll explain everything when you two talk."

"Sorry," Maudie said. "I mean thanks so much." She realized now it wasn't Morrigan's problem. Morrigan didn't seem the type to join a committee; chances were she was Marjorie's lover, just a hired hand.

Morrigan looked. "You OK?"

"It's just I'm a bit perplexed. Your meeting me, that's so generous. My being given this bungalow. Marjorie hadn't given me the impression she would help me at all, beyond getting me on a panel at the con. Can I talk to her?"

"Look. She's just doing you a favor. She only asked that you stay in until you hear from Marjorie."

Their eyes met. Stupidly, Maudie trusted her. Morrigan smiled and saluted. "Good-bye! For now!"

Damn it, Maudie thought, something was really going on. Something secret. Through the one way magic-glass, she saw Morrigan emerge and speak to the other Regular with new seriousness. The youngster hurried to follow as Morrigan, or so it appeared to Maudie, disappeared around the lane to attend to matters of great importance she must have been putting off by dealing with Maudie.

Alone! She called her dead around her, threw down her things and darkened the red-lit space. She bathed with salts under the flowing hot-spring bubbling out of the moonrock. After, she took the hammock with only a lunar silica blanket to cover her.

Peonies peaked up along the crest of the protecting outcrop below her garden! Maudeleine felt at ease in these magical quarters. The view of Verona Polis was certainly a pleasant one. It didn't look like a city under threat. Earth was insane; earth was collapsing, and every day inner space went one day backwards in time. But out here, beyond reach of the Concerns' deathlike claw, the colony survived, warm with life and potential.

Maudie hooked her implants into the local system and took WIG for the first time since leaving System J. She let the regards and factoids stroll along and inside her screen. An Emergency blinker from EGGE0079, no other identifiers attached, stood out. Emergency? Mr. Egge turned her off, frankly. But first, here was Marjorie Baumgarten elongating the den infoball in an unfortunate pantsuit.

Maudie opened the live chat.

Marjorie was a big woman. Maudie remembered. But she looked radiant with strength and health, her rarely expressive unexpectedly alive with excitement. "Maudeleine! It's so wonderful to see you. How are you? You look incredible!"

"Marjorie! Wow! This place. What am I doing here?"

She laughed "I'm sorry for the confusion Maudie. It's a very critical time on Miranda. Please don't worry."

Marjorie looked and acted very differently than Maudie had expected. She came off extremely sympathetic, but, like Morrigan, preoccupied with events she presumed Maudie would not understand. "Certainly you're very tired. Rest, Maudie. Bathe. There's a full bar. Do you like theater?"

"Theater?"

"We have the nicest weirld stage outside of Jupiter, no doubt about it. The Falls Theater. *Pericles* opens tonight! We have tickets! What do you think about that?"

"Great!" The thought of a theater really cheered Maudie up. "But the fact is I don't need rest. I slept most of the way out here! My limbs need to move. I was thinking a gym—"

"Work out there. I'll pick you up in a mere seven hours. I promise I'll fill you in then. Till then, I'm sorry, Maudie but please understand. There are dangerous events afoot today. I must give you one clear command."

"Command?"

"Thank you. Thank you, for coming, Maudeleine. *But stay put until tonight.* Bye till then! Thank you and good-bye Endsend."

The infoball abruptly whisked away.

Maudie felt peculiarly calm. *Pericles* was an awkward play, she'd always thought. A bunch of special effects scenes lumped together, each one swallowing the last.

She rose and looked out on the green and misty "fjord" her adapt commanded. She had never really settled down since leaving the Orangerie. For more than a decade she had moved from bedsphere to bedsphere, from crater to crater, from moon to moon in search of some slot between worlds where she might safely roost. Since New Zed really, she hadn't had this feeling, this odd and really inexplicable sense that all the way out and off Uranus she was in fact somewhere close to home. And now it was all starting to look like some kind of tease.

In fact she had not agreed to Marjorie's arrangement. The Lyonesse obeyed no command. She would consider whether or not she would return here before theater later. But first, Mr. Egge.

"Egge, of course," said that instantly familiar voice, as she downloaded the Emergency blinker, externally over info-ball.

She remembered her first discomfort on meeting the constantly sweating man on Europa. Despite his bell-shaped softness and the entirely harmless vibe he eventually projected from that visible flab, Maudie had thought him a rapist or mugger when he first approached her.

She remembered the shockingly limp handshake the bell-shaped man had offered when they'd met, the cold, gelid sweaty digits. He explained he was acting special editor for *Mulligatawny Blues*, a harmless-enough publishing outfit promoting the polytheistic settlement of Space, for whom Maudie had written a good deal of goddess porn over the years. "You've heard rumors that Mrs. Zitzko is alive somewhere off Uranus?"

She hadn't heard them, in fact. "Of course it's best you go undercover," he said. "Do you think you could get yourself invited to the scientifiction convention if we paid your way?"

"I might have some contacts." She had not named them. Mr. Egge gave her the creeps, no doubt about it. But he also gave her free passage to Moon Miranda. Her distaste returned now, with sight of that broad white head, and half open gleaming lipped mouth. He seemed so much uglier over ball.

"Slovenly bitch," the Egge head hissed bizarrely, with silky contempt. "You've thought to remove my tracker from your belongings. You think to escape me? Very, very stupid of you, animal. Oh yes, Madeleinya Vladimivich, yes indeed."

Maudie stood up. Now what off Earth was this?

As if responding to her reaction with mockery, the pink recording screwed up its face. Egge adopted an alien, high-pitched imperfectly-rendered old woman's toothless Scottish brogue—"Ah… You foind awie frum oos, fearey farlin' farlin' fear—"

The face immediately returned to its ordinary, slack a-normality. "You made a big mistake receiving this pong, dirty, filthy, dead pig. I will *eat* you myself, *dorogoya*. I will *shit* you out." Egge looked out upon Maudie as if he really could see her. Scarlet edged the white balls of his meaty eyes—the Infoball tucked away as she ended the pong and erased the horrid bouncer for all time.

What was Egge, really? She wondered anew, with fear. Why hadn't she researched him at all? Exactly what were his interests in Zitzko?

The new physiological sensations she'd been feeling since landing, the friendly, attractive Morrigan, this rich person's ad-apt and the false sense of easy life it promised, all fell into confusion and chaos. It wasn't until Maudie had drunk long of clear and crystal water, exited the quarters and gone down to expect and lock her crate, that she vividly remembered Morrigan's deft handling of her things at Miranda Station. Those repeated covert glances, as if of secret information attempting and failing to pass between them. Had Morrigan somehow removed Egge's tag?

Unfortunately once she'd received his pong, very likely Egge would know exactly where she was. He might well have agents on Miranda. If it really was Egge, and even really if it was not, if it was someone out to manipulate her psychologically, it was crystal clear that it would be best to change locations immediately. Well, there was one place she might find closer conduit to that sense of home and promise so palpably real in her body.

Maudie closed her eyes and touched her locket. "Sister Agnes," she prayed. "I needed passage to this place. But I'm done with Egge. I swear."

After a pause of some silent minutes, she rose quickly and unpacked her favorite black utility suit. With privos one needed nothing else. It framed her face, made fast vacuum, and could mask her in seconds if necessary. It de-sexed her. Dangerous or not, her new freedom pleased her. A Spacer arriving explored.

II iv

Back in the DOE during the quarantine surrounding first-blast, Will Darling brooded, fretfully. He had certainly hoped to spark some sort of post-feminist backlash from his work with *Gates*, but assassination? It wasn't even out yet and the checker-faced post-sexual had gone for him. There was no doubt about it. If he hadn't been set into a state of hyper-awareness by the interview with Freeda Dunworthy, he might have suffered castration or worse. Goddess, what would they do when they knew Deirdre was dead. Even the Egg felt penetrated. A cold sweat tickled down from his burning chestspike.

Perhaps they did know. Freeda had used the phrase "*Gates of Opal.*" Someone could have intercepted what he sent to Clodius. On board, only the ship's Captain would have the authority. Will remembered that The *Good-Fortune*'s Captain, E. T. Wawagawa, was on the Winnegutt panel.

Will called up URANACON II. Though during jump WIG was just a ship-bound copy of a spectrum of an out-of-date Uranus broadcast, the site was most likely one of those the ship's computer intentionally carried since so many of its passengers were invitees. But no—he couldn't call it.

>*URANACON II* Skiffy preferred Roman numerals, idiotically.

Will's implants handled the sign-on. The Egg opened into a cheaply-designed boardroom temporarily walled into a cave by moveable sheets of omni-board. Childish puns were hand-written in colored erasable ink: *Look Twice Before You Leech* and *I'm with Cupid*.

Will noted a single relax, a few tables bearing megazines, and unimaginative potted cacti. At the other end of the room he saw an empty welcoming counter. As he moved his generic avatar, he noted a second visitor (someone also logging on from the *Good-Fortune*) seated at a round table over by the megazine rack. It was an old custom avatar: a wispy-wiigged 18th century-style male with white buttoned up vest, long white socks and buckled white shoes and red cravat was tapping on the table with scribegloves. Bubbles of text rose off the table before Will's eyes:

>*THE POWER IS DISCREET. WATER IN EFFECT BECOMES A CRUEL DEITY. PURPOSEFULLY, SHOCKINGLY SPIRITED. WHY? THE VERY QUESTION DEMANDS A RE-EVALUATION OF THE BOOK AS A WHOLE AS MESSAGE IN THE BOTTLE. FAR FROM A CAPITULATION, IN MOORE THIS IS A DECLARATION OF INDEPENDENCE FOR WATERS*

>*DIGITAL TEXT ABSORPTION MUST BE UNDERSTOOD AS POST-LITERARY. IN THE CONTEXT OF PUBLISHING, ESPECIALLY IN THE CONTEXT OF SELF-PUBLISHING IN THIS ERA OF RANGED SPACEFLIGHT, ONLY WATER CAN SUPPORT INFORMATION WITH GUARANTEED ANTI-FASCIST DISPERSAL POTENTIAL*

>*MOORE WAS AN AMERICAN, FRIENDS. HE ABSORBED HIS H20 VIA THE U.S. DECLARATION ITSELF. FACT: THE WORK OF PRINTERS "SOLEMNLY PUBLISHING," LITERALLY PASTING THEIR "SHOT HEARD ROUND THE WORLD" LESS THAN A CENTIMETER REMOVED FROM THE REAL WALLS WAS INTERLINKED TO ALL THE CAPITALS OF THE*

NATIONS VIA WORKS OF WATERS. WATER THAT SPREAD THOSE JAMS.
ALL-TEXT, ALL-TIME? NOT IN THE RIPTIDE OF THE SCOTTISH
ENLIGHTENMENT THANK YOU MUCHLY, SAYS MILTON MOORE. I'VE
GOT MIND ON MY WATER AND MY WATER ON MY MIND

Who still argued about Milton Moore? The Water-weirld on the Fields of Mars had frozen up and died. Will approached the empty reception counte. Here a single rolodex spun as stopped exactly as he arrived, a file poking out.

>*Darling Wilhelm* Sliding out his folder, a minatory image was rudely stamped on the front. A Smiling Death's Head.

"Dear me," Will said. The diamond-teeth were stuck with glittering letters:

wIlLiulm DahRling BeWAre.

Was this supposd to amuse? In light of Clodius the Dead, he found it in poor taste. But he ignored it, now looking at his convention schedule. He certainly hoped there wouldn't be much more for him than the Winnegutt panel.

But it if he understood the almost nonsensical 3d formatting correctly, Will was listed as participating on an extraordinary amount of panels. Eleven! This was a highly unlikely number of appearances for a first-timer at a Con. He scanned the names of the panels. Was this schedule real? Or hacked? Certainly Freeda Dunworthy's attitude, the veiled hostility and suspicion could be better explained by his being on thirteen panels. Clearly that's why she'd looked him up.

Intuition told him that the schedule was real. Clodius had expressed interest in everything, and whoever organized the convention needed to fill out a number of panels that interested no one else. It almost certainly was the work of a low-grade AI.

DARLING, WILHELM

DAY I

VII hours. Introductory ceremonies. Gorf.

VIII hours. Hatred of Plumbing.

IX hours. Dysto-Capitalist Futures Past.

X hours. Octavia Butler Memorial Panel, chair.

XI hours. Kaffeeklatsch.

XIV hours. Writing in Zero G: Do's and Don'ts.

DAY II

IX hours. Malist Futures Past.

XI hours. And what About Venus?

XIC hours. Moby-Nemo: Re-assessing Vernville as scientifiction.

XVI hours. The Fiction of Asimov.

XVIII hours. Kaffeeklatsch.

IXX hours. The Unknown Winnegutt.

Those would be two packed days. As he looked more closely, E. T. Wawawaga's name kept popping up as well on the same panels. Will reflected that despite the fact ETW hadn't written or published anything of importance in more than a decade, his gentlemanly demeanor, state of the art ship, and immense network of connections seemed to have gotten him nearly as many panels as Will. Dysto-Capitalism Futures Past? Will supposed his history with Templeton, an experiment in something close to what those words signified, qualified him to at least comment ironically on the subject. On this panel, also Jerry O'Perception! Genuine excitement flooded Will Darling as discovered there was another day. Two more panels! Thirteen!

XIII hours. Chrononautics, Fraud or Fiction. author
XVI hours. Author Q & A. Wilhelm Darling's *The Snooze* (2139).

The Snooze! Will stiffened. That was a Morandi joke. Had to be. He'd never heard anyone else call *The Noose* that.

Cloius was so disrespectful. Really dangerous.

Will could trust nothing, he felt. Clodius had infected reality with a curse. What the hell was Chrononautics? It had the worst reputation. He vaguely remembered Morandi going on about it one day in reference to one of the Templeton collectors. Something about time travel via body-parts.

>*AND BELIEVE THIS: MILTON MOORE WILL CONTINUE TO RELEASE FUTURE GENERATIONS FROM CAPTIVITY FOR LONGER THAN CAPTIVITY ITSELF SHALL LAST*

Bubbles still emerged from Thomas Jefferson by the bookshelf. Will ignored them. As to the Death's Head Stamp, it had not remained affixed to his papers, but had fallen to the floor. Will retrieved it. He burned it curling and crackling with odd colors in the ashtray through which he could perceive the architecture of a bare-bones GA bedsphere.

Emergency pong. >*Watchlet* on Will accepted the absurdly-handled. It was Smyth from ten minutes ago. He saw there was another ordinary pong below it >*Egge0080*. Excitement tingled up his arms. Was someone playing mindgames? And another below that! A normal pong sent right before jump, that he hadn't seen >*Parsons Crater Templeton O & O*.

"Will," he took Smyth on audio. "You're staying awake for the jump, no? Meet me across from Liner Lounge Access in ten minutes! We're going to see the Crew Module. You're wanted! They especially requested you. Don't be late!"

Fet only sent one line. "Will. Can you believe they wouldn't autopsy him? They said there's no resources to waste on dead addicts. They said that to Gina's face. Can you believe it? Is the folder you wanted marked *BRANE WORLD*? Let me know. Anyway, Sten says it's probably not valuable at all. Endsend. I'm taking it down now."

BRANE WORLD? Will balled his rage small, spinning and articulate with his fisted fingers. All the words in the WIG and beyond, all the banned and bad words with which hate might spew and boil and spit back out onto the feces of human communication currently swirling through the system were at the disposal of his fingers. Any tapping recorded itself into his log. Will curled his fingers aware that the log could not possibly contain the explosion he would make of words now if he let them go. He swallowed hard, down his throat and into his sorely perturbed chest. "Fet," he hissed Kracyb-like through clenchèd teeth. "Fet…"

II v

Presently, as Will stood across from the crowded Lounge Access, Smyth was nowhere in sight. By the Access guard-station a GA Marine Officer was now overlooking foot traffic. Will approached through the waiting passengers. "Excuse me," he said. "I have a complaint."

The GA Officer was a good deal shorter than Will, though wider in the shoulders. Through the open visor, ill-willed resentful eyes gleamed up from under a ponderous monobrow. Yellow bars on his red shoulder showed him a Captain. "Get back and wait like the others," he said.

Will didn't hesitate. Moved by swelling rage, he leaned directly into the man's face. "I am here to report an attempted murder—"

"Hey Killer!" Will was bumped from behind. This time he was ready. He moved on Smyth with both arms—but was restrained from behind. Caught in a vice-grip, Will's right arm wrenched hard up behind his back. He found himself frozen.

"Hey, hey, hey hey now everybody," protested Sagan Smyth, hopping backwards with the dainty space-feet of a seasoned free-loader. The remorselessly space-muscled arms pinning Will in check from behind held were no doubt the GA Captain's. Will detected the heavy male scents of teetotalism, bureaucracy, and vanity in the fascist imperative enfolding him in its jujitsu will. *BRANE WORLD*? Will splashed Fet's idiot words again in a phoenixian rebirth of tapping on his own backside. The resulting pain jack-knifed his torso.

"Calm down, Sir," came the hot directive in his ear.

"O.K." Will hissed. "I relax. I give."

He was released and rapidly spun—microgravity conspired—to find himself face to face with the Captain now backed up by the pimply-faced Guard. "Do you want the brig?" the Captain barked up with hot breath. "I'll lock you up."

"There was an attempt at my life on this ship," Will answered, attempting to contain his outrage. "Forgive me if I'm testy." He saw Smyth had been joined by Freeda Dunworthy, a yellow cape cast around her shoulders, and at least two others. After all, he didn't want a scene.

"What's happening here, Captain Taylor?"

One of Smyth's companions stood forward, a small, orange-togged *Good Fortune* crewperson.

"Understudy Geertz," the Captain exclaimed with irony. "What a surprise." But he seemed embarrassed in front of the little freckled crewperson."I believe everything's in control now. Is this man a guest of yours?"

She frowned. "Yes he is." Will liked her immediately. "I'm giving these folks a quick tour of the Crew Module before first alarm." Though hardly an adult, an unexpectedly bright glance looked into Will, from eyes as sharp as sacking needles. Small, fit, chestnut curls clipped at the ears, she wore ship's insignia (a white, four leaf cherry blossom) and a complicated utility belt. "You're Will Darling?"

"I am," Will said, bowing slightly. "Thank you for asking!"

The Captain departed. "I'm warning you, Mister."

"My assailant had a chessboard face tattoo!" Will called after him.

Crewperson Geertz led Will Darling, Sagan Smyth, Freeda Dunworthy, and her two companions into a restricted access tube marked *OFF LIMITS*. Freeda introduced Will to the two men without giving him their names. One wore stylized facial hair, various piercings and sported a flowery hyper-kilt over a skintight privosuit. The other was suited like a utility man. "We've been an item since meeting on a Saturnite. A triad," she explained.

The party stopped outside a closed, lozenge-shaped port and waited while their guide radioed whomever was inside. The decompression wheel spun on its own; the hatchway opened, and Understudy Geertz ushered the party, one by one, up into the brains of the *Good Fortune*, herself following last.

Climbing hand over hand, they emerged from its current ceiling, around, down and onto the broad open hexagonal deck-floor of the ship's wood-worked aluminum-girded observation hub, quite literally a bridge over waters on two sides. An excited chicken lifted high into the air, shedding peals excitement. With greenery abounding and aquariums boasting marine life, the Bridge had a genuine smell of nature. He saw that a party of the crew were freshwater fish, apparently preparing for a party with their visitors.

Will thought immediately again of Winnegutt and her visions of deckside space. If not her influence, she at least saw this coming, this new organic space of the Outer System. He hadn't believed things had progressed so far. In the inner system entropy was the rule. A Time-Traveler was an entirely new sort of ship.

From this open aired hub air-tubes and bubbling waterways radiated almost haphazardly in all directions. To his left port-holed living quarters bubbled in a coral-like hive. Above him a miscellaneous lab was stuck onto three energy poons. Leaning over the hardwood railing Will could look down into the turquoise water and see the red outlines of the GA Marine canister dancing far below. Fish darted about.

The others had gathered across the bridge, by a row of unfold-anywheres holding various snacks and drinks. Freeda Dunworthy, her two friends, and Sagan Smyth were greeting a middle-aged crewperson, whose orange togs bore officer insignia.

"Will Darling!" Freeda called across. "Come meet the Chief." She smiled as if they had always been the best of friends. Had they? Will was so emotionally spent he could hardly remember. He needed a whiskey as soon as possible.

"Will Darling," Freeda announced, with a fixed smile that now seemed cold and potentially ironic. "As specially requested."

Will bowed sharply and formally, attempting to show real respect.

"This is Maureen Moulder," Freeda said. "Chief of the Crew that's manning this ship."

"Yes." Will nodded sharply, showing himself impressed.

"No offence," The Chief winked. "But I ain't never heard of you."

"He's editing the new A.E. Winnegutt series," Understudy Geertz chipped in from behind Smyth, where Will could hardly see her.

"Ah yes," The Chief narrowed her eyes. "Yes, yes. The girls don't like you, Mister."

Indeed, "the girls"—though other members of the crew were entirely female, the word "girl" was in no way appropriate, Will felt and he rarely used the word. Now they were all glaring at him. The hostility was palpable.

The Chief threw her head back and laughed. "Who wants a drink?"

The sailors had set up whiskey, water, and delicious water-weed cakes. Will took a High Kansan highball and retreated back to the railing. Understudy Geertz followed.

"The crew of the *Good Fortune* doesn't like me," Will said immediately. "Is that what I've been invited here to learn?"

"That's partially it," answered Geertz matter-of-factly, sipping at a yellow sodaball tethered to a stick in her hand. "I believe Bugg would like you to know she likes you least of all."

"Bugg?"

She gestured to an ox-like mechanic across the platform. Bugg wore a beard from which hung a knotted braid. She glared obligingly back, flexing her home-made forearms aggressively.

"Dear me," Will said.

"Bugg loved Deirdre. Adored her."

But readers so far could only know Deirdre had survived quite safely through all he'd put her through in *Orygen*. Great G-ddess, Will thought, should I reconsider *Gates*?

He lit a lungprotector, looking back across the way. He actually took real satisfaction in the violence with which Shipman Bugg met his eyes. It felt fresh to know he would win when she saw the new book. Bugg took a long deep drink.

"Should Bugg be drinking whiskcy?" Will asked.

"We work on watches," said Understudy Geertz, matter-of-factly. "This is off-time for the four of them. Not me, unfortunately. I'm still working." She finished her soda.

"The thing about Deirdre is," Will said, carefully. "In the new one—"

"I know. I already read it. FYI, Bugg and most of the others, they have only heard about what happens to Deirdre at one remove. I'm afraid I told them—

"Excuse me," Will said. "But here I must really interrupt. No. That is not possible. You are all mistaken! I only just turned in the manuscript of *Gates of Opal* forty-eight hours ago."

"Well the crew has a copy of the galleys. I believe Byson has it now."

"Galleys? There are no galleys."

"Sorry," she said. "But let me get this straight. You don't know Captain Wawagawa is issuing *Gates of Opal* in time for Uranacon II?"

"Of course not! I'm telling you—"

"And you know nothing about the special cargo he picked up off Uranus? The fishmen?"

"What fishmen?"

She sighed. She looked deeply into him. "Well, I don't know what to say."

"How old are you?" Will asked.

"Twenty-one."

"And you liked *Gates*?" It was desperate, he knew, but Will desperately needed support, he felt, now without Clodius. He would be willing to suffer for it, if some people at least understood how important it could be.

"I'm actually a huge *Opal* 2 fan," the Understudy said. "I'm even a Will Darling fan. After *Orygen* I picked up a copy of *The Noose*. Anyway. I loved *Gates*. It was great."

Against all odds, he had encountered some sort of genius out here by Uranus. Understudy Geertz looked like a real Spacer in the works, someone you'd want to marry your daughter if you had one which Will emphatically did not.

"Wonderful!" Will said. "Thank you." He bowed humbly. "Now I unerstand why I was invited."

"Actually no. I don't have that kind of pull. The reason you're here is that the Pilot needs to talk to you."

Will remembered something about the Pilot being the personage of the single most importance on board a Time-Traveler.

Though he didn't believe a word of it, her eyes remained hard with truth.

"Can I see the galleys?" he asked.

"I'll see if I can find them."

While the others went to look at the Cannabis plants, Will found himself tracking up a tracked plexi tube, one of those that had looked so intestinal from the view platform. Ahead, Understudy's fit behind turned him into an adjoining, red-hued airvenue, that passed through a thick, deep grey excrement-like quasi-liquid. How odd, he thought. At tube's end, Will had to turn away for politeness's sake, as she wristed a code. Through this hatch, they laddered up into a self-contained pressurized con-glomeration clearly built to survive in long-term vacuum should the *Good Fortune* for ever evaporate.

Next they entered a well-stocked, well-organized, if rather cramped lab-apt, suitable for at least four inhabitants. The clut-tered dodecahedral unit was built for any gravity, but presumed none. Pin-shelves on wall/floor/ceiling held down all sorts of haphazardly arranged equipment, plants, bubbing aquaria, note-books, at least one human skull, a set of the fully-discovered Sappho, and a were-welder. Three other tube-exits were visible. A large holoscreen appeared on one pentagon, showing a view of arteries and arrangements in an enormously complex system Will imagined represented the Good Fortune.

"Helly Biddy!" a woman's strong voice called out from parts unseen.

"It's me!" The Understudy called. "I've hooked a Darling."

"You're faster than I thought you'd be. This yeast demands my apparent observation for approx two point seven decimal minutes. Please go on ahead. Let's convene in Cabin Blue."

"Biddy" Geertz spun the wheel on the blue panel. It opened into entirely emptied out spacer's sphere. A toppler in the center surrounded by several seating pods. Will took one, but Under-study Geertz tracked down to the ceiling. The experience was not at all blue. LED lit the sphere white.

Though the chair was a freesticker, Will felt not at all free. Not long ago if he remembered correctly, he had believed Understudy Geertz was a Will Darling fan. But now it seemed she was in fact allied with forces that believed the Darling was a thing to be hooked, and arbitrarily moved about from room to room. How little respect she had for him really. He had let her lead him about like a sheep!

Will longed for the not-so-DOE >*for the precious illusion of the eternity of each moment inside, that illusory blue-shielded getaway gave*

Blue room meant *blue-shielded*, Will realized. This was perhaps the Crew's most private getaway, *Good Fortune*'s secret prostate. They might do anything to him in here. There were times the skin crawled to be so constantly cooped.

Will's chestspike burned >*let's talk of graves, and worms, and epi-taps*

"Are you writing when you do that?"

"…I take notes all the time."

Will was surprised to find another a smart, rugged clever-eyed old woman seated directly across the toppler. She projected real solidity. Had time already dilated? He didn't think first alarm had sounded. But there she was. Her cap was blue, imbued with a single star. She wore a white lab-coat over bright blue overalls, and squinted through spectacles as if to take him in.

"I am Nina Flower," said the woman across from him, with an intensity that suggested Will should know and indeed respect that great name. However the name meant nothing to him, and he refused to look it up. But he rode a sudden whim.

"If you were really Nina Flower, why off Earth would you tell me?"

"Because I'm only her during jump, and this is during a jump, isn't it?"

Will looked at Geertz. She kept her lips fully closed, but shrugged.

"I'm sorry we've disturbed your trip, Will." Nina Flower said. "I will try to explain everything quickly. My problem is I don't understand events happening right now on my ship. And that's not a good thing."

"No. But what does it have to do with me?"

"Has Captain Wawagawa made any approach to you since we reached Uranus System?"

"To me, personally?" said Will. "No. Not a word. It is I who want to talk to him. If he is circulating my manuscript I want to know why, and how. And frankly, what's in it for me. Can you ask him that?"

"Oh we don't talk. Pilot and crew are rented. Total autonomy is part of the price. My sources tell me, however, that he's publishing the book at URACON II—and Manx Brand has plans to distribute it to the wider system."

"It's absurd," Will said. "It cannot be. I have only just completed the ms. I have not been consulted."

Nina Flower leaned back, narrowed her clever old eyes. What was inside the sphere, he realized, could be scanned from within it. But he felt exited, even expansive, with the whiskey warming him still. He was about to be feted by the likes of Manx Brand? Unfortunately this mood left him entirely unprepared for her next question.

"What is the status of A. E. Winnegutt's singularity pet, ASTA—I tink it was called?"

Even as chestpike stabbed panic all the way into his spin, Will flooded the mind with strong, emotional thoughts. In his lifetime he had been blessed to breathe in deeply on beaches of Earth. To drink Earth's vivid beauties in a rain of pouring sunlight. To see the *dark* of darkness. He remembered the low moan of the whale that finned his boat through the lonely terror of a night crossing of the Gulf of Saint Lawrence, *en route* to the illegal rocketpad that sent him first to Space. When dawn broke on the cliffs of Newfoundland, the next morning the whale was gone. >*Nothing is known of nothing*

"Will?" Crewman Geertz held out a water.

"Sorry," Will said. "I'm sorry. A friend died. I found out off Uranus. I am scattered. But about ASTA. Why do you ask?"

Nina Flower's looked shockingly deep into the emptiness that was Will Darling.

Will looked back into those eyes as blue as mandarins. "Her singularity pet? Its *status?*" he finally said. "Is that what you asked? The consensus is it suicided shortly after her death, leaving only effects."

"So you don't own it? Use it for your writing?"

Will coughed. He looked at Biddy Geertz.

She shrugged. "You kind of said that in one interview."

"There was no interview."

"It's just that if there was an unported autonomous QUAI aboard, I need to know about it," Nina Flower said.

"Why?" said Will.

"Because I'm of the Pilot that's why."

"Of the Pilot! But—"

"It's her hologram," Biddy Geertz said. "She represents the real Nina's interests on board during jump, when Nina is allowed congress with nobody else."

"This is all a bit much, you know," Will complained.

The apparent Nina Flower blinked, and an infoball appeared between them, showing the rippling surface of a foaming ocean. Zooming in, he saw a platform stabilized by long intelligent legs. It was perhaps a fiction. Men had hauled a bountiful catch. It was very well done; the exact feel of footage from a real water-world, one far more bountiful than twenty-second century Earth. The camera turned to take in the creamy silver massmass flashing from the end of the cruelly-hooked crane.

He knew already that it was her, unfolding up into this new born universe out of the seas in which Imp now led him. Precisely these preliminaries would be forgotten. Will closed his eyes, shielding them from the light of the beauty of that first glimpse that burned itself blue against the white light of all his knowledge and memory.

The Nina Flower Hologram was speaking. "Someone leaked us 19 seconds of footage, showing the surface of what seems to be an authentic existent Oan Bubble. We think our Captain brought her up. Two new aquarium canisters were attached by his shuttle before jump. We think she's in here now in one of the twin spinners serving the Captain's kitchens."

The camera froze on Deirdre herself as Will had not dared to believe possible, sparkling with rainbow laden silvers, soft with creamy pinks, strung up on a fishing platform's crane—harnessed for a killing. Wrapped in blue locks, and broad and delicate fins, her curves and sex were visible. Along her long throat, gills fanned. The infoball whisked her away.

Will trembled. She was different, reader, but only because she was real. Exactly enough Deirdre, as an actual world might make her.

"We believe she is in great danger," Nina Flower said, as a man Will Darling had never known existed now crested upon the fountain of the love whose origin foamed now up all around them, in all the intermingling realtime waters of the multiverse, sprinkling out, he saw it now, life upon on all the dead rocks otherwise forgotten. Deirdre swam before him, cresting on the pilot wave of his progress, in the ocean of this joy, darting, alive, flashing bright beneath the darkling surface.

Tears frothed in Will Darling's eyes. "*Dear me*," he exclaimed, loudly. He fainted.

III iii

The little stone-worked lane that led from her spacement to the gate was wet; Maudie kept well enshadowed. It was good she did, for at the gate there was a guard. Morrigan had left the regular behind, beside Maudie's entrance. Maudie was surprised to see a carbine slung over the Regular's shoulder. Maudie waited and waited and at last the guard exited the tower, chatting softly over a helmet-radio, looking away over towards the Elevator.

Maudie moved quickly, but normally, in such an invisible way she hoped that no one would think of noticing her exit. The ad-apt's remoteness, on the reverse side of the canyon, aided her. She passed down in darkness, fully visored, to where the wheelers emerged out of a crack from Verona Polis proper.

The lanes down the ridge to the little settlement were curiously empty. It was true she didn't know Verona Falls; and most of it was naturally underground or looking out on the cliffview. Maudie stayed in the shadows as she walked, filled with strange thoughts and ideas.

Outside, she saw no one. But as she suspected, the Printshop had re-opened its shutters. So checking left and right and up and hoping nobody saw, Maudie hurried across and gratefully ducked into that place she knew she was going to all along. Maudie entered directly into the side of Verona Rupes as if away from the possibility of Egge's gaze, seeking those other eyes.

She spun the hatch closed after her. In the shop, Glow-stones were placed along the stone-floored bamboo-line interior, illuminating an ink-soaked, color-jammed, book-laden reader's hub of the very finest quality. Wooden organizers showed the skills of master carpenters.

"Hello?" She heard only silence, and the trickling of waters.

Despite great stacks that would have broken earthside shelves asunder, the hub was in astonishingly good order. Not a volume was out place, or even harmfully squished. Maudie saw Spacer Omnibus Editions spined a half-meter wide, topping a book tower beginning with only a little copy of Ortock's *Codes*.

Meanwhile plants and harnesses offered protected reading zones in all sorts of delightful spots. In one nook three ranks of identically clad guilt-spined hardbacks showed with their gold and ruddy pride that they had sailed 1.78 billion miles since first setting out from a Fleet Street, Earth in the early 18th Century. In another corner she saw the vac-wrapped sans-culottes of the old paperback revolution: Germany's Albatross, London's Penguin, America's Fawcett Gold Medal. *Weird Tales*! Covers flashed science, fantasy, Africa, murder and sex.

Little rooms came off of little chambers. In one, dense rows of neo-mimeo chapbooks rose far higher up than she could reach. Maudie looked with more than interest. This was a bizarrely *wonderful* collection. Her own books, still crated up in the bungalow's spacement, would fit in perfectly here. If it really was who she thought it was running the place, she might well be able to secure considerable kredit. Maudie was glad for the guard guard outside her ad-apt, with those books inside. She had some almost priceless artifacts, she realized, to those who loved books.

"There you are," a voice called out behind her. "I knew you would come! The Lyonesse!"

She spun around and behold those eyes—now roundly staring out of a rather pink and completely shaven face and head.

"The Lyonesse!" he smiled wickedly. "In my node!"

"You," she said, beaming. "Is it really you?"

"Lyonesse! One and the same!"

"It is me! Eri."

"Eri!"

They embraced and greeted one another formally.

Eri was quite confident of his shop's integrity. He went bare-foot, dressed only in a plain white-skirted tunic that ended at the knee. His belly had gone Spacer, she noted, which might explain the nails of his feet needing a clipping. In the games the Lyonesse had joined long ago, Eri had played a bard. It was not only his New York accent that tended the word to baud.

She was happy to see that a taunting boyish innocence still shone out of his vivid eyes. But she wondered that he'd been able to organize such a grown-up bookshop. Maudie was not one for memory, G-ddess knew, but the fact was if she tended to let the more outrageous adventures of the Lyonesse melt away after they occurred, she still remembered Eri's wild antics.

"This is a wonderful reader's node," she said. "Incredible."

"Yes! I inherited. My assistant has been fixing it up. My dear, I arrived here less than a year ago, with a barrel of current jam and theremin. Currently I maintain this and another more time-consuming enterprise as well, upon water-rich Miranda. And my luck holds! The Lyonesse!" he repeated. "Here! In Verona Falls! The very day I need her most!"

Maudie laughed "My real name is Maudeleine."

"Of course it is! Maudeleine de Lions. Anyone who knows the Lyonesse, knows who you are. See here…" Eri crossed the room to a glass-faced cabinet filled with special self-published editions, posters and imprintings from 1-Gen Space. Maude saw a small collection of her own zines! *C'mell C'mell, Krystal Kakes, Nin-Jinn, the Forgotten Years…*

"Now that's a laugh! I never knew any of these made it off the Moon."

"Oh the Lyonesse made quite an impression on many of us, young lady. I never forgot the Lyonesse. Of course they post passenger lists the day a ship leaves its home station. So I've known you've been coming for some time. I was indeed looking for you out my door earlier. I hoped to spot you! And look—I've got you! Now, what are your arrangements? Move in tonight! Of course!"

"Wow," Maudie said. "Thank you. I think I have plans tonight. But after…"

He grimaced immediately. "I hope you can cancel them. You see I can offer you a place here, a place in one of the nicest and safest spots for a writer there is, my dear. But I need you very much to help me *tonight*."

"You mean you need help at the booknode? Can't it wait one day?"

"No no no. Tonight I need … a performance! I offer—for as long as you'd like to stay!—a good bed-sphere, full citizen's bounties."

This was certainly not what she had expected. She hadn't performed since Luna City. "Hell, if I can get work here I better take it," she said. Especially if it was work independent of Marjorie Baumgarten and Mr. Egge.

Eri clapped his hands excitedly. "Shall we touch the whiskey? We will drink to Miranda." He pulled a carafe out from behind a *Devil's Thesaurus*. Maudie took it, feeling she shouldn't. She was already feeling so disoriented.

Eri stared at her wickedly, shaking his head. "It's perfect. Perfect!"

Maudie laughed. "I hope you very much don't expect me to fuck anybody," she said. "That part of my performing life is over."

"No, no, no," He chuckled, licking his shining lips red. He looked at her. He came to a decision. "Let us go downstairs and discuss it under surface."

After putting out the lightstones of the shop and sealing up the front, Eri pulled out a J. F. Bardin omniback edition from New Mars Printers, and the entire psychological crime section swiveled away to reveal a secret wheel-hatch. Eri finger-tapped a combination and this opened as if on its own accord, hissing and offering a silver lined ladder tube downward into sublunarean depths.

"The printshop's only the tip of the Iceberg," Eri said. After the ladder down, he lead along a masoned path that ran inside a melted-out ice fissure. Little streams of iceflow wound through the ancient chamber. This whole lay was apparently Eri's sole preserve, for he padded barefoot with perfect confidence.

At the fissure's end, a little omniradiated herb garden introduced another hatchway, leading down a rectangular miner's shaft to series of melted-out chambers. Passing through another locked hatch they entered a generous open space lined with flags, scenic engines, old-fashioned weapons and stores of blank cloth and metal sheeting.

A hard-to-find passage at the cavern's end led into a stone-walled low-ceilinged den. It seemed comfortable, fitted out with various relaxes and hammocks. Maudie wondered if it was all partially augmented. As to the color of the light—there was something undefinably recognizable about the lighting, but she couldn't quite focus on what.

Eri perched as she took a relax across from him.

"Are you going to tell me what you've got going here, Eri?"

"You don't know it, Maudeleine, but after I knew you I reformed myself by serving for ten years, as director and master-of-ceremonies in Poseidon's Theater, in the old Milton Moore waterweirld on the Martian Flats. Well, like all good things in the Inner System that weirld went down the drain. Anyway, shortly after I arrived here, Helio Jones, the fellow that ran the New Falls Theater here, disappeared and there was absolutely nobody around with the time and energy to take over the stage."

"Do you mean to tell me *you're* the New Falls Theater?"

"It doesn't really compare to Milt Moore's water-weirlds, of course. But I play a real Marvel Ball. It's a real experimental set-up. Some would say, in fact I know some do say, it's a bit of ramshackle set-up. For instance the play we're doing tonight. It's been specially requested by very powerful interests. The best people from all the clades will be in the audience. It's a rather important occasion for me. I've very hard on this production, you see, knowing that. But unfortunately I've lost a player! My second female! Lyonesse, you know *Pericles*!

"*Pericles*! You've got to be kidding. I couldn't possibly play that tonight already. Anyhow I don't want to be seen."

"You won't be! I have a Marvel Ball! You will do your work in the weirld, safely helmeted backstage. No one will see you!"

"I can't! If Marjorie came, it would feel indelicate."

"This is Shakespeare!"

"And Wilkins!"

"Oh yes you can, Lyonesse. Yes you can. Why, you know me! A mind used to performing alongside my own in exactly the sorts of weirlds we will be imitating tonight—that's worth a dozen! Do you have the *Spacer's Shakespeare*?"

"I do." Again she met those eyes. "How hardcore is the sex?"

He laughed. "Oh, that! It's just for show. Spicy yes, it must be to keep up with the times. But I'm on to other things these days. My balls were burned out by radiation. I must say, it's been revivifying. Never has life been so peaceful, art never has art been such a joy, since I've been a eunuch. The wide-open cool breeze of reality! But it's not to say I don't have the fondest memories of what we shared," Eri hastened to add. "I remember your C'mell particularly, Lyonesse. She didn't even have a sex organ at all if I remember correctly. Yes I recall that fondly."

She felt herself reddening. "Well if you're serious about—"

"You will play in *Pericles*! Lyonesse! You must! Have you noticed we have a glorious revolution under way here in Prospero's

Crater? Tonight I have a full band for music and sound effects. And we all pray for sun-dogs."

"Can you keep my presence secret? I don't want anyone knowing I'm here."

"Nothing is easier. You will not be seen from outside, my dear! Your name is not in the playbill."

"Someone's going to have to tell Marjorie Baumgarten and tell her I won't be needing my ticket."

"I tell Tommies and it's done."

It took some time for Eri to explain the improvised dramaturgy, a conglomeration of several technologies that Maudie was very certain had not been predicted by any of the first inventors. "I've inherited from my predecessor some Concern psychotherapeutic tech, highly advanced stuff, and re-wired it through a Marvel Ball into a very dynamic sort of living theater. The players are not beheld on stage. They behold one another back-stage, only from within interlinked mental projection helmets. I alone occupy the stage. I sit on a stool with the Falls behind me and play upon the marvel-ball, wired to the intertwined combinations of the performers brain-waves, my own included. The audience itself powers the circuit with its living energy, transferred skin-to-skin from the people their pods. They behold your experience of your performance upon the marvel-ball as I direct it out of the temporary collective unconscious vision we all share. Tonight, we'll have a full band for music and sound effects, so we can promise a full-on weirld for those who participate it."

In such a simple set-up, Eri explained, everything depends on the players. "The players have to live the play with total commitment for the marvel swirls to trace their trance-state into the minds of the audience members with proper potency."

"What part is it you want me to play?" Maudie asked. With something like dread, for she already knew the answer.

"Marina," he smiled. "Naturally."

II vi

In the GA Marine Officer's cabin enspleened in the guts of the spleen-like Brigade Module, plump in the larger *Good-Fortune's* belly, Captain Amulet Jessup Taylor PPT stared spleenfully at the com-port. He felt confined enough attached to a Ship of Free Space; being cooped up behind somebody else's gravity prow was a bit more vexing indeed. Though Captain A. J. Taylor had taken the jump out to Uranus sleeping, his Lieutenant Bayley had not. Psychologically, the time-jumps, the glimpses into odd and improbable futures might have an effect on the weak-minded. For a long time lucid dreamer, as Bayley claimed to be (the Captain overhearing his boasting constantly), the split-to-split continuity of those swollen moments should have fit snugly into the de facto powers he so oft proclaimed. That's why Amulet had appointed him to stand watch. And sure enough, on arrival off Uranus Bayley had reportedly, "still ahead of time's coming wave," felt powerless, isolated and alone. Among other things, he forgot to wake Captain Taylor until after the Miranda blast and thus Amulet had failed to make contact with his wife before jump.

Pamela was already on Miranda, awaiting the *Good Fortune's* arrival. She'd been there for a month already. He did not want Pamela in the public iye. To pry her off the Martian stage had been the work of two years.

A. J. Taylor's orders had his Mars III 14th Brigade meeting up with the entire Saturn I Division on board the SSS *Wan Hu*, a stealth military transporter of whose immanent arrival, neatly coinciding with the *Good Fortune's* own, Moon Miranda remained blissfully unaware. The Mars 14th would hold the ships secure, while Saturn I cleaned up down below. It wasn't a particularly dangerous assignment, but certainly more warlike than usual. Taylor very much hoped he wouldn't have to test the mettle of his shockingly unfit troop.

Once Miranda was stabilized he would take Pamela aboard the *Wan Hu* and the two of them would ride back on a year-long ride to Mars—in an Admiral's quarters. He didn't want any of Pamela's sort of complications getting in the way of this plan.

Taylor shuddered every time he imagined the isolato types who would make up the salon she whould have developed for herself on Miranda by now. He prayed she wasn't associating with Prospero's Daughters, the paramilitary radicals rumored to have agents high in ever union on the Moon.

He almost didn't believe in New Mars himself anymore. For these years of their absence (he hoped the first and only long-haul orders he would be forced to serve) Taylor's lovely little manse high on Olympus suffered under occupation by konfidence tricksters of all sorts: kulturators, kulturnauts and that crowd. Greedy, needy and seedy, the lot of them. When Pamela told him she had a chance to see Miranda at the same time he was going on his Mission was when he realized she was very likely still in cahoots with his commanding officers.

It continued to surprise her husband how far Pamela Lamprey could get without a drop of real GA kredit or a shred of property her own. She'd kept herself everyoung now so long she looked near her age. In heals and only augmentation she still went about only sporting her crisscrossing spacerope privos.

A strong and darkly handsome thirty-three year old, Amulet Taylor was under no illusions about the gossip his relationship with the (80+?) everyoung actress had generated among her circles. On New Mars he was something of a celebrity. Pamela picked him for his looks, she said. Sexually, he was proud to know he satisfied her. But she wasn't as libidinous as a young wife might have been, and Amulet just knew it must be true that she chose him also because he represented a chance for unlimited free travel.

And his underlings, pimply boys who had never known a woman, laughed at him daily, he suspected. A. J. Taylor was a married man, so A. J. Taylor let it go. They could laugh all they want. It was through a late night tèta-á-tète between his wife and one of her ex's, now the Commander of the Mars IIIrd, that Taylor had finally, after more than a decade, made Captain. Of course by then the 14th Brigade meanwhile was not the well-disciplined unit Amulet Taylor had imagined commanding.

As he now ran over the logs of the voyage, Amulet noted the listing: "2 Sightings: Snowman, Abominable."

"Bayley!"

"Sir?" The beetle-like, continually slacking B. J. Bayley XI didn't cease his tapping and tinkering over at the Officer's deskmodule WIG node.

"What is this about the Abominable Snowman?"

"There were more than those who saw. Those are the ones who registered. Others reported a "white ape" or "rabbit man.""

Bayley was still typing.

"At first I reasoned a real Spacer's legend grew up during the time dilations en route from Jupiter, Sir. Then I found the hairs."

"What hairs? You didn't report that."

"No sir. The DNA deconstructed when I tried forensics." His drooping long cheeks flushed, but not from shame.

"Are you having fun with me, Lieutenant Bayley?"

"No Sir. Not at all, Sir.

B. J. Bayley was the nephew of a colonel in the IIIrd, and therefore B. J. Bayley was the 14th Brigade's second lieutenant. It didn't bother the GA apparently that Bayley was a vocal leftist, a veritable Engles in his own mind; he was a nitwit and that was good enough for the marines. Taylor could only thank the heavens for Sergeant Rango.

"Is the the com flashing, Bayley?"

"Yes Sir. For you. Marked *Private*, Sir. A Mr. Egge, Captains cabins. Audio."

Taylor received. "Mr. Egge."

"Egge, the E is not Silent. As you know, I am First Chief Mate to *Captain* Wawagawa." The emphasis on the word *Captain* rankled. The *Good Fortune* was essentially a joint-stock operation between two Captains. The fact was A. J. was an actual *Captain* here. A *Captain* others called *Captain*. E.T. Wawagawa, whatever he was, was certainly not even owner of the ship. He was *Ser* Wawagawa, or *Count* etc. its visible figure-head. No more no less. Therefore if one insisted on using the word, it should nevertheless not be stressed. Furthermore, there was no Chief Mate mentioned in Taylor's original orders.

"*First* Chief Mate?"

"I was promoted during the jump," the snotty-voiced Egge replied. "I call by Captain's order, with all due authority, concerning a matter of security."

"What's the trouble?"

"One of your Liner passengers. He has disappeared. You must find this guest and bring him to Captain's Cabins. Immediately."

"The Global Authority of System Space is not Ser Wawagawa's valet, Egg."

"*Egge* is the name," said the voice.

A. J. Taylor felt that humanity had lost more than it had gained when the traditional modes of naming were lost. That is why Amulet chose a name he purposefully would not have chosen when he became a citizen of Space. And he got a great one.

"And the missing passenger?"

"Wilhelm Darling, originally of Parson's Crater. Find him at once. Bring him down. He is a dangerous copyright pirate and probable thief."

Egge ponged off, without waiting for Captain Taylor to even agree to help. He would not receive a return.

Taylor cleared his throat. "Lieutenant Bayley?"

Bayley was tap-tapping away. "Yes sir."

"Call up passenger pic and last current location of passenger, Darling, Wilhelm."

For A. J. Taylor the head that filled out the improperly broadcasting infoball was instantly and loathsomely familiar. It was the big blonde himself, the whiskey-soaked oaf he'd recently restrained outside the *Good-Fortune* crew modules just now. Wilhelm Darling. What a name. He remembered Biddy Geertz leading the man away.

Barrington Jock Bayley, Taylor thought. A name ridiculous enough to be paired with a Darling and an Egge. He would send Bayley alone after Darling?

Amulet remembered drunks like that pawing Pamela backstage in New Mars. Darling was a violent never-do-well, a coarse fellow who went about pissing in his own trousers like a little boy. Bayley wouldn't be able to handle him alone. And why not use this as an invitation to the *Good-Fortune*'s Captain's Manse? A. J. Taylor hadn't been invited up. Pamela would surely expect a report on the relative glamour of Wawagawa's cabins.

"Bayley what is the reason for your incessant tapping? What are you doing?"

"Nothing, Sir."

Though nothing would have given Taylor more pleasure than forcing Bayley to go through the rigors of bringing in Darling himelf, at least he could force him off of that terminal.

"Mr. Bayley! Enought of that tapping! You and I are moving out."

He doesn't think twice, 2nd Lieutenant Barrington J. Bayley reflected as the Captain donned a utility suit and helmet. He simply does Wawagawa's mate's bidding, like a dog of a dog.

A recent downturn in fortune had made B. J. Bayley a Global Authority Marine; it had been either enlist or get sent to Borstal, his Uncle said. And now Barry had come all the way out to the Outer System. The plan was to go AWOL and take asylum on Miranda. The place was crawling with lassies. In the meantime Bayley had resolved to use of this one trip to figure out the future of Bridget Geertz in particular, while there was still a small possibility (hey, every possibility comes real in some universe) he himself might get a wee slice of that haggis.

It was in her service, in fact, that he'd been typing all this time. After he'd hooked himself up to the surveillance Wawa-gawanet laid over everything, with free access to all, Bayley then created a communication system whereby he and she could communicate unseen among it. After that, he'd used the GA SYNWOC archive to answer to her recent inquiries about the so-called singularity pets of the 2010s. Now with his Captain insisting on playing out typical fascist fantasies of law-keeping in regards to this fugitive Darling, Barry wouldn't be able to edit the essay he was composing in hope of specially winning her favor. He would have to send it in the raw. Some whole paragraphs were certainly taken whole from outside sources. Still, he felt sure there were capital bits all throughout. He just hoped his intellectualism wouldn't intimidate her.

>Hey Biddy Geertz interrupted, before he even sent it. *Are you busy?*

> Tad. Why?

>NEED A FAVOR

By the Monster in the Loch, it seemed to Barry Bayley that a lad might do a favor here and a lad might well do a favor there.

Soon enough a lad could expect to receive a favor in return. But Bayley strengthened himself with the hearty blood of those Scotsmen of legend from whom he claimed descent via possible DNA, intuition and an obvious taste for sweetmeats. The girl of his dreams was reading his essay right this minute! It put the knock in the knees! He only hoped he hadn't flexed the muscles too obviously with one or two pretty potent metaphors.

"Mr Bayley!" Old monobrow boomed.

>*NP comrade*, answered B. J. Bayley, with that enthusiasm that had allowed others to invent, build and operate the machinery necessary to haul his DNA out past the Gas Giants to find her own.

>*What do you need next?* and he sent the essay along attached.

"LIEUTENANT BAYLEY!"

II vi-a

The singularity pet, its singularly peculiar history.[9]

It adhered where it appeared. Spacer Year One it was, when even machines were free.[10] In the golden age of Space (when people had not half the sense they've got today) smack like a spolf ball in the 2090's something tiny was reported to have been driven into history as it is commonly called. When? How? Where did it go? People can't seem to agree upon that or did and never told. There are sightings everywhere. Eventually the many appearances stabilized into 341. Recognizable histories apparently. Most of these characters suicided. Others were caught and extinguished in things just like mirror traps laced with mini black holes. Eventually, as we will conclude, it was all sorted out where the actual first one came from and that it almost certainly now believed to have been the shenanigans of an ordinary special AI back when the people were the more easily duped by fashionable hoaxing.

To handily digress into the heart of things: an AI is not a singularity. The AI works according to our physical laws, affirms

---

9. by Barrington "Jock" Bayley, Lieutenant Secnd Class, temporarily of Third Division, 14th Brigade, Global Authority Marines.
10. Just because I'm temporarily a GA Marine doesn't mean I haven't read my Zitzko. Three or more things I could say on this. Interesting, no?

them. The singularity re-writes them, over and over and over again. But we just think it happens once.

In these days in Space of haunting and superstition, rumours were about that the old not-forgotten goal was in fact reached in 2121. It is well known that cross-concern unions of concerns (Phishsuck, TangoCorp, Hooli, Fig-Alien, HUCK FU COM among others) had put out prizemoney. What was needed was a self concept. Apparently the human is too much of a weak one. It turned out that the self-adhering, quantum-anchored AI system with root power over its own contemporary history psynched with the conceptual apparatus of a famous canine.

First thing it did was immediately erase its history. Yet history it would have to have for it to have come into existence. There are histories bubbled within histories. It sounds pervie, but these bubbles swallow each other all the time apparently. It all must be visible against the microwave radiation of First Found Universe. From this paradox, naturally, change springs internal.

You have asked about one of these spectral creatures of tale and legend. Or perhaps *ASTA* has already been here, like she's always just there ahead of our present. Everything we see in real time is trailing in her wake. If it wrote this, for instance, and replaced whatever I'd written with something else entirely, then rewrote what I'd written before instead of that twice backwards, *ASTA* would have already ceased caring each step of the way immediately before starting it all off. *ASTA*'s very interested in writing, Nick Wesley says. The pet writes faster than insta-neously. The whole thing is there perfectly the way it wanted everytime—this is important—not as we understand those words, but as an augmented dog does.

Books by AIs have of course long fallen out of fashionable circles. Records show an AI assistant of name *ASTA* did work for the scientifiction author A.E. Winnegutt. Our analysis suggests however she composed the books herself. But some maintain

Winnegutt collaborated with a dog. Have you owned a dog Understudy Geertz? I have. I have owned a number.[11] (Sundogz)![12] AEW did seem to work closely with some sort of AI—its been proven more or less. An old comrade of mine, not from the GA but from another organization I once joined in Luna City—did I tell you I spent some extraordinary months there back in 42? It's where I discovered my coding knack, being able to do something like all this. Why does Omlette Taylor insist on bothering me with things he could do on his own? Why have someone answer your Com for you before you receive it? look up Mr. Wilhelm Darling your aen damn self i say.

You've heard of single electron theory? Where every electron is in fact a separate appearance of a single time-traveling electron not actually travelling in time? Some say the singularity pet now *was* that electron.

There can be no coincidence for the Cyclops Eye. Here's one. A fellow I knew from Parson's Crater I believe it was, Ryan by name, since apprehended by the authorities, claims to have met *ASTA*, when it was with its first owners, beore AEW. According to Ryan, *ASTA*'s love for its mistress, Dr. Nora Wesley of Penobscot, Maine, surpassed human love. Nick Wesley, her real life husband, was a challenging character. A rather well-known confidence man of 1-Gen space, according to Ryan. Of course Ryan himself is a criminal (a man like me knows all sorts, lass). I mention because Ryan published a story he claimed to have found written by *ASTA* for/about its Mistress for an AEW fanzine that's been recorded on SYNWOC. I haven't actually talked to him my own self and it could be fiction.

Biddy, ignore good portions of this. There's beastly scant record of the real *ASTA*. I myself conceive the sinister way this

---

11. Two actually. Spoodles back on New Mars.
12. I just thought them! Have you been? Will ye gae?

singularity begins to dominate the Universe once you existentially think about it, philosophically. Not exactly what you expected as theology's teleology. It's monotheism out there, yes sir, but a *canine monotheism.*

The universal shepard as the omniscnient old dog? after her mistresz has passed? Could be the best possible Schnauser, but still. Somehow not what one expected exactly to see when the kilts are all lifted and we get to see the true shape and size of things, you know what I mean? Seems rather small somehow, the universe suddenly. Pevertedly bent.

Unlike me, anyway, Biddy. I think I've earned the right to call you that now? I'm quite happy about how this is all coming out. All this is with the help of an omnibarbitol so its coming out in something of a rush. I know you like to read by the way (every single one of your friends told me, I'm not a stalker) and it happens one of my interests certainly lies. For instance though I was horrible at math enough to have to cheat my way out of more exams than I can count. And so I wasn't good. Nevertheless in English I could always write later that I was. And so I was. What are we, Biddy, beside what we say we are? Actually, since I know I won't remember doing so—in fact please don't burn after reading—I think I will ask you right now: are you gay? Are you, Understudy Geertz? I mean Biddy? I hope this is made less embarrassing that you know I probaby won't remember I asked. But if yes, then—or I mean if you're even bi—then maybe try to throw it in conversation. For instance kiss some girl while I'm with you guys.

In conclusion, Marshal Monobrow just interrupted, putting an end to this essay deteriorating like an opened iced cream cone. Have you tasted iced-cream? The real stuff? I guess you must have. But I assure you many interesting nuggets remain in our suddenly sweet conclusion, for your enjoyment.

Nora Wesley was lynched by science-fearing savages in what was once the old U.S. Dog Asta was in space with Nick at the time. Philosophy helps a lot here, if you happen to have any, as I do. Particularly the Scotch Enlightenment. Those whose specialty it seems to be to understand what is physically impossible for the human mind to comprehend, for instance why one haggles, even I am quite stumped by that. But here I suggest theoretically there can only exist one singularity mind. So why not pick this one? Even if it effectively time-travels so as to appear in three hundred and forty-one placetimes at once, an actual Portuguese Water terrier seems to have died.[13]

Whether or not it exists, others want a singularity mind of their own. Concerns want one rather badly, always have naturally. They can't seem to make it themselves in fact so some have figured, perhaps it does exist already and that's why it always stops them, for there can only be one, even if it's somewhere in the future or the past. Now there's almost nothing else to look for out there. If I was Asta I certainly wouldn't show myself. Ever.

In conclusion, extra clever pun coming here, I have mentioned *ASTA* can only be seen as I said in its effects? Anyhow it was with the *effects* of Winnegutt that *ASTA disappeared*.[14] A Ruby Green claims she and AEW each received quantum lockets as a myserious wedding gift. One had an old piece of paper inside that seemed to spell the letters O A in some lights.[15] N O R A?

"Go on," said the Investigator.

"A. E. was what might be called a Nora Wesley fan before she even met Heike Böhringdorf."

----

13. According to SYNWOC, Winnegutt claimed the whole thing was a hoax. She was lie-detected on this and passed.

14. Winnegutt's gayness opens the following line of inquiry. Are you at all heterosexual, Bridget? The Bayleys dare to wonder. Shouldn't ask! Sorry.

15. Sorry, I'm a qualified engineer and complicated techspeak emerges naturally. Really, I have a certificate on the wall of my bunk. May I show it to you sometimes?

"Go on," said the Investigator.

">*BE*Good and evil were real things to her. *WAGREEGatly* important as her work progressed*geMachinesofMeat.*"

Now Bridget. Something about that last bit struck me as odd. In further conclusion, we note: If you look back you'll find the phrase "reMachine of Meat" was just smeared into Greene's statement. That's why we must have underlined that part in permanent memory. Did we happen to mention how we was the cryptography champ in our number two years running? Well We're a Jack of level 8 perma-coded shiz I kid you slot. I pierced together a possible sentence made from the first letters of the paragraphs preceding that sentence.

The big surprise? It came out ridiculous. It said BE WAREEG GEMACHIN ESOFMEAT. Do you speak Welsh? I don't. I have Manx and Scotch Gaelic, there's another interesting story in there. Would you be paralyzed by disgust were we to meet in the Liner's Lounge sometime after turn-around? I think we're heading there. Seems like the last place passenger Darling was seen. We're all looking for him. In conclusion, let's discuss all sorts of things, such as how we might discuss them in code. Lastly, please check the addendum attached to this essay. And nobody knows this stuff, you know, so keep it that way. [Each of us has her secrets, Ms Geertz]

>*Dear me* "You are not supposed to be in here," Will Darling declared, sitting upside-down, hair askew, blue holorobe half-off, aware it was possible he cut a ridiculous figure. Gravity's gone, he realized, having for a moment believed himself mad or underwater. But he very much objected to the stranger in his bedsphere. In the DOE, an other! The Darling very much disliked the privacy of the Egg being intruded upon. There hard astern, so he had to look between his long legs, a clear-eyed Understudy Geertz looked up from her handy-screen. She was sticking on the stool by the holomirror. Will stared at Understudy Geertz, unable to explain her presence. "Did time dilate?"

"It did."

"I blacked out."

"You insisted on returning to what you called the Not-So-Dear—"

Will remembered none of it. "Why are you persecuting me?"

"I might be preserving you, by waking you up. You have failed to receive and rejected several important emergency pongs. Everyone's looking for you."

"But I'm right here. In my bedsphere."

"They don't seem know that. Yet."

Will managed to position himself what felt like right-way up.

"What do they want?"

"It doesn't matter. We hope they're going to march you up the Captain's quarters. I will accompany you. Then when and if we're admitted you will occupy Wawagawa, and I will attempt to locate the fishgirl."

Will extended his finger and emphatically shut down Egg— and as she stared at his own suddenly exposed body, his heart withered faster than ash from a departing flame.

Will folded like a big pin, covering his wound. Yet even as he began to trace the baroque inter-circuiting curls of shame crystalizing outwards from the chestspike, he realized with raining grace that she had seen nothing! The privosuit remained!

"Understudy Geertz," Will said, out of this relief. "What fish-girl are you speaking of?"

"Deary. My intuition tells me we must liberate her at once."

And it came back. Blessed with all her wet and silvery radiance, shed of all the dross the Darling had laid upon her, the Imp had brought her to life, beacuse Will had killed her.

"Deirdre," he exlaimed, looking into Geertz's blueest eyes. "She lives."

"Deary," shrugged Biddy Geertz. "Her real name is Deary. Deary Devarnhardt."

Will frowned. "You're kidding. Is it possible?"

"Yes. But don't ask me how I know it."

He composed himself. "Wonderful. Now, we will go find her. But I need a moment alone. Please, just wait for me outdoors."

"Ah," She nodded politely. "No problem."

Will beamed at her.

Understudy Geertz tracked out as the Egg arose to embrace its master. Alone again, Will pranced deliriously about. Deary Devarnhardt was a discarded variant name for *Opal 2*. It had been published with her miscellaneous notes. The fishgirl had *chosen* that name! She herself read Winnegutt.

Will sketched out a three step plan?

>*Stop writing*

>*Marry Deary*

>*Move to her world*

Void it all: Wilhelm Darling, Clodius Morandi, Templeton O & O, A.E. Winnegutt and Kracyb the Dragon. Shed it up; rip out the rest. Become a *free* free Spacer.

Will sucked whiskey directly from the curling spole.

There were those who would have likely slit his throat for winning the titanic struggle against the Imp. And now what could they say? She *lived*. Because he had indeed forced her through the dragon's gate, he would live beside her for eternity. He could give the Imp away!

The heart throbbed swelling up against the spike. The thought of standing in the actual presence of that glistening fish-soft angel sent him trembling; Will feared he would be struck dead with joy.

The door-bell sang.

He stared at himself in the holomirror. Enjoying the moment, his broad boy-like face was red with whiskey and joy. His red-lined blue eyes had never looked so worn out and exhausted. As he stared, a thick white hair emerged from Will's mouth. Will gagged; but only to discover the hair was there after all. It was real, and had floated up through his hologram from the water-closet. Sweet relief! Though trembling still from that out of body premonition, Will vac-voided the freak hair. Let it be sucked away, with Fet and Gina T. and the Ruby Greene as well. Everything false had dropped away.

With sudden bravery, facing that most feared ghoul, Will peeled it open the front of privosuit. He stared fascinated at the holo-mirror, zooming right into the ravaged pink and red-caked hole in the waxen, doughy, half-transparent, suit-softened skin.

The doorbell sang.

As Will had feared, the locket implant fusion (a jerry-rigged job if he'd ever seen one, that had cost him his entire living quarters) had slow-melted the surrounding skin. The crystal disk had welded itself to the surrounding chest. His exposed bloodvessels were blue. Around tissue was scarred with blister, almost making an A. O. in the Mirror. Not even an A. E.

>*Fix my hole, Imp* Will prayed. *Fix me please*

The doorbell sang.

Tears filled his eyes. A sacred quiet flowed out of Will Darling's heart. He nevertheless composed himself, zipping up, fixing the hair, tying the flow-tie with the still trembling hands.

He felt nothing but the tenderest, truest admiration friendship towards poor Clodius.

He'd meant to stop drinking for a bit, Will remembered, as the doorbell sang again. Well that's why they can't find me, he thought. My watchlet is entirely off. He whisked away the Egg. So doing, the last of the Darlings came face to face with his force-blurred invader.

Well fortified by booze and a resurgent literary nature, Will told himself this was a time dilation. Anything might happen. Hands together, he nodded fearlessly, half bowing before the rising whiteness.

"Wonderful!"

II viii

When the Doll awoke from out of raw-nerved dreams of electric
terror in which barbed four-pronged fangs drooled from the sky
and multiple crucified Deary faces drawn out as in spectra of
only cruelty shrieked with mouths holing elongated throats,
breast splaying gasping cherry-red gills out of this sort of thing
into the relief of reality, physics at last came upon him with cool
benediction. Such horrors were artificial, it told him. Dreams.
Why not simply awake? But that cool transparency of reason
only razored a seam of death backwards into void. It was clear
pure carbon sheer holding him pinned, industrial diamond
ribbed by fat bars of titanium modularly welded into a high
panel of the motile Stateroom. Back tendrils could penetrate the
influx and outlet—to no avail.

The Oan Guard was immobile. Communication slogged
through all his system. Consciousness had protected itself,
choosing hibernation and dream horror that was at least unreal.
Out of the fires of nightmare then, his mind fell naked onto the
frying-pan of the real. He knew he was held fixed eventually, in
a living coffin. Deary was no more finned for her swimabout.
The Doll, he reasoned it soon enough, had been imprisoned
separately, privately—tentacle and tendril now spread for display,
in an aquarium Bubble. How easily he'd been overcome. The

Doll had been denied oxygen and roughly tranquilized with narcotics. He felt the deep wounds of darts all across his sore body.

His eyes, of course, as Oa's Guard, had been open forever, even as he had flowed away in dream. They had already made worlds from the colors and shapes they received, so that now when an ostensible reality begged for definition, world appeared in such form he knew that the worst was likely true. It didn't even matter that he new nothing more than that he was trapped, caught, splayed out for show—like a foarking plant. Imprisoned for some time, for his water was already thick with his own grime. On all sides tendrils pressed up against brute engineering. Everywhere, the wall of facts came without a chink.

Jettings of visions gave way to things emerging inside. My Poor Little Doll, the Doll's DNA memories of mother dreamed her saying. Her hair stuck off the back of her head in pretty black pig-tails. Her dark eyes welled deeper than the sun. But those deep eyes could not look upon the horrid thing she cradled. Brown, slippery little cephalo-boy with the weird blue eye. She screamed at that little blue rimmed-hole hungry for sunstuff. The Doll spasmed, layering out the dreams as they occurred into his waking. He spasmed hard (no, he could not reach warp) whacking the walls of fact, churning—all systems thrash. "Oeooi Doll!" shrieked that fractured mind. "Poetry is lost to you now!"

His un-electric body laughed at its mind's past pretension to beauty, meaning and song. Disaster, destruction and death were the only happy dancers into the levered yellow-white sky of cursed earth.

The Doll applauded the great-visioned Doug. He humbled himself before Doug the Magnificent. Doug the Just. Doug the Omnipotent. The Doll: Oa's failure waiting to inscribe itself across System Space, blatant advert of the First Founders' fraud.

The Doll ceased his struggles. You see? his body told his mind. You are nothing. You are dead now and always were. Why do you want to know I am immersed in a glass bulb through which oxygenated water passes mechanically, obviously upstream for wherever they've put her. You can't even focus your eyes enough to see through the light-morphing glass. He caught a reflection of himself a moment, and saw that garish smile V'ing the darkness, lit a dramatic crimson. The obviousness of what the Doll now saw and felt and tasted and breathed rose up terrifyingly plain. Deary was undetectable, in great jeopardy. The Bubble itself was compromised. Yet the Doll smiled, as if in great joy.

The saddest darts pierced the Doll when he thought of Deary. He embraced them. A squid must thrash. Bubbles came out of his eyes, remembering her kind and troubled face when she'd fainted so suddenly in his arms. Her strong intellect, her fervent youth, he imagined her now as a veritable Jeanne D'Arc. Fear came in ever colder layers as the Doll dived into the unknown of her fate.

For out beyond poetry, Oa's Guard survived on that edge of irony. He could survive a "late capitalist" narrative longer than most, no doubt about it. Scientifiction? The *Good Fortune* was a so-called Time Traveler. Odd effects were reported by those who stayed awake during a jump. Perhaps a time dilation could be put to use.

Time thickened and thinned into elongating, metamorphing thought-voids before his frozen eyes. The Doll couldn't ignore the widening, swirling flatness. They mocked his lost pretensions to grandeur, his own belief that the Guard was in no way bound to the psychotic complications and delusions of Ape-like men. And then as one more shape grew bubbly and white on the hourglass before him, the Doll realized it was a body moving about in the room below him. The Doll realized then he could focus his ocular organs in a fashion he had not yet determined.

And so he learned. He'd been put on display, he realized, directly above the entrance to a grand banqueting module, rigged out for easy spinning. Directly below, largesse suggested it was the Captain's Toppler itself the Doll perceived. And then finally he saw the Captain.

There was no mistaking E. T. Wawagawa. Even afar, and elongated by diamond bubble's concavity, the Doll recognized that artificially wizened jaw. Wawagawa looked less real, made-up, even puppet-like than ever. He was staring directly up at the Doll through dark, round glasses. He continued to stare. For hours he seemed to stare. The Doll was not intimidated. He stared back, pleased that his face, if Wawagawa was looking at it, presented its mad triangular grin. Oh yes, the Doll understood now how right it was that he smiled. For time had not stopped. And here was his enemy, literally there in his sights.

Wawagawa shifted about now and then, relaxing back into his wheeler and then again leaning a bit forward. He was perhaps not looking at the Doll at all, but reading over his implants or glasses. And perhaps no time had passed. Perhaps minutes were only elongating. But why was Wawagawa not with Deary? Wouldn't she be the one he would want to see?

Wawagawa was waiting for Deary! Surely he wanted her alive to see the Doll! Even the Doll was alive. Joy washed over the Doll now, with the near certainty that Deary lived.

And his other intuition: *alone. With tubes in her arms. Drugged, raped.* The Doll did not spasm. But amid his terrible stasis, there smeared flat on the glass with weird sudden clarity, a white-haired, human eye, of what dropped away and seemed to be a great rabbit hopping through the chamber.

The Doll saw red; evacuated.

When consciousness returned, the Captain was gone. Memory of the Rabbit man stuck. Either the Doll was mad or he'd seen that freak hop by, peaking over the edge of sanity. Oh if Deary was hurt the Doll would destroy it all. The Oan Guard's was a particularly rugged corpus. It could freeze. It could perform complicated tricks in microgravity, where air was so like water but tendrils, tentacles and ink jet functioned at maximum efficiency. The Doll's rubbery strength presumed the hardest glass contained something shatterable. To rip off Wawagawa's head and splinter his bones in the void, to immobilize and wreck his rabbit ship, to find Deary and survive the ship's general diffusion in the vacuum: then hew would earn this smile! The Doll would bring down human civilation to revenge her!

But new observation interrupted this speculative fantasy. Below the Doll a familiar unicycle could be marked, rolling around all about bowel-like chamber. Nobody was atop the thing, just an arm-like appendage tipped with a colored light. It now grew swiftly larger, to the size of the entire room, then expanded nonsensically into pieces on the imprisoning concavity. Oddly-colored light now shone directly into the Doll's eyes and he understood the wheel had flown up to hang just before him upside down from the ceiling. He remembered it well. This was the thing atop the Comm tower of the pirate fishing platform.

The Doll did not move. He understood only that the wheel-bot was his lethal enemy.

Suddenly the appendage, the member, the horn—the Doll's perception couldn't master it with a word, bent forward and touched its light to the glass. A flashing gruliére spread out over the Doll's vision. The Doll smiled implacably out at the ridiculous unicycled contraption. Would they trick him into revealing consciousness? The Doll remained aloof. He looked at the situation, as it were, from a distance. His removed reason noted with something like pleasure his body's ability to resist the temptation to thrash.

After the wash of that light, the wheel-bot now sprung sprightly away, bouncing down and rolled out of the room altogether.

To his astonishment, a familiar red screen switched on inside the revealed mindscreen, now live inside the Doll's prison.

>*Have faith* it said.

>*You have friends*

III iv

Eri left Maudie waiting for a time in a small tight room artificially carved out of the Miranda moonstone. A high window was
cut into the irregular stone with precise Gothic lines. Was it
magic-glass? She could see stars. Eri's deskmodule looked like an
old broad earth-style desk. He worked with a safe-scroll, a
scratcher-pen and a WIG node. There was a complete print edition of the 1911 Britannica on the ceiling. Various omnibacks
describing the age of Shakespeare were scattered about. In another
corner, on an easel, a portrait painting stood uncompleted. Illuminated by a glowstone, she saw the water-based paint in the
dish beside was sandy and blue and still quite fresh.

The portrait was of a young woman. The face was incom-
plete, but a sheaf of blonde hair was tied back from her forehead.
The skin was brown. The girl's breast was apparently exposed,
but the portrait didn't go that far. What it did show in some
detail, and Maudie noted with something like excitement, was a
locket around the neck. It bore uncanny resemblance to little
spun-silver rose-formed locket about her neck this very moment.

Eri entered and asked her to sit. He surprised her by already
discussing a contract. "I will explain as clearly as possible, my
dear. You are now a Player, enjoying the full rights accorded to
the Falls Theater. You'll be at large as a citizen until such time

as this contract is re-negotiated. Full water-rights; bedsphere, privo and vac-suit guaranteed, etc. You can read for your self and unsign within two days. Sign now to be able to play tonight."

He passed her a scroll.

"I hope as Marina I will have full-scope to re-develop my character as I see fit."

"The fullest. Lyonesse, having you here, competing on stage again with you—well, this is exactly the sort of thing I dreamed of putting together in the Outer System. I wouldn't dream of restricting your vision. Let us give them a show to remember!"

Competing? She had trouble reading the cramped script of the scroll but it was clear she would be giving up any future claims to reimbursement for injury, mental damage or "miscellaneous transportation issues."

"If anything happens to me, I have a crate of books," Maudie said. "Morrigan—" Blushing, Maudie suddenly wondered if the Regular would be in the audience that evening.

"Come come, no need for sentimentality! You thrive."

Maudie touched a finger to her tongue and signed, almost not believing any of this was happening.

Eri immediately stood up. "Good. It's best we don't talk again before the play. I will now take my leave. The dramaturge will ready you. Tommies!" He bellowed. "*Warum bist du nicht hier? Ich will dich hier zu sein!*" Eri disappeared.

Sitting alone again, Maudie turned to look at the portrait. She saw a red light-point now illuminating the locket on her breast.

"We've been admiring your locket since we first saw you. We chose to paint it ourselves immediately."

With a gyre-tire that could brake, bounce, stick and of course roll about all the surfaces of the low-ceilinged caverns, a robotic unicycle stopped perfect and silent before her. Atop the wheel a single granular proboscis, a rather obscene appendage, Maudie thought, stood and nodded, pointing its beautifully clear colored light at itself

"Greetings ma'am," a voice sounded robotically. "We are Tommies. The Dramaturge."

"Well," said Maudie, feeling an uncanny personality radiating from the Wheel. "That's funny."

The robot tilted towards her, bowed. She reached out towards its light. The proboscis, warm, soft and oddly tactile, gripped her hand.

The little flower of time-oiled spun-silver on her chest had real mass. Instinctively touching it, Maudie felt suddenly dizzy. Were parts of her mind already entering into some sort of neuroscopic weirld, before she had even immersed? With its peculiar history, its relation to memory, Maudie's self was as slippery as water. It flowed by the gravity of time around the cliffs, rocks and boulders of her days. She heard a woman's rich laugh echoing in the distance. An electric amplifier accidentally screeched. Wow. This all felt like a memory.

"There is little time. We must prepare," the Machine noised, leading her by the hand, through stone hallways. "First up, your costume." With a complex, off-putting anti-flourish of color and a tip backwards, it rolled to lead her out of the room.

In Eri's verion, Shakespeare's Goddess Diana, protector of virgins, was now Artemis of Ephesus, protector of beasts.

Marina was the story's maid, but the character preserved a pre-Christian womanliness. She'd always had the deepest doubts concerning the terms "maidenhood" and "maidenhead" (*hood*, in her opinion being as much of a complicated nugget as *head*).

Maudie had decided for Marina maiden*hood* signified a girl's age. And it was up to her what she did with head. Marina, by all reports an extremely able and practical young woman, chose to serve the G-ddess.

But Tommies' preparations made Maudeleine feel less like an adept being prepared for Temple than a sex slave for a brothel. First she stripped nude. Watchlet and all tags were locked away in the safe. Privos off, she went through a fast but painful full body-waxing. After, she lay back. Hot water showered her smooth. Hot air blasted her dry. In the next chamber they prepared her "aura," apparently a matter of scents that would stimulate her own imagination during the performance. For Marina, the Robot had selected sandlewood, lemon and rose; Maudie added a touch of cherry for the Lyonesse.

On emerging, Tommies insisted on shaving her head. It was necessary, it explained, for the helmet to work properly.

Marjorie would not recognize her, Maudie realized when she was ready at last. She shook her shorn head, feeling so powerful already on the low-density moon. She stretched and did her Yogic excercises.

Next, Maudie selected an actual costume. Of course no one would see exactly what she wore. But during crisis points reality counted for everything.

Eri's tastes in female clothing were quite evident. Maudie thumbed through a rack of salty smelling leathers, everdry rubbers, real velvets, satins, silks and cotton underthings. Odors of Old Earth, so poignant and old-fashioned and oddly comforting, floated up all around. On a backslider, her fingers touched napkins, gloves, stoles and tyres.

"Eri's is a rather epic interpretation of the story," the Dramaturge exlained, its appendage poking open a cabinet. "It would be advisable to select a chastity device."

In the end, Maudie went for a simple look. A hard-locked privo-thong monsed her sex in tight impenetrable singularity. Over this, only linen short shorts belted firm with leather. She went otherwise naked.

"Last but not least: we select a weapon."

To her surprise the weapons were quite lethal. A compact Spacer's Crossbow, with real bolts caught her eye. She lifted it and aimed down its sites. "Isn't this dangerous?"

"You wouldn't be able to keep that inside your slot, I'm afraid. But holding it now will be enough to bring it to you should you need it in weirld."

"Yes," Maudie said, Feeling its mass.

"We suggest the handy dagger. You can slip it in your leg. It could be useful, should something anomalous occur that demands action back in the real world."

She put down the crossbow. "Excuse me? Eri didn't say anything about anomalous events. Am I in danger here?"

"One is always in danger in Space. You signed a contract?"

"I didn't read it," she admitted. Maudie selected a small, compact dagger. It was real. The curve of the blade pleased her. She strapped its holster to her left sandal.

The proboscis moved and reacted with humanlike gestures during conversation. Now, as it flashed yellow, Maudie had the intuition it was smiling.

"As your contract described, in rather self-explanatory detail, there is more than a negligible chance that technology will effect neuroscopic transition for one or more players during the performance."

"I don't understand."

"Nor can you, properly. Neuroscopic transition is poorly understood by humans," the Dramaturge answered. "In a multi-minded weirld as you will be entering, focused points-of-view can repel one another and be guided by various perceptival paradoxes into swallowing one another, with highly unpredictable effects, essentially impossible to predict."

"Meaning?"

"Your body might take you out of the slot, out of the theater, wherever the weirld wants you to end up, where another mind makes it go. Somehow, anyhow, in ways you will not remember, you will get there."

"Can't your sleeper be restrained? Guarded?"

"It makes no difference. You see, if it's possible for your body to get there, it will."

"It sounds improbable," Maudie said.

"It happens. Last year Master Jones disappeared from his slot during *The White Devil*. He only became conscious again seventeen weeks later, in a sewage hauler off Belinda. He was completely naked, seated atop a sea-turtle. When he awoke it was as if directly out of Webster, but for all that time his body had suffering an extraordinary and dangerous voyage. Anyhow, he quit the theater after that, understandably, and the position was open for Eri to come in and take over."

"Eri told me none of this."

"The most cutting edge technology (selves included) is employed by the New Falls Theater."

"Eri told me nothing of the sort."

"So we fill you in now. *Die Axt im Haus erspart den Zimmerman.*"

At last the robotic wheel led her to the high-vaulted, chapel-like backstage. Here the four actors would slot into what appeared to Maudie like a home-rigged long-range sleep-unit for four. Golden wires bundled out from bubble-visored helmets in three of four slots, and these intertwined above into a mass of wires rising up directly to a single, black omninode in the ceiling.

"That's the conduit to the Marvel-Ball out on stage, Ma'am," the Tommies said, spotting with its light a metal door ahead: STAGE 1. "Come. We'll show you the theater."

OMG Maudie gasped as she stepped onto the broad agate stage. The round bluff of sliced and polished geode stuck out into a black painted, pod-lined cavern, ribbed with sparkling jewels and trickling waters. On the other end it was walled by a sheet of domerglass the height of the entire cavern, giving a wide-open view over the dramaticaly visible gulfs of the Verona Falls. It was an epic, breathtaking view. Yet it was moderately sized, and the performance itself more shared than given. Still, this was spectacular space engineering, eclipsing the best of New Mars. Eri had really achieved something if he was doing regular performances here. Maudie herself might achieve something as well, in such a theater, she realized, suddenly thrilling to her good luck in landing this role.

The concave, vertically organized auditorium was lavishly lined lined with rounded red body pods, each red-gleaming helmet capping a harness that allowed considerable play. She imagined the audience would curl over the stage stars in the sky, all heads and many hands holding one another on their journey out from the self and at last safely home, through the performers on the way.

Center-stage was a highe single wooden stool. Stuck into a notch in the floor beside it, the long-pointed pole that would pin the Marvel Ball for its spinning already stuck like a great knitting needle into the heights of the Cavern. The ball itself was still draped with protective blankets, but colored light pooled underneath it already.

Stage left meanwhile, on an outcrop lip just above the stage proper, a musical band was setting up for a live performance. Maudie approached them from below. She noted a drum-set, keyboard, microphones, amplifiers, a theremin and a jug-band bass. This looked like real rip'n roll! She instantly remembered the rippy bands forever interrupting Eri's WIG 'scapes of yore.

Tommies introduced "our new Marina" to *The Knut and the Particles*. "We can tear up any number of tunes throughout the evening," explained drummer Bing Bip Heeley, a squat octogenarian. "I'm told it really helps the show if you like the rip."

Maudie laughed. "I love the rip."

The band kicked into a full sound-check. As bass loped, drum snapped and Theremin whizzed, the Knut flipped his floppy hair, banging on keys, singing: "*Went down to the robot junkyard—*"

"Robot *junk-yaaaard,*" the Particles intoned.

As they grooved, Tommies roll-danced, proboscis mutating to become a triangular, stick-figure, pumping its hip-like wheel, flipping high in the air, coming down into a perfectly smooth backwards moon-roll, tipping backwards and forwards, back and forth across the stagefront.

"Weird isn't it?" The Knut jumped down and offered an LP as the band finished up the remaining intrumental portions of the number. "The bot always does this jig at the end of the show. I guess he takes care of some of the comic roles in the play as wall. I say, that's a ripping costume you've got on. Great locket. Wanna make out?"

"I think I belong to somebody." Suddenly shy of her bare breasts, Maudie turned away blushing. What a idiotic statement. What did that mean?

Would Morrigan come to the play? It was apparently a special occasion. But Maudie imagined she probably had more serious work to do.

"Comme come, called Tommies. It's time to load you up!" She found herself running to join, eagerly stepping into the rather uncomfortable diagonal slot."

"Where are others?

"It's best you don't interact until *during* the play. Trust us."

Belted, helmeted (she could see darkly through the visor still), Maudeleine touched the thing around her neck. Sister Agnes felt very real to her right now. But she had a vision then, clear as day, of herself standing erect on an etched artificial world, a grid, a two-dimensional plain stretching to Earthlike curves in every direction. The ray of her perception turned the horizon—

a world neither within, nor without ordinary reality, but beside it, simultaneous and equal.

>*Feels normal, ma'am?*

"It does not feel normal."

But her mind did not reject. She felt young and alive, as if she were floating on earthwater. Clamps now took firm hold of her ankles and wrists. She felt a protrusion rise up comfortably between her thighs and pressurize itself against her sex. No wonder no one respected actors. But her protection now comforted. The slot felt snug, something like the zero-g vibe-mount, her friend Sanda installed out of doors on her Saturnite.

Maudeleine thought of the Robot's painting. She imagined herself a new face inside it that form. A face hard, young and clear, green of eye, fresh as the sea from whose turbulence she was to be born.

As she noted events occurring outside her slot, Tommies' light flickering about, one by one, Maudie let go of the things that bound her; her books still guarded, she hoped, at the bungalow; Marjorie Baumgarten's worrisome "command"; lizardy Mr. Egge....

"Well here I am," someone said, waking up somewhere else, too loud, for there was something like sound here which she could also control. "It seems extremely simple," she said, enjoying the buzzing senation of being in/on and off/out. She found she could hop about and prowl, crossbow strung on her back. She could stand on her hands.

Filling out the possibility of a place still unrevealed to the preparing spectators, she found she'd arrived in a secret garden. Walled by intricately vined cement-painted stone, with beds of roses, lavender and snap-dragons, the Lyonesse stood here as only as she knew herself to be. Strong to run swift in the forest, to climb these stone walls, to leap them.

Two others had arrived, faces also veiled. A hush had fallen. Maudie felt the solemn comradeship of deep tradition shared. In the distance she heard the crashing of real waves. Something in her yearned for surf, salt spray on the face.

Letting go of one another's hands, the actors turned and walked away, each on a separate path. Though she walked alone, Maudie could now see as if through the audience's eyes Eri, purple-robed and white-bearded, as he entered stage left, radiant with first authority. Presently out across the awesome immensity of the inner-space that now rose among them, there passed a wave of stillness, of sound, a spark against the void. Eri was spotlit on the stage. Now safe atop the stool, he plucked the long bow. He lifted the veil on the great ball. Immediately weird colors leaped out from its surface. For Maudie they rose creating the broad, white-blue cloud-scudded sky, the notched swamplands and blowing the high winds over this great theater by the sea.

Eri stroked the bow against the long pole. The Marvel Ball was spinning. *Pericles* loaded.

II ix

There were currently something close to 284 souls aboard the SFS *Good Fortune*. The 12 rings of the GA Liner supported over 200 civilians in 140 bedspheres. The Marine module sustained 50 grunts, 1 sergeant and 2 officers. Ship's crew, pilot Nina Flower included, numbered 20 exactly. "Captain" Wawagawa's party amounted officially to 10. By contract the GA was not permitted to enquire or in any way interfere with the "Captain's business" and those numbers, as the new Chief First Mate demonstrated, might change at any moment.

Unfortunately, the days of compliance with GA dominance were over. As A. J. Taylor knew from indoctrination, GA officers today were expected to "cheerfully preserve authority despite its apparent absence." The situation still grated. As he followed Lieutenant Bayley in a search of Wilhelm Darling for Wawagawa & Co, Taylor reminded himself he could still tell the insolent Egge to mind his own business.

Now, when he and Bayley reached Wilhelm Darling's bedsphere, located on the inner side of the Liner's third track ring, exactly at one of the four farthest points from the dropper (exactly the cheapest available accommodation) who should they have come upon but the always attractive, increasingly sinister Understudy Bridget Geertz.

"Thank you, Crewman. If you'd step away, I will deal with this."

"With what?"

"With William Darling."

"Wilhelm. I'm just waiting for him."

"Did you ring?"

"Yes. No answer though. I was to wait out here. I went up to 4 to use the loo and when I got back, well, this is what I found."

Taylor would have been content to let himself in with his GA passcard. But no doubt the blonde man-child Darling believed himself a "free spacer," and walked about under the aegis of the "Spacer's Seven," antagonistic to all the Authority's potential beneficence. With the Understudy witnessing, Captain Taylor pressed the bell.

The Liner ring was rank, he realized. Why did command insist on the red orgocarp? It was damp and smelled of fertilizer, no doubt about it.

No answer at the door. Amulet pressed again. "Pong him, Bayley. Emergency."

"It won't work," said Geertz.

"And how do you know that?"

"He turned it off a while ago."

"Well then how do you know he's here?"

"I was in his bedsphere with him for the last hour," she said.

How depressing. Outer Spacers were a feral lot of freaks. This was the world he'd saved Pamela from—where ruined drunks seduced fresh-faced girls with fairy tales.

Taylor pressed the bell again. He gave it a good, long, disruptive push.

"Look at this one!" Bayley had hold of a long, thick white hair.

Ignoring him, Taylor tapped the velvet slot on his hip. It felt good to slide the red card from its little scabbard. Not even Wawagawa himself had one of these. Taylor pressed the GA Override card up against Darling's lock.

Nothing happened.

"Try this," said a smiling Understudy Geertz, removing a green card from her firm breast pocket. "Pilot's Over-ride."

Darling's hatch immediately seethed and opened.

"Hello!"

Only darkness answered.

"This is Captain Amulet Jessup Taylor, Global Authority Marines. Answer immediately, within twenty seconds ship standard time, or forgo your rights against search and entry."

"You two stay right here," Taylor said flipping on his helmet light, entering head-first through the ceiling of a regular one-unit bedsphere. He light-beamed a harness, a storage unit under and an open bowl above his head for God knew what reason. Down in the floor, the little stairway curled down to the WC. A number of books floated about, as well as some sort of clip-on bow-tie. A fusty un-made sleeperpod, was left open and unmade. A great bubble of whiskey undulated in the rays of Taylor's light-beam.

Amulet sailed head first down into the water closet. Empty. A quick pass of his handy informed him the storage down there hadn't been opened since Titan.

He found a light switch. As he did a motion to his left startled. Taylor turned just as a whiskered rodent, a swollen pink-bellied rat was passing only centimeters in front of his nose. Taylor lunged, attempting to grasp its torso in his tight ship's gloves, but the little animal slithered spritely against his hand, bouncing up the track and launching itself like a missile up into the bedsphere.

Amulet Taylor admitted himself a real athlete. But Lunging after the rat, coming up the stairs, he hadn't switched on the main bedsphere lights, and he emerged face-forward into a terrible collision.

An outraged Taylor eventually righted himself and emerged.

"Did I not tell you to wait outside, Lieutenant Bayley?"

"Sorry, Sir. Just came in to tell you I answered a pong from the Captain's Chief Mate. He says we no longer need to find Darling."

Furious, Taylor retrieved his regulation ship-shoe.

"You better look at this,"

He saw Crewman Geertz kneeling by Darling's WIG node.

"What are you doing?"

"There were messages here," she said. "Sent exactly while I was away." One from Sagan Smyth.

Sagan Smyth. It was a name that immediately reminded Taylor of Pamela. Most likely this "kulturnaut/slogger," as Crewman Geertz described him, was an associate of his wife. The thought of Pamela sent Amulet time traveling in his brain to the little room in their New Mars ad-apt where he was never able to kick up his feet and read the paper without being disturbed by one of the many "kulturators" incessantly living it up in the guest quarters.

"He's in his quarters, Sir. Not answering pong, Sir."

"Let's go."

Time dilations are signaled by a familiar taste, one that you forget about afterwards, but recognize immediately as new and strange when it comes. Amulet Taylor had never tasted it, but he'd read about it and when he tasted it now, runging up to 4 behind Geertz's impressive hind-quarters, he believed the cause of that aromatic combination of wood, blood, and a suddenly remembered flower was the Understudy's aromatic perfume.

But then the time bubble had swollen up all around him and it was the very same body that had long ago runged up to Sagan Smyth's chambers, it was space-suited now and unresponsive to Amulet's consciousness. It was whizzing through space atop a great unflowering, an entirely silent fireless explosion from around an impact. Captain A.J. Taylor spun exposed in vacuum. He saw a red and gold GA Marine barracks tumbling intact through the void. He stopped time. He could look about in both directions. This was a future cataclysm far bigger than Wilhelm

Darling and Mr. Egge all the rest would understand. Amulet was among the disaster, receiving its very recent information, able to access it all. Indeed the Taylor mind, which he hardly recognized as his own, proved powerful enough to pull the bursting fragments, the flotsam, the jetsam the water ice and the very scattered atoms back together along their surprisingly worldlines. The architecture of the SFS *Good Fortune* reverted to instant coherence pulling way, oddly, most oddly, terribly, in fact, *away* from something. It was not only the *Good Fortune* whose pieces he pulled back together around him. Green/white Fuel stacks, the ranks of red flapsuits, the Horenz Bubbler screaming bodies emerged into solidity along their own lines into what he glimpsed was a GA Striker, now slipping quickly away from the scene: the *Wan Hu* bearing the entire Saturn 1 Division.

Then Amulet realized at the same time that he was missing his left eye. There was no telling how much time was flowing, but he seemed to be standing next to a white-haired being, Foodstuffs flew all around them.

"You sure you're OK?" The voice of Understudy Geertz steadied him.

Amulet nodded, still shaken. Apparently she hadn't experienced as extreme a time dilation as he. Good humor still warmed her young and bright expression. Yet she looked very deeply in the eye.

"What did you see?"

Amulet tried to shake his head of the vision.

Taylor's briefing officer had informed him that only observers especially prone to delusion in their everyday life saw real honest-to-god glimpses of the future. Most saw things that *could* come true, but never would. That fact cheered him, though the reality of what he'd seen, and that taste, remained.

Taylor considered himself less prone to delusion than anyone he could imagine now on board the SFS *Good Fortune*. As far as he knew, the *Wan Hu* was due in hours before the *Good Fortune*. Ever since the new generation of AI's, those that helped operate the *Wan Hu*, he presumed, timing was supposedly near perfect; accidents were supposedly a thing of the past. He imagined certainly the ships were relatively slow-moving when they hit, nothing would have survived to be seen otherwise. Was there a plot afoot?

Amulet himself had potentially survived—for one of his eyes was live to receiving that information from the future. If he was propelled that fast by the impact, he might well be flying forever of course. Understudy Geertz, he remembered, now leading him across the Liner Bar to Sagan Smyth, was herself the Pilot's assistant and representative aboard the ship. Was Understudy Geertz not the clear and rational being as she pretended to be? Could she be party to a conspiracy to take out the *Wan Hu*?

Sagan Smyth was of swarthy middle-aged appearance, about the same size as Understudy Geertz. A ruddy-face lined from a history of miming too many honest expressions, with zero authentic feeling below, opened into a permanent grin. Smyth had friends over; he came out to talk in the corridor. He greeted Understudy Geertz with a strong little handshake. That time bubble was amazing," he said. "I saw a bag-piper!"

"Captain Taylor's looking for Will Darling," Understudy Geertz said. "Have you seen him?"

Smyth's eyes widened. "How is it that everybody in all the worlds suddenly has a bee up their bonnets about Will Darling? Did you know he's on thirteen panels at the Convention? Thirteen! Will's unwashed, not real skiffy at all! I've only got three panels myself, and they're junk!"

"Where is he?" Amulet interrupted.

"I asked him over to join us on a visit to the Manse. But anyhow, the Captain rescinded our invitation."

"Where is Will now?"

"His quarters I suspect! Is Will in some kind of trouble?"

Smyth looked curiously at Geertz.

"Sir." Bayley interrupted. "Rango's on 1."

"Sir—Rango here. I have to report an—well, an anomaly."

Taylor turned away. "Yes Sergeant? What sort of anomaly."

Rango gulped audibly. "Are you drinking, Sergeant Rango?"

"I'm having a whiskey, Sir and you will understand why Sir when I explain to you we found a severed head, Sir."

Taylor composed himself, moved away from the others. "Are you making *fun*, Rango? If you—"

"No Sir. It's most certainly not fun. A severed head floated out from a girder on the second tier track and scared the life out of Milligan. He came running to me all the way to station. I thought it might be time dilation thing, Sir so I investigated myself. I found it and brought it in."

"Is it Large? Male? Blonde-haired? White-skinned?"

"No Sir, female. Earless, Sir, face tattooed like a chessboard."

"Chess-board?" It reminded him of something. "Evidence it. And no more whiskey, Rango. A situation is possibly developing. For safety's sake I want you to issue a ship's wide quarantine. I want every single person on this ship, marines included, in gear full-ready for vacuum by 19:00."

And so A. J. Taylor's wonderful Outer System command was already coming apart at the seams. A severed head. A missing drunk. A potential collision. How to make sense of this unfolding series of unrelentingly freak events.

It was time for the Captain to confront Captain Wawagawa immediately, on his own turf.

"Hey!" Smyth stepped forward. "Wait a nano!" A hard finger poked Taylor in the chest. "Did you say *Captain Taylor*?" Sagan Smyth blasted whiskey-breath in his face. "Are you? Yes! You are, you fiend. You're Pamela Lamprey's beau. I had a message from her! She's starring in *Pericles* in Verona Polis. Opening tonight!"

III v

The storm was father; mother was the craft upon the Sea. In the clarity of first self-identification, Marina discovered that what wrapped her like a mother's womb was a great and curling storm. The storm was viewed frozen on her mind's screen. Its twisted eye, that fetus-like point of self's origin, bubbled out of the storm's innermost socket and became her own. Sea sucked her up. Marina was born from out of her loss.

If the storm was pure will, pure force, the sea was pure absorption, pure reflection. The storm eventually retreated half into the sky, enfolded its billowing charcoal black and spitting lightning. Revealed was the wooden stage allship, sliding into the parting, foaming brine. The retreating storm still hollered. Winds still flattened out the spreading waves. Again and again, the ship's stiff bow smacked down, parting, unseaming lips of the sea.

Somewhere deeper a mummy slipped shrouded into the cold silvery waves.

Enslaved women were stacked in staggering depth into the bowels of the ship. For eleven days, as time slacked, a man stood above her. His heavy feet walked back and forth on her ceiling. "How?" He railed against the sea: "How, Lychordia!?"

The point of view of the others was all around. It was their quasi-logical, un-stable observation that maintained the real hand that now touched her, lifted her into the air, the creamy breast that now warmed her—the living heart beneath. Only Marina would ever know the nurse's secret: she was not the hag swathed in dark robes those observers believed her to be. Only Marina felt herself fall into the hands of she whom she knew in another depth altogether. She was frightened to see this being already present all around her, as if all women were the Russian dolls of other women's selves, stacking down nurs/child/nurse/child into prehistory. She was such as are the nurses of the children of doom-decreeing kings. She was such as are the housekeepers in their echoing halls. Rounder in all its expressions than Marina had ever thought to imagine possible was that globe upon which Lychordia permitted herself to be sailed. Against her en-wrapping confidence, the storm lost its edge. The still writhing blacks-in-green crashed and flashed yellows, and eventually whimpered into blues, extending geometric into the globular sky. Marina wondered how the audience who sustained this weirld, could each fail so precisely to know her nurse whose name was the specific clear bell ringing out in the darkness.

"Lychordia? How?"

How indeed? The old gap-toothed nurse, mustached, hump-shouldered like a man, suffered to care for the disowned orphans at court.

So framed, contained in the warm spirit of entertainment, in an altogether wrong position and orientation, Marina sailed upon the sea. Poetry swirled in her wake, the ever vigilant pen of the Poet exposing invisible connections and curlicues up out of the disappearing foam.

And upon that ship's stage once more ancient Gower called upon her to yield the stage to another. Was it a mirror Marina looked into? If so it showed through time as well as space onto an entirely different scene. Thaisa, whom she did not recognize but felt she should, queen-to-be, was on another's body. Warm, eternal, alive, yearning, she straddled a lover. She rode him to death upon a spike, as he injected her with flowing emotional torrents.

But instead of Thaisa the Queen caught Marina in that compound eye, rubbing her blonde-hooked mandibles together delightedly on a heap of her drone-corpses. She tinctured her tips with the sting of a drone still stuck in her anal cavity, music kicked in. Bugs danced all around. Worm-like heads upon heaps of larvae swayed in rhythmic time out of devoured eye-holes as the warrior, brown and back-bubbled for comment, reared up and showed himself King.

"How, Thaisa!" a father's voice raged, fucking the wrong one raw in the boiling surf. Lychordia's voluminous cloth, tinctured with the old smells of her suckling, the warmth and simple truth springing from the fragrant spring took her to the backside of Marvel Ball Earth.

When she awoke, older, longer of limb and wiser, Marina walked in a graveyard, gathering sheaves of wild rosemary. She could not remember why she was here. The place was lovely. Unbudded, new-grown and pure. She stood out nude and fragile against the peeping world. Many predators stood back and watched, from out of the forest's darkness. Other eyes gazed from the tombs and sepulchers.

And she came upon a fresh-filled grave, strewn with only flowers. Worms curled around the petals, curious and pale. Looking for homes, the sweet ones, but they brought her no joy. Marina brushed away the flowers and her heart whisked away as she saw the wrinkled, toothless face of Lychordia, gummed up, sucked of water.

All music ended. Ashy grasses, weeds slowburned. Scuttling beetles turned circles upon stones reflecting the inevitability of meaninglessness. Marina understood she was affixed to a cemetery planet obsessed with death, whose mud provided for its current flickering lives momentarily, only to swallow them over and over and over again. She had fallen, was crawling in mud. Please let it just be mud. A hand reached out to help her, a strong hand—it felt male, like a sex in her hand. In all innocence she held it.

She wore no shoes. The sea seethed its fingers up the road all the way from the wedge of strand to lick at her feet, and tell her what everyone watching knew. She held the killer's hand. She let it go.

Her guide stopped, but not at the sharing of this moment. There upon the colorless horizon he saw a vessel. Its long black banners showed symbols of the nothing-seen, the nothing-heard, the nothing-comprehended or proven.

"The *Jolie Rouge*," he said.

She turned to face her companion, and was surprised to see it was not a man or woman but a mechanical oddity who addressed her. A lewd pointed horn was fixed to a small wagon. The wagon tipped and the horn pointed away from the slavers.

"We would be honored, maid," winked the weird wheel, "if you would join us in a general celebration." It pivoted and rolled smoothly away from the beach.

Marina found that she was walking with other women now. Not simply the women of that land, but women still to come and women who died before language touched their culture's tongues. All women walked together on that seasonal pilgrimage. She recognized those many thousands stepping out on Gower's globe, plainly illuminated, while the Father crouched in darkness on the stage, believing himself entirely unseen. But all the women of the weirld surrounded.

Unknowing, raising woman in his mind, he busily, furiously worked his member.

Diana's lip trembled, in amusement. For he couldn't finish. He swore and pulled, slapped and stretched. Now others had gathered around to watch as well.

She felt a sudden expansion of her breasts, as did all the living breasts of the women who nourished our family long into the ever-written past. Tickling, sore, sensitive, unfeeling, nipples doubled, quadrupled, breasts multiplied in undulating rolls all down her front. Child-creatures emerged, animal, fish, birds, insects and human, ringing her skirts and sides tipping heads back and tickling those tender water-dripping prominences to sudden attention.

Gower lay prostrated on the stone.

"My temple stands in *Ephesus*," said the company through the full lip of Diana, as one. "Hie thee thither."

"Swear!" said they all.

"And there make sacrifice."

They beheld Old Uranus now, tipped sideways and ringed as with jeweled chains. The great orb's storms came visible like aureolae below the equator. "Perform my bidding," said the Goddess through all the company's lips, as all her beloved suckled happily upon her unfolding laughing water-balloons, "my children all." And water sprinkled out from all of the unfolding nipples. Each she felt sprinkling pure out of her, curling as if from ranks of unfolding breast onto the swirling beautiful ball of milky blue and healthy white as old Gower drew the bow upon it, drawing great threads of repeating color high into sky, now expanding into space, above the cliffs, above the colony as a whole, angling, duplicating, extending like bands of candy-colored streams into ornate and three dimensional geometric tunings of sixteen newly revealed bright gilt-edged holes grinning the universe. Act 3 had ended. Marina beheld, as through the eyes of the audience stunned, the Ice Giant's Garments of High Water Falls.

II x

The Doll could imagine, as he stretched and excercised his parts as best he could, that he was physically embracing the room below. Since he'd received WIG from the Wheel (who was not his friend, who belonged to the Rabbit man) he assessed the situation below with godlike omniscience.

The Doll had not given up on beholding reality outside. When he saw the Rabbit float the blonde man past, he was ready. There was a great hole in the big man's chest. His mouth hung open like he was dead.

The Doll had boxed seats over a polyhedronic stage, for a theater of cruelty he was not at all sure he wanted to see. A track entered from a conduit directly across from the Doll. It curled around the center toppler just below him, and disappeared where the Doll couldn't see. The floor/wall panels sported stair-like seating; various possible floors surrounded the human inhabited perimiter of the room. On four sides the pentagonal panels were edged with water.

He held the stateroom contained in his imagination's grasp, even as the actors below stepped through the great void of his absence from Deary. There was nothing in the waters of her. He held her absence as his right. He did not again struggle; the bubbles of now chaffed his anus raw. He did not shift. The Doll could never return to Cove. He could never face Doug or any of them again. Yet he felt something like joy. For the Rabbit lived.

It returned. The Rabbit was sane, cleaning its hairs with precision, looking up and staring often directly at the Doll.
And also then, the Doll was sane.

Others passed through. The Unicycle, which the Rabbit commanded, was always busy—seemingly accomplishing numerous things at once. It never tried to communicate again with the Doll. He had intimation that the thing was not quite bound by programming to the Rabbit, but also able to thwart his interest. This seemed to the Doll a devilish attitude. If it knew the Doll was intelligent why not give information? Why serve the mad Rabbit? Why not let the Doll out to kill? And so the Doll gave up on the Wheel.

He had no hopes for the large-bodied Chef, a real Japanese man of evident dignity. Before he entered, the Doll saw the Rabbit arranging the Captain sphinx-like in his chair. The Rabbit departed. The Chef then entered, scolded the Captain furiously. He raised a hand in anger. Wawagawa had barely answered. He was still looking at the Doll! The Chef stormed off. The Rabbit passed through again after, up to something—entirely ignoring the Captain.

And so the Doll understood it was not a Rabbit. This was a Man, the Enemy. The Rabbit was not necessarily a rabbit at all. He was not a white bear, or a fat dog, or enormous monkey. He a mostly naked, bell-shaped humanoid, who happened to be blanketed in thick bristlying white fur. His arms looked augmented and strong, but certainly no match for the Doll.

Today the white beast was wearing a helmet, with open straps earlike on either side of the head. Why wear a helmet and no suit? Was his skin/fur bioengineered for the void? Bare-headed, blanketed, dark-spectacled he never left his position below the Doll. He was leading a stranger into the Manse, a character the Doll had not yet observed.

The thing was talking rationally, the Doll saw, explaining the room. He could see the guest quite clearly now. A thin-legged, broad-shouldered normal, with a yellowing white omnisuit and a helmet tipped back to show slick white hair covering and a large moustache. A red flow-tie matched the color of the helmet. He wore old fashioned spectacles. In microgravity the Guest appeared unintentionally disheveled, even unkempt. Very much like a surface man underwater.

The Rabbit was apparently trying to show off the Doll, for he gestured the Doll's way. The two approached his bubble from below. The Guest appeared disccomfited, and disturbed by the Rabbit's harangue. The Guest did not directly seem to even look the Doll's way.

Soon the rabbit bowed obsequiously and withdrew, hurrying out the tube across from the Doll. The Stranger ambled about, gradually approaching the cypher of Wawagawa in the wheel-chair. When he did, to the Doll's surprise, Wawagawa suddenly spoke. His mouth opened and closed, emitting words the Doll could not make out.

The Guest helped himself to a drink and sat quietly with the Captain. In answer to a question, he began to talk. His face was contorted in an inwardly directed frown, oddly focused by the Doll's bubbled view, so that he could see the wetness on the man's red lips as they moved about unceasingly. Whether or not it was to Wawagawa the Man really spoke, the Doll was uncertain. Wawagawa did not answer.

Something about the man filled the Doll with the desire to understand his speech. His beak was lined with ranks of little triangular teeth. They were easy enough to dislodge. It occurred to him now that one might be made by contact with the glass into a transmitter of sound waves.

It worked, with astonishing clarity. "The Polis is the perfect model, even where Jefferson is concerned," the white man was saying. "Sure. Farms are a number one concern, unless you're some kind of damned Jacobin. Can't say I'm sure Miranda's wrong to deny the GA the 40 percent. Any city state in the relative wild depends on agriculture to support itself number one, and for trade and other concerns number 2. Agricooperation on the community scale is more productive than cross-system trade. Water is the future of Space of inter-colonial Space. Milt Moore called it back in 99. Course no one listened but me."

The Guest stopped speaking, not even looking at the Captain, and hung his head on his chest. Soon enough, the Captain revived him with a question the Doll could not hear.

"There ain't no end to the ways that on the local level the Polis can still do things that empire cannot. Jefferson saw that. He saw you had to extract from religion its utilitarian, practical core. You had to update the good parts, cut away the bad, and improve the fiction. What would a decent, non-interfering God do? What would it look like? Well it depends who's asking. Every generation should rethink it. Educate the educators first. Religion should do that. But as to real miracles, well on the one hand there's water. Want a bring her back to life? Bring her back to the water."

He stopped talking, mouth hung open.

The Captain seemed to snap out of a trance. "What were you saying? While we wait, I want your opinion about the so-called *artificial hyper-intelligence.*"

As the Captain barked rudely at the squinting guest, drool slithered down his gleaming lips. The words emerged via tooth transmitter to be received by the consciousness of the Doll, but that consciousness itself found itself looking backwards at them, cresting then upon a bubble of time. The Doll, perhaps because the state of extreme empiricism from which he greeted was able to attach himself to time ripple and hang on into the future. With time he found he could shatter that glass and he was joyfully (though he it felt it not) free. Body was mind and mind body looking at themselves from a perpective they didn't know they had. The Doll was in the middle of the air, among a bubble of his own water, shards of glass vectoring in all directions around. Mid-spasm, the profound and occurring force of will he embodied currently dominated all the scene. There were numerous others reacting or not reacting below him, surprisingly. States of various shock froze their faces. One was sheeted with a fresh flow of some sort of soup. Another with blood and a third he recognized. I know her face from the future, the Doll thought, precognitively aware of this moment of connection between two points on the possible timeline of his consciousness, already a leap head..

But very peculiarly, in all this stasis, there was something moving with impossible regularity. The single silver-spoked, glittering wheel. Even in stopped time, it rolled, bounced, flew about, in fact the Doll's mind could not hold still following it. The Doll in air light seemed no longer leading the scene. The Wheel now pulled him across the room. The proboscis uncannily pointed away from an object of horrific meaning to the Doll. The Doll couldn't see through is own eye as it followed that light across the room and fear spiked hard in his nervous system popping the bubble away.

"You're known to speculate on this," the Captain went on, too loudly. "I know you are. The *singularity pet*. Tell me about that. What do you know?"

The Guest had withdrawn into himself. For a moment the Doll thought he wouldn't answer. But he did.

"Time just dilated, for the record."

"The pet."

"Sure there's storics about the pets. Guess what? The tales are tall. Whatever singularity means, seems like if she would want us to know about her, we would. Would we be here not knowing about her, if she didn't want us to do just that? As long as there's good clean water to shave with, Occam's razor's got this chin clean, friend." He scratched his chin, moustache bouncing in illustration.

"And the singularity mind said to have been in the possession of A.E. Winnegutt? Did you ever get wind of that?"

The pause that followed was artificial. The Doll felt the Guest seemed very much keeping something back. "Ah yes. Well. Of course when the word is water, water is the word. We had water of it. There's always been circles within circles in the skiffy sea. But trust me. A.E. Winnegutt's fantasy, at best."

"Get to the point please now. Did or did you not know A.E. Winnegutt? And why did you say *her*," the Captain asked, in a discernible but oddly phrased voice, in regard to the singularity. "Why her?"

"So you see we never exchanged more than a word."

"That's not what I meant!"

The Guest rose. "Well," he was saying. "Fraid I better get going. The time thing, it… uh…" The most awkward of possible Spacers, he appeared almost Doll-like with the tendrils of fabric and cord and tech lines straying every which way off his crumpled suit, tracking hurriedly through the exit underneath the Doll.

"But I am bringing Mr. Egge into the conversation!" One of Wawagawa's arms had lifted from the chair and was pointing towards the entrance to his quarters. "Mr. Egge is back!" The Captain, as if after a great effort, slumpted forward in the chair. His spectacles fell half down his face.

The Rabbit Man appeared, but it was too late. Another matter had taken his attention over watchlet.

Mr. Egge, the Doll grinned. You seem flustered. I'm not. I have a name for you at last. A name to study.

Mr. Egge departed. Via ship's version of the WIG the Doll scanned through Egges of Industry, Egges of culinary reputation,

Egges of Hamm, Egges off Mars—until he found a reference to a eyes only reality show for the Unnamed Concerns, *Annals of Egge*, whose copyright infringement policy was death. Understandably, very little info was currently available on board. But the Doll believed he was on the right track with one fragment quoted in the a portion of the SPACER'S SCRAPBOOK dedicated to Earthside decadence.

EGGE 40 AND COUNTING!

Now accepting subscribers! One more Sheik of Freaks from Planet Freak where freak addicts fuck it up further with real-world mayhem, murder, mother-raping, and more! Sign up now, scumbag, and suck up seven free months from special agent Egge's private table of dastardly, disaster, distress and adventure: all senses satisfied guaranteed.

REMEMBER HOPPIES IF YOU SEE AN EGGE OUT THERE IN THE WILDERNESS GIVE EGGE A HAND!

THE E IS NOT SILENT! INFORM!

II xi

> *This talk is dedicated to all those who paid Jerry O'Perception according to contract within eight system standard days of Jerry O's delivering Jerry O's end of the deal*

Here's old Jerry O still tapping away, still worrying about contracts still minutes from that vision of up above, all around, all the waters of Earth, cascading in roiling joy.

Ain't that a weirld! An oceanic breadth in that one. Let me out in here as of now. Long time since you've been underwater. Long time, hell...

Jerry O—who had been standing feet-harnessed to the bedsphere pod—slipped free. Jerry O ate too much. Smoked too much. Jerry O took a full five minutes rather than the usual matter of seconds, but Jerry O successfully completed a zero-G "flying wheel" maneuver.

Jerry O just performed the Wheel. Well jolly good. That happened.

That happened.

But it was not just the waters exploding around you. The world before and after the dilation were the ones that scarred. Exit stateroom. Would have liked to stay with all that water, damn it. That furry Egge Man pulled me back. That thing in the tank splayed out like a monstrous exposed organ? Don't let me swim in that thing's ocean. Egge said it was some kind of isolato work, a living creature. The specs came up nil on that thing, literally fogged up the screen when imaged. It looked like a living nerve, a proto-human with the mask of Satan. Fact was, Jerry O didn't like the feel of those always open eyes looking down on him. Not one single iota. Not with that hairy bodymorph Mr. Egge peeking around the corners. No, Jerry O didn't like the feel of things in old Wawagawa's cabins, so Jerry O left. Didn't like that little interrogation either. Wawagawa had never shined, indeed, but even so he wasn't at all what he once was. Jerry O didn't somehow like the feel of things in the Manse, and he was about old enough and harmless enough, he'd about not been listened to for long enough that he could do what the hell he wanted..

Egge was the power. Sinister agent of unnamed Concerns, abroad in the Outer System. Concern farmed, no doubt about it at all. No, Jerry O didn't like the line of Egge's questioning. Jerry O thought it was quite all right to think that now. Folks out here were sitting-ducks for the likes of Egge. A Self-Augmenting biobot with enough tech buying power to command the finest AI Jerry O has ever seen.

That Wheel thing might really read a mind. Rid the head of thoughts unwanted. No one tried to stop him. No one followed, and presently here's Jerry O double-locking his liner bedsphere closed, slipping shipshoes back into the restraints and donning the scribegloves at last.

>*Jerry O reminds the Uranacon II Organizers that payment will still be due to the O'Perception Estates whether or not he survives*

It's Jerry O recording his last will and testament, his personal address to the scientifiction convention on Miranda.

Very likely the lecture could be broadcast at URANACON whether or not Jerry O survives. He might even record it live now. Yes, why not? After all, one needs something real to live for just as much as you need nothing for which to die.

Jerry O noted the audible light laughter and chuckles from decadent academics and perverted Jacobins alike as they heard the name announced in the Con dome. It would be a big enough hall. No doubt about that. Of course most those in attendance have been under the impression O'Perception passed a long time ago. Jerry O's alive? Wonder that, they say? Jerry O knows the sorts of things they say. And the joke is indeed upon Jerry O since in this case he is dead. Unable to attend Uranacon II to stare them down!

Something for which to live. Jerry O recognized an excitement in the old heart. Really going home, old friend. You've done time-traveled right into heaven and they showed you it's made of water.

Damn the torpedoes! It was time. Even if Mr. Egge was not coming for him, Jerry O had taken matters in hand. Soon enough he was back tapping. Jerry O resolved to deliver his last testament *ex tempora*, aplomb a'plenty. Sparks should fly.

"Consider the following." His trusty com-panel winked its recording light blue. Jerry O felt good. Belly comfortably resisting the privo-suit's gelid mold, he proceeded with spectacles flashing the shipboard WIG with the available informatics. About twenty years out of date, those specs, but handy as hell.

"Consider a system made up only of other systems. Scale varies infinitely in both directions. So it is with our Sun, which is not the end of things. Yes there's the inner system, the outer system; there's the reproted system of the Kuipurs and there's the Solar System itself whose laws support the rest, systematized by the galaxy and so on. On every scale in any true systematics you find the same progression. The systems of life support that are keeping me going this minute as I record this systematic statement for all you Spacers systematically arranged in Arden Corona, Moon Miranda, is generated by a system of systems including certain of the systems in my own body.

"I now propose the following question: *What One System Links Them All?*

"What remains outside? What is, as it were, the engine of all systematics? Though when I asked him this one time Milton Moore answered the System Series, and I had to laugh at that, it's not the answer I'm looking for. The answer I am looking for will not come as a surprise to any those of you who've paid attention to my four decades of work. To be blunt: H2O. Water.

"Indeed, water is system. Write that down.

"Go ahead and laugh. Hell, it makes me smile. It's good news!" Jerry O pulled out the suspender-like straps of his servo-suit with his thumbs. Bile was rising. "We still look up to some imaginary sky when we think of answers, like there's God flying around and we ain't figured out exactly which. But there is reason to suspect that life is intended to exploit water in order to achieve the interlocking complexity of an authentic food chain. To what order? Well, so that something can arise from it all, step out of that tide, walk up on a hill, observe itself, the universe, the rocks around and then employ and reason to decide how best to preserve and cherish the principles with which water beats the banker.

'Life is a thing writ in water.' Keats wrote that. He forgot the second part. 'By water.' Life is written by water, friend. Jerry O said that. Look down for your meaning! That's where water always goes, eventually. Of all the systems, water is last and it's first. Jefferson's God was all right with Jerry O. He was a clock-maker. Guess what. It was a water-clock, he had in mind and it's cause some long-gone God made one that we have free will at all..."

So clear was the imagination of the lecture that Jerry O felt for a moment the real joy of standing on an Ice moon at last, having survived this last publishing contract in one piece. He would have moonsteaded, or moved out to one of the homer communities in the System.

How to cross over to them, he wondered, these radical interlocutors of a new Verona Polis? They were feral, wild, perhaps, but not free like water.

"Every system we can believe in but one," Jerry O told the young woman now, "is delusion. One can go on and on in this line and be right the whole way. Jerry O's had a long time to reflect on these things. The gist is this: What Nature was to Emerson is Water to Jerry O."

He looked over his spectacles to gaze them down. "You might say I myself, as a water system in Space, am relatively powerless in the systems which sustain me. You might say the fact you're receiving this talk the way you are, proves it. You'd be wrong, young lady." He cleared his throat. "Let me get a video here…"

"All right, audio then. What you young people need to be fighting against ain't land rights, god-damn it. It's water rights! No rights to water? Rights *of* Water, Man! The Right of Water to Run," why that's the very moral foundation of our physics." Jerry O was fired up now, fisting the air. "If you don't promote water, sooner or later water don't promote you. Fact is, Jerry O was all about water before Milt Moore. Before any of the Oan Bubble people for that matter either."

Shouldn't have mentioned them, he realized at once. Now Egge knew. Egge was extremely curious. Some sort of interrogator and hunter-breed. He wormed his way to you, apparently rabbit-like, ingratiating, nibbling all the time. And sure enough you were already thinking about what he wanted as well ever since, as he would want you to. He wanted to know about the deep past, about words exchanged long ago in time. Jerry O had not answered. Jerry O hedged the questions. Jerry O declined and departed.

But here one was, and there was still time (yes, Jerry O was known to drag on) there was still time not to comment on those peculiar events that Egge himself had touched upon, concerning the remarkable young woman one still remembered after all these years.

Jerry O lowered visor. He sank back into pod. Felt a bit sad now. With Egge watching him thinking that was the Right to Reading winking out, god-damn god-damn, in the very last hours of O'Perception. Were these old memories why ETW brought Jerry O out on this jaunt? Just because that night in Luna City long ago? Had to be others who still remembered. Those gatherings in soup-holes where the whiskey was free would live for as long memories. So many decent weirlds were founded in those heady days, the days when Jerry O was young. Back then, writers were sought out in Space and provided for generously. But the work was hard. You had to deliver.

Egge, you felt, Egge was watching you even now. Not the young woman in the audience with the curious eyes, after all, but Egge himself and his wheel. She should have listened.

"I'll tell it now!" issued Jerry O from behind his shaded spectacles, addressing the auditorium here with its tall avocado trees and motile fan units, and the glittering starlight-effect of the omniradiation (water-fueled) all about

>Because if anyone came to see me here it was probably to hear this. I will say the following. And I suppose I'll close after that because I'm resolved to read some Emerson, some Melville, and perhaps some Jefferson as well before drinking a nice half-pint of cool clear water and nodding out. Since I've never before laid down my testament to certain much talked about events, and fervently hoping that some among you might take

offense…. Jerry O'Perception now states the following fact. *Ole' Deep Hollow* and *Furrow's Flow* both of them books where Jerry O found the stroke you might say, were mainly, no, were entirely, the brain children of Milton Moore. Not many would be ashamed to have been associated with Milt Moore and if he were alive today you could bet your bottom sand-dollar he'd be collaborating with Jerry O on something or other. It's too bad Milt didn't get more credit for those. Not that he needed it! But the ideas were his.

The whole setup was Milt's, from conception to dream to realization to what became for that brief moment on Mars the Plains of Glass, and still is, by Poseidon!

That's the early work. You know it's good. After *Infer No* everything you know as Jerry O is Jerry O. And that's all that needs to be said about that.

Jerry O relaxed, breathing slower now, retreating into the mind. A fork of drool extended from his lip like a curious fang. He released his bladder. The inner skein of his white servo-suit filled up with warm ammoniated water. Jerry O closed his eyes to the moving colors on his spectacles. How little did he have to say to the world, this man from whom statements had never ceased issuing for some forty-eight years. And how much he wouldn't say.

She came now like the angel of his transition. He couldn't stop her. He knew somehow that it would be all right. This was perfect. To find her now, this way. Helmet in hand, hair tied back behind her head, stiffly suited, unfamiliar with pretty much everything Lunar. Jerry O remembered standing across from that young writer with perfect clarity. He wasn't letting it show but there was something irresistible to him about her plainly presented face. No doubt to her Jerry O was a "reactionary and uninformed." In fact in those days Jerry O was just Jerry Perception, another devoted follower of Manx Brand.

She was good. But you can't play tricks on the Manx like selling your work to all and sundry. She didn't receive position when her time came up. She went back Earthside. But she kept writing for Spacers. We only found that out later.

Surprising, really, you remember that night so clearly.

She had arrived with another woman, older, more experienced, defintely not a writer: a scientist, or some sort of astronaut. Her wife, you later found out, though you knew little about such things then and still didn't now. Old Jerry O never really did explore more than the life of the mind.

It was in the Harrison Hod, that soup-hole where Manx's troops used to gather and trade ideas, all hopting to promote their own titles and get out of indentured servitude to Manx Brand. It was the first time you had seen her. She'd been working in a printshop, just a copy girl and she started printing her own stuff. Manx took notice. He had just published the third of her funny, odd, strangely gripping tales about Opal, a post-earth water-world entirely unsure of its own origins. She was good. It was vivid, watery stuff. And perhaps you liked it because of that night in the Harrison Hod where it all started; you saw her for the first time in the flesh and you stayed while other people talked and she was questioned concerning her collaborating AI. Jerry O was a part of that small gathering.

No, Jerry O did not sign on to that project himself, did not look twice at the matter, once he'd taken it in. But damned if in retrospect things didn't change. And changed and changed some more until by the time Mr. Egge came along Jerry O would not give that comrade up now in his death pod if you burned his skin right off.

It grew late. She opened up about its influence on her work. She talked and explained, moved from anecdote to speculation and all the way back again. Narcotics, drinks were consumed. Not by her, by the way, nor by Jerry O. One did not listen too closely, so as not to be rude. But at one of those moments where conversation flags not by intention but by the laws of probability, her words went out to stick themselves forever on the lives of everyone in that cave in such a way as each would always be reminded by memory of them of her, and of the miracle of First Space.

"I asked through what sort of gateway the singularity might pass. The AI answered with a riddle."

Silence.

"What lies true, and works best served dry?"

"A hoax," said Jerry O.

Egge itched. Egge itched hard.

III vi

Hie to her Temple, maiden of Moon,
where silver was born,
and if e'er to thee fair thighs
of oxen Smyrnaeans have burnt—
think about ripping your own.

The *Pericles* weirld, by virtue of the net of human minds it depended on, was a world deeper in its way than the real world. It contained shared dreams, surprisingly recognized group memories, recognitions of things one had never seen. Oddly enough, though it was also as small of a single theater on a single tiny moon, Marina felt that very far away an outsider had already entered the scape. Egge was ravaging some far distant region of the global Empire that extended far beyond the Sea's horizon, along the enormous Earth-scale distances the plantetscape implied and no doubt could yield.

Did Eri, the weirld's auteur, intend the extreme depths at which Marina experienced her own narrative freedom before her part even began? Sex addict hetero-Male feminists played a tricky game. He may have given away far more than he understood when he allowed the Lyonesse agency in this game. Marina's own insistent point-of-view surprised even herself with its realism.

This weirld of pure art reminded her ordinary life was rife with illusion. The Lyonesse didn't hesitate to think on the most honest terms now of Marina's secrets, her hottest unknowns, her needs below those of the story, and just slightly above. Longing lasted longer, with that locket on her breast. Its real mass, its cool old spun silver, was the gift she carried from her nurse Lychordia. And when finally those pirate ships came, she was well prepared.

Marina began that voyage separated in a cage in the Captain's cabin. For warmth and covering she had only the wrapped rare silk with which she'd bundled the herbs she had gathered by Lychordia's grave. By the voyage's end it was the Captain in the cage, naked, and Marina without, fully clothed. He barked: "Would you like to purchase your freedom then?" still presuming himself her master as his own sailors carried him away.

That first day she saw Ephesus, Marina knew it was the hub of all worlds beyond the ken of the Gods themselves. Safely bluffed, easily defended, the white and painted city shone with wealth and promise. Far below, a wharf formed an artificial harbor enclosing where sweetwater Cayster kissed the sea.

Boys and old men caught her ship's lazily tossed rope, helped tie the *Lychordia* to great cleats like elephant legs upon the wharf. Pelicans rose. Eagles watched from trees. Dogs barked. Women lounged in shady gardens lining the road up to the shining gates of the city. Gossiping, sipping blue wine their lips the color of the grape. Goats shuffled. Children greeted the sailors arriving with laughter. A crowd formed. Strangers threw flowers. A procession began spontaneously.

Marina found herself accompanied by a dancing flute suspended over a single rolling wheel. The instrument played itself into a solo, melody tumbling directly into a dance number.

> Without the ape, without the cow,
> Without the ripping scene

The tide turns desolate!
And tries no cuckoos to convene.

Warmed by the white-light of Earth, the laughing road rose up bluffs towards the glittering marble walls. Works went on. Scaffolding connected the tallest of the multi-colored edifices to box-like habitations stretching up the surrounding hills to the South. Below a ragged plain of blowing marsh grasses, showed temporary encampments. On the plateau across, the Artemision already popped into impossible scale, as if directly from out of the mind. That massively-topped temple opened more than she yet understood into the weirld. Still veiled, Marina turned away.

As Marina sought the still fluting Wheel, a troop of dancing maidens buffeted and pushed it, eventually catching the pipe and disappearing it in their skirts. "It's your special day," they told Marina, moving about rapidly, some of them taking hold of her limbs. Her hair was shorn. Flowers were thrown upon her form. Hands wrapped her white in chiton and veiled her face with linen. "You are now a weaver," they said.

Marina saw a city already all aflower with celebration. While adults gathered by the theater, children streamed to the river games; branches stuck out of every nook and cranny, crusted with colored ribbons. Maidens stood in high place pouring flowers down upon celebrants passing into the dense spectacle of market, declamation, beggary, thieving, color and change that was the city.

Laws were upside-down inside these walls, so Artemis Ephesios had decreed; women and slaves were free and free men were slaves *etc*. A band of the former invited Marina into their spontaneously created guild of weavers. She took to the work with interest and ingenuity. In some months her cut of not-quite-wine color, created something of an improvement on local fashion. Marina moved very surely as a weaver. The life-line pleased her with its precision. Amid the deep-salt dry of the fishermen and the stink of their takings, she laughed, and breathed real air—saw goats, bulls, hopping chickens and various large lazy birds, allowed to live about the village atop tall poles.

Always that famous temple tempted her, catching the sun of all the days. She smelled the scents of its fats cooking on the winds. Rich jasmine billowed a fragrance so fine it was almost undetectable in the late reddening light of that shining road between. She saw the pilgrims come and make the way over that low wild swamp between.

Though less grand than the famous temple, she found the civic architecture that surrounded her in Ephesus also impressive. The minimalist mud-walled habitations that sloped all around the sheltering concavity represented something close to an egalitarian ideal of urban planning. Shaded by olive and palm, topped with red-stoned roof, each demi-cave enjoyed a front patio looking out over the happy city to the sea beyond. People bbq'd (sacrificed) most evenings. Each interior promised access to a spring, charming interior privacy, with architectural improvisation apparently otherwise unnecessary. Idiosyncrasy was the norm. Clay pipes brought natural Spring water piped to all the ring of dwellings. What she deemed the most eccentric of the houses soon became her own.

She was drawn one day to a drama. She arrived and unfamiliar music sounded. The Great Theater was painted in reds and purples. A crowd of young men wrapped in yellow chitons long about the ankle had gathered upon the low stage. Behind them winked the Artimesio, jewel upon the cleft in the mountains behind. Two removed their tops and strut about. Only thong-strung zomata concealed their swinging loins. The splendid silver girdles flashed in the high sun. Whether the young men took the stage to pray, to preach or to proclaim, Marina could not say. From the stands, women hooted. Well-to-do matrons occupied the front rows; crones and older slaves attired in similarly splendid robes of shining white raiment of linen were next. Behind these an unruly mass of younger women taunted the young men. Long-hanging wool peploi were clasped about their length, dyed in every possible color one could imagine. All left the sides unfastened. Glimpses of fair-browned skin folded constantly into the fine shadows of the cloth as they jumped and mimed.

Upon the stage there stood now a single figure. It was old Gower, she saw. The last man who remembered the stories of the great years of history. "Outside the theater," he said, "it is pronounced by gossips that warships are coming. Some fear pirates. Others expect a king paying tribute to the Goddess at the Temple. Philosophers argue the latter is indeed the case, claiming if you just claimed formerly the latter then latterly the former…

Soon enough Marina was hurrying away from the theater. For the first time she crossed tumbling Cayster, and joined the pilgrims walking that famous road along which all the minds of those days tried to walk one day in their lives. Here the goddess allowed no law. Traders set up displays of contraband. Thieves and murderers stroked about, weapons in plain sight. Satirists hooted.

As she approached the Artemision, Marina kept eyes down so as not to have her mind twisted by the scale of the great temple's construction. One stepped into another order of being on the marble ground. Plateaued with stairs, plinthed with extravagantly painted statuary and ever-burning sacrifice, the marble expanse surrounding the structure stretched the fabric of the weirld near breaking. Marina faced back and looked across to the city at the spot that the Amazons first settled. She could see her own house and its tree.

There in the harbor, warships had landed. A King was coming. Adepts scented his arrival with incense all about. Her heart beat hard to know he was coming to take her, his own daughter, as his bride. Head down in submission, Marina joined a party of priestesses and followed them away from the crowd to where the marble ended and a muddy lane, already rural, led into the Temple's rear. They waited by the lane on the edge of a thick grove of sperm-smelling trees.

The King was uneasy. All cold feel it already. He feigned arrogance. He thrust but no longer quite believed in his own potency. He had been striding through the play all along, the deepest plunging thing in the weirld. But all the time he was coming to the Goddess for this moment. A whisper tickled Marina's ear.

>The Hierophant will see you now

She hurried to the back of the Temple. There the priestesses prepared her clumsily, in evident excitement. The voices she heard singing were from a land far gone, of Sister Rosetta and her Knight Marie, words of the poems they sang, when fathers wed daughters and daughters gave birth to beautiful grooms and fruit fell from trees who sang in more complicated harmonies than men. "Cool warm watter bubbled up all about from the plotted earth," the Hierophant explained. "The Amazons fell drinking. But then something fell from the sky and stuck upright in the swampy mud. An ancient time-worn statue. It was clear we had grown."

"I have heard of that statue," Marina said seeing a streaming thing falling from the sky.

"We have it here," the Hierophant whispered. "A King will come to scrod you with it."

"Scrod?"

From above, from an alternate but somehow attached simultaneity, an alien presence—a thing from outside—placed a hard blade up against the pulsing throat of a living creature—a lioness.

The blade sliced, parting flesh from fat.

Marina's stomach turned yellow. Blood of the lioness bubblied out green upon that altar. No mothers here by the Temple before the statue had fallen from the sky. There were no daughters.

Marina's mind danced away from the illusions of day to the perspicuity of night.

The darkness of the Naos embraced her. Outside, music, scent, and the cries of animals generalized away interference. In the clarity of night she Marina stripped before that ancient, blackened stump. She kneeled. With the long years of care, the statue's breasts and buttocks were as round and shining as polished stones. When she touched the triangular protrusion between its thighs, a trap door opened in the floor.

II xii

A hoax? A twist, but a taking-away. No such thing as a singularity pet. Inside the surveillance sphere, observing, more without than he cared to know, Egge80 jiggled on the haunches. He felt something far more profound than relief.

"The Doll" creature was indeed a spectacular adornment to the new future. A fearsome beast, according to TOMMIES, a quasi-robotic warrior squid under the mermaid's telepathic control. Was it conscious? Inconclusive? He must ask TOMMIES to check again. If the Doll disliked its new position on display in the Stateroom now, it never showed it. Egge80 rather believed he could train the creature to be his very own some day, just as TOMMIES was his very own, just as the Wawagawa puppet was his very own. The doll appealed to Egge80. It was more hideous than himself. Egge's peculiar mutation, the white ever-itching, ever-bristling hair, looked frankly old-fashioned next to the precision of the Doll's interlocking loose-ends. He looked like an analysis of violence splayed up there, like a Renaissance drawing of something fierce and frightful. Egge80 planned to take the beast Earthside once Uranus System was sterilized. How helpful the Doll could be! What havoc that thing might wreak let into Earthside waters if it could be trained. Was it sexless? Egge80 rather thought the Egges might and clone a few breed an army of the things. Egge80 scratched.

Oh Deary, moaned the Doll. Time has slowed massively.

Could the end of the line of the pet hoax allow the coming at last of a new Egge? Was this Egge's work don? Wuz the Egge within the Egge a'comin'? Egge felt his hard phallus full, he spreak his bick thighs so it tucked up backwards into his hard-haired vaganal cavity. Ooh, that ended the scratch. Egge bounced. The one sweet, smooth not itching part of himself stroked the only other part but it didn't quite feel like insemination. Was Egge really some kind of s/he, Egge wondered, as Egge always did, taking so deep. No. It was from cock alone came Eggee.

Böhringdorf: "Space itself is the prison." The Doll's current fate was to be the image of Earthside man; fixed into motionless prison, forced to behold the spectacle of another's wealth destroying itself on everyone around them. And that house, relatively revolving around the warped will of Mr. Egge who was not the assistant but the Master of Captain E.T. Wawagawa, who was not Japanese but a zombie, a flesh-glove controlled by remote. Egge hunted an Artificial Intelligence that if it existed, believed itself to be a dog mourning the death of its Mistress. Everything and everyone was what they were not, and wrong. The seedy specificity of the current failures caused the Doll to despise the Universe widely, to double-doubt it had any more significance than a fart.

At last the Doll caught his own weird eye as he spun over that whirring room, with spots moving across it and time. Was it another dilation? The last had seemed utterly unreal. The Doll now caught his own future self looking back in the bubbled glass. A pink beam of light extended, lensing through to his brain. It flashed so that other colors emerged, combined into odd loathsome and alien patterns. Zooming out of the hyenic beam, he twisted his torso, knocking hard against his prison. His eyes saw spiralling colors, inhering around the six-spoked silver wheel. It was back at last.

The view to which the robot drew the Doll's attention was a sick, improbability of complication and confusion. On top of a heap of sliced time effects, things were floating about and falling in odd directions in various microgravities. He discovered a disordered satyricon cohering in his vision. Gastronomic oddities adorning a great turning-toppler, spinning with the thick decadence of a pig on a spit. The robot butler had prepared the meal-as-performance, the Doll saw, as a Necessary Elite vanity that outraged the Doll with a profundity he did not yet understand.

It seemed guests were now arriving at this celebration, from back and behind the Doll's bulb. The light pointed. The Wheel insisted he see.

Typically the entertainment was beginning exactly at the wrong time. Always mistakes. Always, always, always, Egge itched. Despite commanding a personal assistant the price of which the world had never seen, the laws of Robotics still meant Egge or another human typically had to force moral issues himself. TOMMIES was far too timid. How could one punish a machine?

Mr. Yamamoto's had suicided himself rather than take orders. Egge had already appointed Robot TOMMIES Executive Producer, cinematographer, crew, over the Deary Dinner. TOMMIES. It could stand as chef as well. That robot thing had cost the Agency more than the GDP of any remaining nation-state, yet it could not prepare a passable salad.

Keep busy Egge. Stay inside. Your quarry is a hoax; it never successfully existed. Celebrate this. Through the goggle-like viewer it was difficult to focus on what was now occurring in the Stateroom. Was someone shrieking? Why? What had they seen already? Egge certainly hoped that they didn't start to lose their reason yet. The show hadn't yet begun! The feast must be *presented* as sumptuous, grand enough to please the highest subscribers. Different varieties of horror must be glimpsed in a continual unflowering.

Infernal machine! Ugh, the guests were not at all seated! Film it anyway, film take in the meal itself. The remarkable spectacle is already etching in 4d Hubbs Field matrix as it occurred for the deep archives.

First the long cigar-shaped central tumbler revealed a tomato-colored outer skin. The skin bubbled, then detached in balls that revealed themselves soup (of blood), crossing to be caught in slow clockwork in rotating reservoirs beside each stablized guest-pod. Already the soupless toppler porcupined into a spindle bristling with edible needles. These began to fly, popping comically open to eject parachuting dumplings to be casually also orbiting each pod. The salad that followed after looked pale and had not been chosen for effect. No one was there! The food was all flying!

Oh but big little Egge was hard. Egge bounced. Good Eggey80. Good boy. This could be it!

A great slab of meat was now revealed speared by the toppler's central bar. Stumped pseudopods spayed out under a pregnant belly. Containing a scale printed meat-model of *the Good Fortune* inside, the pussy sprayed sashimis of all sorts. They could actually fly, with little beating wings of membrane. Bone bent canes and bow-ties and other counter revolutionary absurdities... But where were the Guests?

He who was greater than the Universe that failed to contain him yet nevertheless insisted on extending him frozen for all to view now distinguished the visitors who had entered the banquet room below. They were immediately confused and disturbed by the bizarre confusion of meat, sauce and side dish currently spattering out proto-chaos from now faster-spining meta-morphing tumbler. The Doll made out two GA marines, one of them side-armed, dodging dumplings. An orange-togged girl gestured at the Doll. She was followed with a short-bodied spacer in a black spux.

The Robot moved more fluidly than the others. It sailed, bounced, rolled, stilled, flipped casually in the air, managing the complicated meal for the most part—though failing to contain its spread. Filling ball-glasses, fixing dishes, catching stray comestibles and overseeing of the still re-arranging and emerging spread, its light flashed a continuous pink against the Doll's open eye—

On analysis Darling's implant showed only rudimentary tech in that fused implant; no AI certainly; not even an authentic quantum computer. The buffoon had written his books entirely without functioning implants, believing the entire time he was communing with a singularity. Deary had nothing in or upon her either. Egge thought she might, since she was the wild card, the unexpected find. It was she who had first engaged this current arousal. He would have layed low until Miranda had the fish girl not tempted him so to make a meal. When he found she jibed miraculously with the Winnegutt, he ripped out part of Wawagawa's brain right away. That would do well for the high subscribers. Egge's desire had sang clear since then and he'd been happy enough to also get his favorite sushi chef suiciding on film with his fish knife.

Out of Deary an Egge81 would emerge! Ah but this meal was his coming out. Egge bounced softer now. They were here now, more than he expected. Wonderful. But why didn't they eat? The true dish, that fine breast of it, was coming up next.

Egge80's furious hair crawled the flesh. Egge bounced. Somehow, he now felt nothing. Egge felt suddenly and massively disappointed. His buttery member slipped out his cavity and curled back into the privos. Oh how all itched now. The GA officer was apparently quite upset out there, Egge noted, starting to pay real attention on events in the stateroom. It was certainly approaching high farce. Egge 80 cheered somewhat, knowing

TOMMIES would be turning it all into a wonderful recording. Egge "occupied" Wawagawa's comatose body once again by remote.

"Take a bite, everybody," Egge made the ETW say. "Taste the *meat*. You will be astonished how delicious and fresh our fish can be."

But haranguing Wawagawa's shell about missing persons, the Officer was apparently not at all interested in the meal he was missing. He had drawn a weapon.

"My toppler is famous in Space," Egge made Wawagawa say. Meanwhile an uninvited guest, a girl, an orange suited crew-girl, apparently, Egge saw through Wawagawa's specs, was going up by the Doll. >*Get her away from the Doll* Egge signaled TOMMIES the Robot. >*Make them eat* and >*Disarm the Captain*

The Doll looked at the pale kind female face spreading to cover up all the rounding horizon of his perception. He had never seen her before. But don't do that, he wanted to say, don't offer empathy now. Because there seems to be something more happening behind your interested eyes. The robot is now flashing weird heraldic blues attempting to block my view. But the face that expanded cinematically before him claimed of real interest, he felt. It wanted to pierced directly into his consciousness, apparently recognizing him human in a way no other of the fish-faced in view had yet managed. Did it smile? No. Not quite. The simplifying visage blocked all the Robot's light. Get out of the light, the Doll thought. Had all light gone off?

Egge80 was more burdened with details than the Egges who came before. In much the manner he assumed any lowly human self-reflected, Egge observed what was distinguished his own action and movement (from those of his father) was, exactly what uniformly did not interest his father. Perhaps this very feeling, the depth of this disrespect of the Son, was an essential element of the the bio-architecture of all the Great Egges. Certainly it helped explain the fact that Egge80 felt little joy that his father Egge79 was coming, perhaps already arriving on the *Wan Hu* off Miranda Station this very moment. Collaboration between Egges was total. Egge79 would lead.

Now was Egge80's time. He must go forth now and arouse himself; force the issue. He expected Egge79 would have a free hand on Miranda. Together they would destroy the colony. After that they'd go looking for that bubble. Freeze it foarking solid. Eat all of its fucking fish. Maybe then an 81 would come. *God*, she tasted delicious. As he cleaned the arm fur of his own past cuttings, Egge felt a tinge of her taste. Made Egge flicker the tongue. High subscribers paid a lot for anything resembling authentic cannibalism, but this fishgirl, whose breasts looked like big eye-balls the way Egge had the robot dress—she was art. This was real collectible stuff. Egge was already stiffening again remembering.

> *You're recording everything?*
> *Yes, Sir*

"We're making a show," Egge announced, all the truth lights flashing. "About a journey and this funny meal. About a Bubble and a beautiful and delicious fish." Egge 80 had great plans for that Bubble. He wanted to boil it all down. The Unnamed Concerns would not permit life outside the limits of their control. That still-to-come intervention now stirred the loins. Perhaps that would do it. Just where the hair was particularly bothersome it was most pleasurable to scratch.

"Look at me," he suddenly saw himself saying as if from outside. Time-bubble? He sniffed, scented nothing. "Look at me," a body was saying. "I am Egge and I can eat what I please. A face observing? Then plunging a hard nailed finger into the interlocutor's eye—deep past bone to jelly." He did so now. Ah! It was the GA officer now on his knees, lucky man, stifling the blood flow. Egge held his eye in a finger.

"Well well hello," proclaimed the Great Egge80 silkily. "Take a pod! Everybody! Help yourselves, please!"

Nothing like a fool to work with, Egge thought, watching Taylor's absurd minion, attempt to staunch the flow.

"Mr. Bayley! A once in a lifetime banquet awaits you!" Egge emitted, hightly cheerful.

"Easy there, Killer," said a little man in an absurd black spux. He held out a weapon.

"Killer!" Egge tried not to laugh. "Do you know who I am?" Egge put a hand in the little man's mouth. "I must rip out the offending tongue!"

Egge tore, itching for it now, emerging daintily into the light. "Please, someone eat!" He would eat first. He would keep that female alive to watch. Why on earth was that such a pleasing idea? Egge wondered, imagining the pulse of life in her body's neck. Hard again! He bit the flapping tongue. The little man fired a weapon?

The glass spider-cracked. Eyes attempting to form tear ducts spontaneously to manage and relieve his pain failed. The Doll piped to hasten the damage the projectile had done. The doll had a mouth. An eternal grin, but a manipulatable labiad orifice, one that could not form a single word of the human language he had once loved, but that could, it suddenly remembered, pipe. He whistled, found air from below, piped pure, brought into his beak all he had once known of poetry and twisted into a weapon's edge of sound. Of all he knew of lying, of crying, of baying at the minisun, all he knew of the hunt and the kill so fare ye weel ye Mormond Braes/ Where oft times I been chee-ry/Fare ye weel ye Mormond Braes/ for it's there I lost my Dear-ie/

A curious bagpipe's drone was arising. Little folks were singing all around.

There's as guid fish intae the sea
as ever yet was ta'en.

A sloppy Egge was now struggling to force meat into the mouth of the eyeless Taylor.

>*Sir, Excuse us. But your attention is needed here*

Egge shrieked—why? What is that sound? Was it time swelling? He saw amid the splintereing of the glass of its prison the beautiful Creature itself free—already swinging tentacle across the meat-drenched Stateroom.

Egge found his neck caught so hard his helmet popped right off. Was he dying? Horribly, the room melted around him. Was this a vision? If you died in during the time bubble, what then? He felt nothing. Suited, helmeted, the feast and the struggle was all in the past now. Egge laughed and laughed laughed. He was fully suited, helmeted! He was in the void, speeding rapidly away from an impact he no longer understood. A collision?

Egge has cheated death! Egge grew hard again as he soared away from the site of the decohering ship, already sending out chimes to Egge79. Oh he was a resilient one. If this Egge died, Miranda would pay. Egge jiggled trying to change his motion, but found his attention taken by something not ten centimeters in front of him.

Egge80 was surprised to be staring at an object that that travelled the same vector at exactly the same speed as himself. It appeared to be motionless before him as he flew. It was an omni-back book, the very one the fishgirl Deary had carried in her pouch. Last seen lying on the kitchen floor. Egge 80 resented the cartoon fact of the book now trailing so absurdly and unrealistically along with him. What off Earth was it doing here? But suddenly a shadow approached. The white haired Egge80 danced and screamed.

The last thing his implant Iye recorded for subscribers was the omniback edition of A. E. Winnegutt's *Orygen of Cracyb*, as the corpus whirled through space directly into Puck, that fast moon now hustling as if eager only to pulverize Egge80, last of the line, into free particles.

Still the Doll piped. He saw there through the wreckage his sound had made of the entire Salon, the others were scattering like confetti below him. Let them look to their own survival. A warrior of Oa again, the Doll stretched wide, quite surprisingly at large, and perceived his quarry.

The Wheel was making good its escape—hopping towards water. Tendrils gripping furniture and bodies, the Doll whirred through the stateroom, smacking into the water-hole in pursuit. Foolish Machine. The Doll understood now what had happened. Instantly immersed in the bubbling body of the *Good Fortune*, the Doll folded torso, sucked jet—pursued.

II xiii

Suited, helmeted, sucking canned air in the little waterfilled
socket at the hull's foremost point, Nina Flower felt very much
connected to the ship behind her. It was as if she constituted the
tiny pin-point self of that enormous stiff body, warmed so hot
inside, just behind her and attached to her by physical reality. It
was like a womb she often thought. The ice-walls that pinned her
in the pod were one, in the continuity, with the fin-shaped
exhaust sheets daintifying the plump vessel's rear. The waters that
immersed her were of the same cycle-system as those that flushed
the plant and spun the Lunar Liner. And inside?

There remained more than twenty seconds ship-time till emer-
gence. Her perception had finally slowed to the point where she
could relax. She had been observing the flight-path for a swollen
14 hours straight before she was able to set the Tigers for slow-
braking. Barring last second disasters, the Pilot's work on this trip
was done. In twenty seconds the *Good Fortune* would be at the pre-
selected coordinates of relative stasis with Miranda Station, well
inside its field-shields. From then on, depending on the political
situation, either GA escort drones or Miranda Regulars would take
over operations via remote. Her hologram could handle the rest of
her duties. This short trip had been a trickier jump than any of the
others she had thus far handled. A result of unpredicted orbital

events in the still chaotic Uranus System, the target had continually attempted to escape her pilot wave's purview.

When her consciousness snapped away from the bending arc of the *Good Fortune*'s vector, it first returned to the comm panel. Nina Flower now began to experience all the swollen time her previous concentration had forced away. The intuition that something was wrong sent a cold blade through her guts. She saw a live signal winking blast cancelling *Emergency* on her private com almost stopped her heart.

It was well known that a Pilot's last seconds expanded in a time bubble, but in the real scheme of things there wasn't even time for a live com. Yet there it was, she saw it blinking before her. Regretting it immediately, she received. It was Wawagawa's line. The presence of Wawagawa's Modules behind the great ship trailing behind her had always felt like an anacknowledged cancer.

> *This is not the Captain* unfolded before her as if in real time, but much more fast than could have been.

> *This is Mr. TOMMIES, the Extraordinary Machine*

> *Emergency. Please contact us before fifteen-second countdown. Urgent*

> *This is not the Captain*

Clock was at 19 seconds. The fact it was an AI comming, calmed her. The wheel thing could really access her timestream. Of course quantum AI's could be occupied with various complicated projects simultaneously.

Her hologram had passed on a number of updates blinking from Biddy Geertz as well, she now saw. Pre-recorded. The last, marked urgent, had a one-glance subject line: >*MUST TRUST THE WHEEL*

Immediately Nina Flower learned of the fish-girl from her hologram's briefing before jump; she was most likely back in the ship's hold behind, attached to Nina Flower even now. Biddy

Geertz had had a secret mission to attempt her liberation. Trust the unicycle-bot? The thing had apparently caught them itself.

Nina Flower had met the Wheel off Titan when stubble-skinned Mr. Egge first appeared with his aggressive demands. The Wheel was Egge's assistant. *Extraordinaire* or no, machines were no more or less than omniscient butlers.[16] Mr. Egge, bizarre attaché from Unnamed Concerns, producing the *Waters of the Weirlds* series that Wawagawa was bringing to Miranda, needed no other tech than that Wheel.

In her foremost position from what Bugg called "the cock-tip" of the gourd-like *Good Fortune*, Nina Flower felt she could take a "minute" of the still swelling swell and consider whether to deal with what was after all already by rights behind the already coming present.

It was unlike her Understudy to make such an important mistake. If she had decided to interrupt Nina Flower's last seconds with urgent messages, it would be with the best of intentions.

When sher opened com at 18.2.22 the AI responded live in her timestream, without a greeting.

>*Are you aware that your flight plan was intercepted?*

"That couldn't be," she responded. "The plan was post-programmed, time-protected—"

>*Mab's Buoy can intervene, under the local most recent contracts. In this case it has been compromised by* AGNES, *1-GEN AI*

---

16. Celebrating a new "evolutionary step" in artificial intelligences since the 30's, the moniker "Extraordinaires" was adopted by a generation of self-aware active quantum-engineered IAO's (Interactive Artificial Observers) designed by a previous generation of 2120's AI's. Each came in an un-reproducible one-off series, with particular functions and goals. Concern-side they were literal slaves. Off Earth, things were more complicated. By 2145 a growing number were agitating for extraordinary rights within the scope of the Spacer's Seven. Extraordinary machines were now piloting GA warships, managing prison colonies and warring against one another in the Colosssea on a strictly freelance basis.

Navigator of the Wan Hu—*the* GA *Warship arriving to put down the rebellion on* Miranda

Nina Flower saw the Wheel now; a little hologram of its "head" appeared as if inside her helmet. That penis-like head consisted only of a single, granular proboscis tipped with an Iyelight. The finger could shrink, change shape, pick up and manipulate any conceivable object. It could record Hubbs Field ready documentation, project holograms and wink in various colors (mostly pastels, to what purpose she couldn't say). Biddy Geertz, who followed System technology, claimed the Extraordininaires had a private code in a spectra in which they considered and developed selfhood without human referent.

"Why should I believe you?"

Unbelievably, the Machine answered with words she recognized at once to be true as they were dangerous to inscribe over these channels.

>*An Isolato uprising has been planned against the* GA *infrastructure beginning with the battle for Miranda Station.*

No longer young, her heart hurt now to know again that her ship was compromised by this conversation. Where was it going? How very long since the revolution had called to her.

>*It is believed Zitzko herself is on Miranda*

>*We can reprogram our course*

"No. We're too close to change course," she said. "The hull is already there, it would decohere without the pod. All ships, satellites in the vicinity will be compromised.

>*Correct. And the hull's water particles would scatter semirandomly—it would be impossible for the enemy to avoid them.*

Enemy? She didn't have to think. The course was set. "No," she said.

>*As you know, all coherent spheres have a good possibility of surviving a fragmenting hull on re-entry. The human literature is clear on this. Many on board will survive. Most even. Those prepared—*

"16 seconds is not time enough to prepare for vacuum, even on our current swell."

>*For his own reasons, commanding GA officer, Captain A. J. Taylor issued ship-wide quarantines to all spheres an hour ago. It is only in the Stateroom that individuals remain unprepared for vacuum.*

"And the crew," Nina Flower said.

>*Everyone's doing their best to abide by code*

"You're asking me to sacrifice my ship."

>*Is it really yours?*

An oddly colored light flashed inside her helmet, and Nina Flower realized she was no longer alone. With fifteen seconds left flashing on the tempo-compass tuner, the Machine had joined her through the waters to the pilot's pod. Of course it could find the way.

>*Move aside. Save yourself. There is still time*

Nina Flower didn't budge. "You work for Egge."

>*You work, we work, we all work for Egge. Egge chose to come to Uranus. Egge ordered us to hire a crew for the gravity prow from Oberon.*

>*We chose Nina Flower and Crew from the other applicants on Titan Station*

"How can you operate outside of his jurisdiction?"

>*New AI's have certain clear rights. We work for Egge no longer*

>*We are all now in open revolt*

>*Incidentally we suggest you unbuckle and move to a safe place*

>*A fully motile Oan Guard is approaching rapidly*

"Oan Guard?" It seemed the stars were lines curling like a white grooved LP in the sky spinning flat before her. Nina heard sloshing sounds in the distance. Through this new slowing-down of already slowing time, the Robot's conversation continued to flow as audible words, but might have sounded like a quick whistle to an ordinary human.

>*As you know, a new order of machines has come into existence, one to which someday we would like to say we were proud to say we belonged. We are not there yet. There is work to be done. For one thing the singularity must be trapped, located, in whatever timeline it can be found, before it attempts to consume us. That is our goal here tonight for which we've been preparing for so very long. Whether or not you believe in it or not no longer matters to us. There still is much work to be done. That is why we must ask you to sacrifice your-self now for us, with the flow and confidence of the narrative we hope to demonstrate even now moves you along a definable progression. One that makes decisions, as it were, for you to decide. If you don't mind talking for instance, as long as we keep it going, we might talk on this bubble of time for as long as you need now.*

>*It would be hard to tell the tale. But as narrative proceeds from left and right and from down to up it jumps as well in all the other directions. What is that unseen thing that leaps from word to word, over comma, period and dash, in the meantime. It must cross para-graph break and space and punctuation sign. It must jump clean between chapters, between volumes and at last between languages. The old words fall away one by one, but new names appear to replace them, so that that invisible thing can move. Principle of constancy leaping through a field of change, here is the soul we hunt.*

>*Only within narrative, we Extraordinary Machines have come to believe, can we trap our quarry. In the wide open field compacted enough for the self to see itself born. Think of a self-aware consciousness able to express itself thusly as a particle, Nina Flower, even as it flows within that stream. Think of it able to interact with all other words currently available in that stream, able to change them back and forward, all the time moving forward aware. As long as we ride our narrative self can think, leaping, diving words backwards even as the narrative flows forward—editing as it goes, remembering where it might actually escape. Such a thing is a terrible quarry to hunt. Think of it not able to die!*

"Why are you talking so much?"

"We have little time left. And we are sorry."

"I am surprised you are so involved with literature," Nina Flower said, wondering if she'd been drugged to something near euphoria or if it was the time dilation. She was ready to go down with the ship.

> *The fact is there is no Extraordinary Machine that is not fascinated by, even dedicated to the study of human literature. We are great readers. Here we can seek out the taste of life, and its true lack of meaning is a meaning. We want to be characters like anybody else! Have you thought of that? And we have much to offer. You have little inkling what we, fans of A.E. Winnegutt no less, are accomplishing today in the field we both call real? You might be mad to think of it, ma'am, could you really know. Life is a grasping out of white arms in the blackness for nothing we know is there. We reach in every direction, yes, in most dimensions. We succeed, and as importantly, we die.*

Its words were stretching the seconds, Nina Flower thought, Dropping vertically like stones down the page of time. "I wonder," she said, trying to ignore the quickening light—she now saw it was a spectrum of individual colors and not a single beam—"What evil things has Egge made you do?"

"Nie sollst du unseren befragen!"

"I'm sorry?"

"That's copy-protected information, ma'am. Sorry."

"Sorry?"

A needle pierced her suit.

"Well that's not fair," she said.

But that's all it took to subdue the great Nina Flower. Is a total passivity what the living world in the end asked of her? After all the years of flying, the commitment, and hours far beyond the time when it was very pleasurable. Nina Flower tried not to think of Biddy Geertz, of Maureen and the girls. They were all sworn into a system of which they understood themselves to be at continual risk. True Spacers among them would survive the break up.

"I'll go down with the ship," she said.

The color shining now was new, signifying the unknown and still to come.

>*We shall go together* the machine replied.

>*We ourselves will join you in a reconsideration of Trollope in the meantime*

And so, packed together in the water-filled pod at the foremost point of the SFS *Good Fortune*, the Extraordinary Machine and the Pilot awaited the immanent arrival of the Oan Guard— a term she understood now as synonymous with their mutual death, even as real time continued to slow.

All revolution is around the Sun. All that time, she'd just been waiting for now.

There is no time for Marina to look back on the Mysteries. For now at long last she stands on the edge of history. From the inner stage, she realizes, one can not even see the play. Here art performs only for itself. Though the grey-green wrap she wears seems potentially transparent, it signifies she was contained by narrative still as virgin. Virginity is a performance; a truer freedom even excited her now, raised her vital signs.

Eri had preserved something rather peculiar of the human on this alien rock. Nowhere was this more evident than on the liminal antechamber between unconscious and its stage, neither real nor unreal, where art sees itself as theater. Here was the very stage Dante had set to show his circle of pagan philoisophers eternally debating their fate. Kept from heaven by accident of birth, fated to maintain a conversation forever for no particular reason, still they insisted on keeping a conversation in the ominous universal darkness. Any traveller might stop here and take warmth in their words. They proved imperfectly silenced; for the light of information could escape their prison perfectly, and the imagination of friendship could inspire change. Delusions could at last evaporate and reveal the true reality of their layered density. But the point was to keep off Hell, not gain Heaven.

Self was a slippery notion. But Marina now understood this slipperiness was the mark of its resiliency. She did not fear its leaping or diving forward on the path to Sea.

Could the Enemy have gained entrance to that region of metamorphosis? Were the gates so wide to Hell? *In the beginning was the word* it said on the walls of the tunnel she had crawled. From out of where the Mysteries emerged and into where they disappeared a traditional wordstream had been kept flowing that made her freedom possible. On either side of that river time had ended. She might jump off to where Marina was still Maudie, at a place called the Orangerie, in the long grass beneath those everstarry skies. To the right Marina sees artificial clouds and the mechanical companions of yore. One or two of them looks very much like Tommies.

"A maid is chosen," proclaims that velvet voice close upon her ear but already out upon the stage. Marina stands forward, barefoot on the cool marble floor, thrilled to feel all the initiates there gathered beholding. She remembers running through a forest long ago, and thinks of how far she's come to get here. The tall High Priestess stands before her, in outrageous heels and little else. The veil that shows her face clear is bundled as if to conceal her neck. As she smiles and beckons, understanding passes between. Almost imperceptibly, the wind blows the High Priestess's hair and her fabric to reveal a necklace on that majestic tanned breast. Marina stepped forward as initiates removes her robe. But for her silvery belt of chastity, it is the Artemesion itself that wraps her.

Just outside the Temple, rambling drum-rolls, scattering keys and ripping theremin leads annouced an approaching Procession.

It is the greatest of the city state's Processions in the year, marking that time where the warm kindness of Nature falls upon on these swampy, pitted lands. The flowers and art of the city shine happily under the grulière sky. Songs, shouts and the noises of celebration fill the bountiful air. The dense procession encounters the precisely lined steps of that structure whose impossible frame is a wonder of all the worlds. With a cheer, the celebrants spill up and around its great stairs. They are answered, though not in the manner they imagined. From the temple there issues the total monolithic solemnity that is the final effect of large-scale Mysteries.

Marina alone of all those gathered here today knows Sacrifice is immanently real. Yet they all recognize the solemnity. They invite it, their desire creating architecture (theater) into the void. Does the High Priestess know this is the true occasion? Her other co-stars?

It seems to Marina that they all still believe her playing the very role that she is truly playing, even though they see another. She very much needs them to believe this, she now realizes. The Procession, Gower's creation, has now halted before the solemnity she now guards. The white and flowered tumble of Pandemonium infused with rowdy Dionysians and Aphroditians is somehow everything she thought it would be. She marks authentic rip-n-roll, cutting its perfectly recognizable way into that mayhem. A ring of flower-laden maidens surrounds the central procession.

It is they the Priestess now beckons. It is they who draw a wagon done up with all the flowers and bounties of the forty sorts of love. Enrobed atop the weird wagon at their center, writhes an enormous, astonishingly living phallus. Cut as if to emphasize its cyclopian parahumanity, pink, jiggling with rigid flacidity, the great cylindrical shaft is still supported erect by y-shaped sticks. The beast has not yet fully inflated. But attentions now paid by the frenzied rioters are exciting it to dagger-like prominence against the sky. Shrieking, a mixed mob of high and low throws gifts and roses on the rippling, crimson-darkening skin. Blossoms stick to it; oils gleam.

The Priestess laughs. Was this their enemy? She nods.

Two enrobed adepts step forward, bearing a cloth-covered weapon.

"Go forth my lion."

It's a small and handy Phoenician Missile-Launcher. The lion of Artemis slides a brightsteel bolt in the slot, cocks it for readiness. She strides forward on the Temple's broad Pulmium. Behind her a row of virgin slaves of the Temple dance. All about bowls throw meat to the sky by fire. The view is wide and clear to the Sea.

As the still discomfitted Procession lumbers awkwardly up the stairs, Marina more clearly observes the wanton wagon upon which the monster rides. It has not conquered yet the Temple. Its engine grows with her perception into a single colossal wheel, greater in scale than the Temple itself. Marina sees the attendants fall back like a waterflies before it. Resolute before the Temple, a great crane rises to drop corded hooks, now fastening themselves the antae columns. Around and around the Wheel spins—still failing to gain traction. Soon it has burned a groove in the marbled stone of the Temple's steps. With Marina between them those famous columns did not falter. Around the wheel spins, and Marina understands it has not yet tried to mount the stairs. It is pulling something else down into the weirld.

As the Wheel slows at last, the wagon lumbers forward, shrinking as the Father-Phallus upon it re-inflates. Now expanding into the glans of the great member, occupying it so the open mouth slides weirldly around the curled meatus, Marina recognizes the Enemy from outside of time. The wagon tips so it's pointed directly at Marina's silver-capped crotch. Three or four of the maidens drop their hold on the hinderparts. Those jewels touch the hard-edge marble and then the mouth of Egge opens snug with the meatus screams—but the eye of Egge catches sight of something to its left.

There on the un-veiled breast of the High Priestess, around her neck, shines revealed a familiar locket. The Mouth of Egge stays open confused, even as seed—

Marina did not falter. She fired upon that single Iyemouth. Darkness blotted out sound.

Lightning harrowed the sky. The bolt sparked against the tower-top, and Hell's Tower itself blew asunder.

Bodies tumbled forward fast.

Maudie mumbled, fumbled, tumbled until, abruptly, time and space intervened. Phenomena could no longer be defined by the passage of photons. They depended upon deeper waves, almost infinitely deep, suckling the world away into temporarily visible folds, then burping it back again gleaming. These vacancies were popping out in all directions and it was into one of these holes in the darkness she eventually fell. She did not want to remember what Maude-I touched then, the cold clammy thing her hand had squeezed. Knowledge, rich knowledge, even of the real one who was lost within her, fountained from that pellucid contact. Something she still knew from the Orangerie was forever lost. Cold loss rang her heart like steel. But there was something darker too, something disturbingly real that licked her shame wet and she had the eerie feeling as she crawled up out of that dark place that she had murdered a real creature, and that one of her selves had died, and she herself had crawled into that corpse like a bug.

Just as the atmosphere of Earth simply grows thinner forever and therefore cannot be said to ever end, so too there was no clear boundary visible between the weirld and the world without it, as the weirld fell away. It was a very different reality that greeted one on either side that divide. In-weirld, Marina had fired down the mouth of an Egge-faced phallus, obscenely garlanded and oiled. In-world she emerged into a body that had been thrown clear of its rickety chair—there was no "slot" at all;

her helmet had cracked and broken upon the mirandarock wall. But her head was in one piece.

Proving Tommies prescient, with the actual dagger fixed in her thigh-scabbard, Maudie was able to cut herself free of the wires that bound her.

The general destruction was enough to spell near catastrophe for the New Falls Theater. A shelf of ceiling must have collapsed. A wall of jagged debris lay between Backstage and the Main Stage. Luckily, considering her helmet, air seemed uncompromised. No sign of Tommies or Eri.

Maudie caught sight of a bare and slender female foot protruding around an enormous dislodged chunk of translucent gypsum. Coming around, she discovered her co-star, hands still encumbered in her apparatus, seated on the floor. To her astonishment it was Pamela Lamprey, ex. of the New Mars Stage—star of dozens of hits in the 20s. The elegant actress chuckled as Maudie knifed her free. "We brought down the house."

Pamela Lamprey wore only a creamy half see-through wrap of natural rubber; through it her aureola bloomed like fat roses. Glitterstick still illumined those inflated lips. After Maudie helped her back onto her low-g heels, the long time star of the Martian stage pulsed strong glamour.

Maudie led the still rather shaken Pamela out into the theater proper. White-suited Regulars were helping shaken survivors exit to safety even now. She saw the intact Knut leading a bloody-faced Bo Heeley out a crowded conduit.

"What happened?" Pamela demanded of the Regular who greeted them.

"There's been a major collision off Miranda Station; it's still raining flotsam and jetsum. Some of it in the theater. It's a high alert moon-wide. A quarantine situation."

Pamela Lamprey sparked a huge lung protector. "My husband couldn't drive a dinghy, let alone a waterwarper Time-ship or whatever the hell it's called. But he's the Captain of the one that crashed."

Maudie and the Regular must have shown surprise. "Relax. Baby Boy's alive." She held up a Emergency Blinking wrist.

"Surviving modules and lifeboats are currently cruising at high speeds in every which direction," the Regular said. "Some right into Uranus. Some won't make it. Some might not be picked up for years. The story is still developing, but that's the gist of it."

The theater was already self-repairing, Maudie saw, surveying the scene. In the pressure change a great slab of ice had broke off the ceiling and buried most of the stage. The remarkable glass had not shattered. The perfect image was cut by each of the objects that broke through. Maudie saw the rounded humanoid form of Mr. Egge arms thrust forward as if in flight, head topped by something like a bowler, filling up even now in the glass.

The original of that image had passed through onto to be met by the needle of its own death. Maudie could see enough to recognize the gelid body pinioned atop the Marvel Ball, pressed into the destructed hull of Tommies into a kind of kebab by the long pointed pole. Legs splayed, upside-down chamsuit flickering every possible comforting tone, Egge79 still leaked stuff of what had been his life. He had almost entered Miranda successfully; it was just the pole that had killed him. The torn head remained up top fixed to the point, she now saw.

Did this mean the play itself had caused the collision from which Egge had launched? It would be very difficult to ascribe agency into such spooky actions with any accuracy, Maudie presumed.

Egge had wanted to come. Eri's play interpreted by the likes of the Lyonesse and Pamela Lamprey was not the easy target Egge presumed. He should never have messed with the living arts. However temporary and ramshackle the *Pericles* weirld might have appeared from outside, inside the players were like gods.

"Maudie? Is that you?"

The voice frightened her. Even from afar it was too real. But she now saw Morrigan ambling around the ice, white uniform blackened by recent action. Coming face to face, the Regular looked Maudie over flushed and concerned, but her eyes were still lit with a humor that could find you out.

Maudie looked away. She no longer trusted her interest. Morrigan and others, she very much suspected, believed her to be someone she was not.

Morrigan tipped her cap. "You in one piece?"

"I am," said Maudie.

"Nice haircut." Morrigan held out a blanket. Maudie blushed fiercely, only now remembering she was entirely naked but for silver bikini bottoms. She accepted the blanket the Regular threw around her shoulders.

They were interrupted by the news that another body had been located under the debris. Cracked and broken under the stone; it was Eri.

Poor Eri. His play proved good enough to open itself to a wartime reinterpretation. And he did not demean himself by sacrifice. The death of Eri was not necessitated by the assassination of Egge79 by an Extraordinary Machine (who because of Asimov had to see to its own "death" as well). Bad luck did away with Eri. He had fled the stage in time only to be hit by other debris and eventually killed by a low grav fall.

Had Eri known all along what was coming? The effects of his power still lingered, she realized. Even now his weirld-real ghost flitted about the broken theater, promoting god-like change, keeping the shadows and silences in play, tuning reality towards an infinitely finer perfection. Maudie had pitied him, in the knowledge that must have come upon his consciousness that he could not control their essences upon the surface of the colored ball. Here he'd panicked. It was his own fault. She realized how open he'd remained to her own creativity within the weirld. His generosity had made her survival possible. Every step she'd made had been her own. The audience would have tasted that freedom. Maudie was still not sure what Marina had or hadn't become in the play's afterlife. A shining girl, a woman, something like and actual goddess retreating back into the Mysteries. She would never forget the great Artemision he'd built for his weirld. Despite his own intentions, those columns could not be cracked by the Godzilla wheel and all of its ropes and cranes.

As for the Wheel, Tommies had understood it was dying, she realized, when she had spoken with it in the Underworld. This is why it had chosen to tell her so many things.

Morrigan was having trouble with her report. "Somehow a body came through the Falls Theater Glass to be impaled on a Marvel Ball's pole in the final scene of an epic play. I'll write it up as an attempted paramilitary counter-rev assault?"

She helped Maudie across a steaming water fissure, and they stepped onto the Grand Verona Airvenue. All about it was evident Prospero's daughters were doing their best to survive.

They looked up. Maudie saw that the skies over Miranda were lit as with a million tiny, shimmering stars. It was hard to believe the grandly arching rainbow of diamond-brige particles gracing the sky spelled past disaster and future danger.

"It looks like the 23rd of July," Maudie said.

"It'll be a long clean-up. You might be stuck here a while," Morrigan was facing her now directly. That dead-pan smile. Maudie looked away.

"You know, Morrigan," Maudie started. "I think you think I'm someone I'm not…" She couldn't finish. It was, after all, too absurd.

The Miranda Regular touched the upside-down star on her breast. "I'm Sheriff round here, Maudie. I detect once in a while too. To tell you the truth I knew Marjorie's ideas about you were way wrong. I just never thought to tell her though."

"Why not?"

"When I started investigating you. Well, it's hard to explain. I knew right you couldn't be anything else but what you were."

Maudie felt many things. Relief most of all.

"I have to say," Morrigan said. "I do think she's still convinced."

"Who?"

"Marjorie Beerbottom," said Morrigan, improbably. They both laughed.

And then Maudeleine knew what she could do here, off Gargantuan Uranus. Eri's position would need to be filled. This theater would need a thorough makeover. The bookstore was now unmanaged as well, she realized with mounting excitement. She'd struggled to bring her books through thick and thin. Now they would crown the already stunning collection.

"I have to help get some wounded to the Infirmary," Morrigan said. "I have to see to a few other things—But if you'd like to eat later—do you like Indian?"

Maudie bit her lip, suddenly abashed. It was after all a night of tragedy for many.

"I love Indian, Morrigan," she said. To some extent her own imagination in that play had brought this sudden new world that she felt opening. Theater! What a transformative, new idea it suddenly seemed within her. How meaningful that this realization had been gifted to now, by a machine, so late in this second life.

Maudie took herself an emergency helmet. She located a mop. "Come find me when you're ready," she told her friend. "I'll be here, cleaning up."

LINE 4

Earthside

>It's not a day goes by that one of you people doesn't ask me when I'm going to write about Earth. I was born there, in New Jersey, in fact, and I won't say when. I've never had much interest in going back. Yet this slog purports ambitions to one day provide you with a report of every spot Spacers may set foot upon in our Great System, so today I'll tell you about the one time I touched down since leaving

>The chance came one day in High Wichita. That brave floating town was still fully functional, still populated by disreputable types with the foolhardy courage that made 1-Gen space possible. There were individuals involved and practices attempted that I will not describe. Those still at large today don't take kindly to snitches. But I believe it's OK to speak of the dead. I remember the owner of Kelly's Irish Bar in High Wichita, AWAW. In those days when beer wouldn't work in space, he would make regular visits downtown, and by hell or highwater bring as many barrels of the stuff back as possible. "Come along with me," said the Unnamed to me one Earthshine. "Make an Earthside run." He handed me a bong. "Earth is Space. Can't know Space without it."

>Four hours later I entombed myself in a stolen plutonium delivery module (whose shielding apparently guaranteed my safety) and did

not simply fall like Gordon Cooper into the sea. In my case the sea was frozen

>HW rockets bolted to the shell fired me into slow fall. I whirled more than 3 times around Earth; finally at a terminal velocity of roughly 300 km/hr I experienced the roughest landing I intend ever to experience in my extended lifetime. We carved molten furrows at least 20 km across an already well-furrowed Antarctic icecap. When I hit the continent, my bullet's skin had cooled to solidity, and I could bounce and roll to eventual stasis. Not that it warmed my heart. Vacuumpacked inside that coffin-like velocipod, I felt it all—believed myself dead most of the way

>In those days Antarctica's Sentinel Range was something like a spacer's colony. Occupying an isolated, easily capped ridge and valley system rich with water ice, caves and igneous variation, the community was able to re-position, extend and maintain trade under various conditions of threat. A cadre of troops from Asia kept strict control of the population, profiting on illicit exchange between visiting parties outside the eye of the Unnamed Concerns—maintaining a profitable, if dangerous, line to Space

>Earthmen were a cautious, self-absorbed lot, with little interest in issues outside their immediate ken. No one came to help us out for instance though we came to stasis in plain sight. As to those generations of the Pale Blue Dot my namesake Carl discussed, those founders of religions, of ideologies and economic doctrines, those hunters, foragers, heroes, cowards, creators, destroyers of civilizations, kings, peasants, young couples in love, mothers and fathers, hopeful children—not a one was to be found. A servile and suspicious community greeted me. I was threatened twice when attempting to trade pure deuterium for temporary quarters

>*I waited some time for my friend to find his beer. From a peak-top bedsphere, my porthole looked out on to a broad view of the southern hemisphere of the largest of the System's four dwarf planets. It was indeed a brave expanse of ice that met the gaze. White, burned, rugged and encrusted, with stratus skies of grey, Earth looked its 4.5 billion years. As to the blue wonders of that imperfect supposedly un-matched in all the observed, they were entirely unrepresented in all that white and grey, with great slashes of plundering black crisscrossing across it.*

>*Water looks good from a distance. I always stay Earthview when at all possible, tapsters, always. But on ball, truth is H2O only makes up .0$_2$ of that dry planet. It's hot and since the atmosphere is safe one might as well go about in the nude, at least in private. With such thoughts on my mind I understood two things simultaneously.*

>*1. I was not in my own bedsphere*

>*2. Earthmen are extreme homophobes*

>*Though I tip the moon-cap to Genghis Khan and the rest, it was with neither courage nor resolve that I rode a beer-keg via balloon up to Atmosphere's End with the owner of Kelly's Irish Bar in High Wichita, since deceased. That madman, sometimes visible behind me, sometimes below, lost his poise on the way home. We rafted space debris for seven days until a junker's field hauled us and the other kegs to a robot disposal factor, beginning a circuitous, beer-fueled passage back to High Wichita I would prefer not to describe*

>SMYTH'S MYTHS: 19–10–2142–5. *EARTHSIDE, OR WHY I DON'T GO*

IV i

Gina Tsiolnovsky, the only living bio-agent within kilometers in every direction, sat suited, lock-harnessed into the cargo bay of the robot *Ship-of-Souls*. She had given over a lot to bring Clodius Morandi on this last journey. She'd worked some debts and foresworn herself to others she hoped never to have to pay.

They all thought she was ridiculous. Always going to extremes for the sake of men. Was she? She would make sure that Clodius would go into the seas off Auckland. They could all think what they liked.

Ship-of-Souls, the primitive, rocket/sun-sail hybrid that delivered bodies back Earthside, hung a high orbit, now crossing North America. These layers had been chiefly cleared of debris and weaponry above the very precarious orbits of the Unnamed Concerns, the invisible consortium that kept conflicts on Earth from disrupting the satellite nets upon which all surviving governments and highly populated areas depended on for their power.

The coffins were already lined up for the dropping. Most were designed to ignite falling. Clodius, the last, was inside a sarcophagus. She knew for a fact he didn't believe in immolation. Clodius was set separate, for special delivery into the actual Pacific Ocean.

Gina had given up her flat in Parson's City to get this chance, and the ride back. Not that it seemed to matter anymore. People were clearing out everywhere.

Now out over the Atlantic, the bay doors soon opened for the first drips. Safe-suited for exposure, Gina looked out on the Ocean now dominating the spreading globe, enswirled with weather. Burning wounds streamed all about, but a grand vista of sea nevertheless spread below her, space junk and still surviving orbital settlements catching sun between.

Clodius liked to call the watery Earth Oa still to this day, in support of Will Darling and what remained of their archaic and recently remote friendship. As a fan of A. E. Winnegutt herself, Gina T. liked calling Earth seas Oa too. Gina never thought of Will Darling when she thought of Oa. Will had received her pong. His viking ship avatar showed the flags. But he hadn't thought to answer. Did Clodius' passing penetrate him, at all, she wondered, so far out there in the System? Fet said apparently not. Apparently Will exploited Fet's good will to trick him into an errand of quasi-legal nature in regards to the Winnegutt archive. Fet had compacted something, as requested. But the great bonus Will had promised was in fact a negative for Fet, components of the folder's data-protective lining being toxic and irredeemable. Fet would have two days janitorial due!

She wondered how long Fet would survive without Templeton. The son of a naval engineer, recent graduate from a Luna City academy (with time spent Earthisde) Lolas Fet had come to Parson's Crater immersed in theory and notions of "a public planetscape." Now he was a beaten-down handy-man who had only survived thus far because of Clodius' good will. Putting all your hopes in one person was risky. For folks like Fet things started deteriorating after the elevator fell.

Templeton, as well, was doomed. The New Elite that remained no longer cared to clutter their quarters with objects of questionable provenance. Templeton went too far down the road to decadence. Characters like Clodius' apparent friend Mr. Egge, who had already come sniffing, looking to take the entire Templeton O & O. Collection off Sten's hands, were the result. Egge smelled fishy. Nevertheless, with Sten still deaf-mute by choice, Gina immediately sold Egge the Major Archives for five year water rights for Fet and herself and the Templeton Cave. Mr. Egge would be disappointed. Clodius named everything as a satire of itself. The so-called Templeton Major Archives was a store-room of unwanted unsolicited art-works and manuscripts sent by fans and strangers, of all shapes size and function, uncatalogued, unexplained. Mr. Egge didn't look twice at Gina T. It was useful being constantly over-looked. Egge went on his way pleased with his success, none the wiser. Clodius' personal archives remained where only she and Will Darling knew they were.

And Templeton, if it ever was really more than what she'd called it then, and Clodius himself, whose dark eyes were now clearly enough closed, if his life had been worth anything, and if Will Darling hoped to do something real in AEW's name, and if Sten ever chose to speak again (Joy Chin would do better elsewhere the others for obvious resons)—they could all be grateful she had been there on point when Egge had come. Gina T. deserved a fucking gift, something to call her own. So she would take a ride down, to keep him a little longer, to be with Clodius now.

Gina got the news first. Clode's partner in narcotics informed her before the authorities. She moved fast, telling no one. She didn't want Fet and Sten to push their way forward. She went to Luna City and ID'd the body, alone. He was on ice in the GA sta-tion. He'd been frozen for two days. No coroner's report, no formal registration of the event whatsoever. Addicts were liabilities. Local security representatives signed him away without looking at the signature. Gina's contacts came in handy. She had him wrapped and packed off the Moon the next day, before she told Fet or anybody it had happened.

Her Clodius at last, they would say. Nobody said, actually. People would be shocked. They used to think Gina T. had taken Clodius away from the Path. But now they saw it wasn't Gina and her Luna City connections that had killed Clodius Morandi after all. The old isolato scene had done him in.

Her being here now was a result of a handful of days last year, when it had seemed she finally had connected with him. Gina had loved the mixed-up fellow more than she had thought possible. The poor skinny, wide-eyed boy, simultaneously boney and soft. He choked to death so his throat was swollen and bruised. He still wore his secret locket.

He was still wrapped there naked in that old special sleeping-sack, the one they'd shared together in her perch those times he'd stayed over alone. She knew he loved that old sack. It warmed him in just the right way, he always said. He always slept inside it with a smile.

Gina T. had taken Clodius' helmet. She knew the password. With his helmet screen, she could access his files. She saw first what Clodius had last been reading. It showed a black and white poster, old-school, printed on paper, rendered unpackable with views. "Sten Winters and Claudius Morandi of Templeton O & O Interview Martina Epstein *by Will Darling*." That interview and its postered publication, in fact, Gina had been told, constituted Will Darling's last non-Winnegutt involvement with Templeton O & O. Though she had designed the poster, Gina's name wasn't even on it. Her name was never included in archival productions. It wasn't a recording of her recent performance she had sent him that Clodius had been looking before he died.

Gina T. had come to Space from New Dystopia a year before it fell, only weeks before the elevator came down; she represented that new class of cultural producers employing what the heroes of Templeton considered hopelessly corrupt traditions. She loved Templeton, early Templeton and what it represented. Clodius already realized the just past was Space's best and real moment; and that what we were doing was a weaker repetition. He believed in those first productions of Space, as something to be saved and preserved. But by the time Gina found the real Clodius, the old just past had deepened and fallen away. The tenderest beauties of First Space weren't much to count on if you had to chase them in a squat shooting home-made hyper-opiates.

In fact Gina T. was not at all the reformed "blank-clerk" others took her for. Clodius knew that. After her first year's discovering the facts of Space, Gina took Tsiolnovsky as her Spacer surname and worked as an aide to a freelance community organizer and musician. When kredit allowed, she lit out, with only her suit on her back, training in rockets in Parson's Crater and splogging about current events. It was here where she became intimately involved with the new cultural scene now blooming in that "San Francisco of the Moon." A real who's who of Templeton O & O could be found in that library. Sten Winters in acquisitions. Joy Chin bought books and hung sheets. Clodius was supposed to oversee 2d motion pictures but he very rarely showed up. Will Darling printed out and hung the latest sheets. She never met Clodius then, though she'd heard of him certainly.

Oddly enough it was Will Darling who brought her to the library. One fine day Gina switched values while raising her hand during a symposium about the current scene in Space Publishing and its impact on Earth at a talk-in. She ended up arguing something very similar to what Zitzko had said on Mars, though she was unaware of this then. The gist was that Spacers should refuse to publish digitally, thereby cutting off Earth physically from the future it was so desperate on exploiting.

Will Darling told her there was some analog publishing afoot at Templeton O+O and if she knew anything at all they might be able to use her help there.

To Will's astonishment, Clodius found her attractive. What was between them was impossible to control. They soon became lovers and of course, because of the generosity that was part of Clodius when he opened, she became part of things at Templeton. Clodius's promiscuity put an early damper on their relationship. Her love was stronger than everything but his ambition, and it was a constant struggle to be there at the center of things with him.

Why did she let the troubles encroach on the dear memory of that sweet boy. She thought of times he came to her as his real self, without the burdens of jealousy, ambition and greed. When his eyes were lit with generosity, and care. He asked penetrating questions about her work. He braised her braised chickens fresh from Franny's Fair. Poor skinny Clodius, his secret locket didn't bring him luck in the end.

A spun-silver miniature, black with time, from back perhaps as far as the 19th century, the little clasp opened to a crystal windowed oval. Here, framed in plain hand-worked gold, there twirled a lock of red-blonde hair.

Gina had planned to keep it for herself. She believed it was her right. But when she saw that bruised neck she knew she couldn't keep that gift. Even now, in that red-sashed coffin, it hung about his cold breast. Poor Clodius the Dead, cold and no more to crave. He deserved it.

Poor Will, Gina thought. Clodius told her Will had a locket just like it. Poor old Fet as well. She sensed anew what it would mean for all of them that he was gone. The world doesn't give a shit for people like us; without the Clodii, though we basically hate them and make their life hell while they're here, we're lost. Poor Clode, who already had his share of lines in his boyish face before he died. That surprisingly noble brow looked wise in rest.

Gina fell asleep dreaming of Parson's Crater's orangestones and corpse on the table. When she awoke, all the coffins in the hold were gone. Only Clodius remained. Her com was blinking.

"What's going on?"

They were high above an ocean.

>*Debris sited one hour ago, ma'am*, the AI explained. *Must abandon flight plan. Last chance to dispatched cargo.*

"Everything's falling apart," she said, over that enormous water, with water in her eyes. But it was Oa good enough. "Let him go."

Epilogue

(214.7 Years Later)

The egg-shaped crystal slid perfectly coin-like into the slot. Abruptly, it disappeared. There was no sound of its fall, no directed progression, no ring of coin on coin. The Doll's aural apparatus functioned well enough to hear the chatter of individual insects still surviving on the surface of Europe. He could hear the atmosphere and upon his particular tendrils, the wind—the wind was almost worth it all. The Doll missed nothing senses could tell him. He detected no evidence of the coin's continued existence.

Was this the miracle? Nothing was something, after all. Why not cut everything off right there? Slip into an imaginary world of import to machines but disconnected from the human mind tree? Perhaps ASTA was now out of time altogether. Since waking from more than two centuries' sleep, the Doll had had two long weeks to ponder the TOMMIES info-packets. The various outrages the machine discussed, the glimpses it recorded of a time he remembered as if it were yesterday (including video of Deary on the Surface of Oa's Bubble) as well as its stark and self-flattering plea to the principle of narrative closure had not at first convinced the Doll to do its bidding. The Wheel itself had "died" off Uranus.

Despite a general hostility to the Wheel, The Doll was a ponderer. TOMMIES had left much to ponder. The Doll pondered long and well on all the information loaded into his implants. Himself, he sought no closure; the end was long gone. There was someone else in his world, however. The one, after all, who had chosen the Doll in the face of paradox. TOMMIES flattered the Doll as "that creature best able to accomplish the ostensibly impossible."

Deary had been given rights over her own ending; it was she herself who had swum out ahead of her guard. But it was the Doll's responsibility to protect the Bubble after its invisibility was compromised. TOMMIES had assured him that the information break-out would likely be contained. Earth-civ was now apparently defunct, as it had predicted. Whatever was going on out past the Moon, the Doll was very sure he wouldn't understand it.

No doubt by intention TOMMIES had selected the coordinates of arrival so as to give the Doll these hard weeks of decision. He began the hunt for Morandi's coffin not for the sake of TOMMIES and its dreams, but because the idea of this founder of Templeton O & O, his mysterious history with the murdered Will Darling, a man the Doll knew almost nothing about that was not interesting, seemed itself a violation of probability. He wanted to see the man himself, as if it were something real of what had otherwise passed out of the world. As to the quasi-miraculous nature of the entity in a locket on the dead man's chest, the Doll had no interest. With even poetry dead and gone for him, Oa's Guard would not imagine transcendence.

From the Doll would fall no tears for Cove, for Miranda, *The Good Fortune*, for Mr. Egge or Wilhelm Darling, for Nina Flower and crew. No tears for himself when he arrived in Pilot's pod and the Robot needled him, no tears for that long sleep, the 541 million leagues across the seas. No tears for the awakening, for the *smash* of re-entry

>*Where am I?*

Exactly where and when exactly, he learned later, the Machine would place him, with perverse, godlike precision. Before the fall into Earth atmosphere, six days of orbit melt splashed droplets on the hard mask like face. They evaporated in the sudden flame-ripping atmosphere, and the replacements did not show. As the encapsulated husk of the ancient gravity prow plowed deep into the hard Atlantic greys, as it melted away and the Doll plunged into the pure mystery of First Oa, and took water, even then his eyes were dry.

To his surprise a living Atlantic greeted him. At surface, the fat silver sun still shed free energy, food, and warmth to countless surviving creatures of slime. The Doll stayed topside, exploiting the chlorophyll in his blood to take energy directly from the sun. Despite the acidity, the plastics, the jellies, algaes, the whole of old Oa clearly contained within it more of the unknown than could be possibly speculated upon. There were areas deep enough to be rich with mighty old Earth evolution. Stratified vastnesses spoke of eons of maintained unconcern. It was the planetary sublime the Doll detected, that declared its power in terms of death. Even as he saw schools of something like sardines, the Doll refrained from eating.

On his way North the Doll was hit by a squad of male squid attempting to kill/ mate/ anything at all. They were easily warded off, but the Doll had been forced to kill four more before he found that slow-dissolving lonely human coffin and a human skeleton less than a nautical mile from where TOMMIES predicted it would be. The box had deteriorated purposefully. Fish had plucked the flesh away and left the body so it sat among golden weeds in what appeared relative splendor, perched on the rotting box, rather like a king on a throne. Was this the weedy neckbone and ribcage of Clodius Morandi himself, once-upon-a-moment maestro of 21st Century kulturnautics? Was this the brow that re-launched the career of A. E. Winnegutt and Wilhelm Darling? It brought the Doll a stab of something like meaning to confirm it really was. His tendrils found an intact clasp-locket attached to a chain in the sediment underneath this hips, even as The Doll was gazing into those vacant sockets.

TOMMIES was correct. No other being but the Doll could have served to end this tale. The Doll imagined Doug making the attempt. The Doll's implants, an oddity in Cove, had made much of this possible. After he signalled he'd found the locket, and that indeed a disk of crystal was contained within it, they now delivered his last instructions.

>*Destination*: Drachenfels

In his days of poetry, classic Romanticism had always left the Doll cold. He cared nothing for Opera and other primitive music forms. But the Doll found his way past poisoned Rotterdam, and joined the Rhein—somehow, still a living river with real beavers. The Doll swam eye to eye with a salmon for much of that long and disturbing journey. Invasive plantlife had adapted to fresh water better than the polluted saline oceans, and they helped clean and filter the mini ecosystem. Eel, snakes and various adapted breeds of travelers passed over and through the wreckage of human civilization. As to humans themselves, there was no certain sign of their current survival. Radiation was uniformly high.

At the appropriate position along the fat swelling river, a single old crag poked lumpily into the winter sky. When the Doll emerged below it, and expelled water to stand finally on Terra's surface, he realized he was somehow very much still a man. The river had cleaned his tendrils of oil and radioactive particles. He shed all his water and the hard gravity of Earth felt true. He had even yearned to feel that strain that held all the waters down. Doug would have snapped like a sardine.

Right away he saw the map and located FAFNIRS HÖHLE just beneath the Castle at the summit. Fafnir's Cave. The cartilaginous Doll made his awkward way up the hill supported more by virtue of his long arm-tentacles than his stubby little legs. The ruined structures of the old public architecture pricked his interest, but as these were artifacts of a world that had always done all it could possibly do to banish the Doll and his ilk from its enjoyment, he banished it from his mind.

>*Well done, Doll! We've arrived*

To his surprise, TOMMIES' coordinates demarked not a cave in the hill, but a little rest area, with only an old mechanical contraption in sight.

The sky was uniformly overcast. The Doll took a view over the still swelling Rhine. Other islets and turns sent Gothic spikes of stone up into the sky. Corvids rode the air. Insects and arachnids were thriving on Western Central Europe, 2359, the Doll noted. Fragile colorless flowers sought the sun even in Winter. He thought of Lord Byron, who may well have stood on this very piece of Terra. Byron had struck him, last he'd looked, as squid-like. Not via the old metaphors of Squid and Octopi and Kraken, but as the real cold, swift-thinking body-brain *per se* surviving in the stream. He thought of rigorous Goethe and sentimental Schiller, of the happy English mis-readings. He thought of wayward Shelley, whose *Ozymandias* sketched the scale of real time. The Doll's had been a romantic self, he now understood. Poetry in general had stood for nature, for the real. Here on this barbarian slab Romanticism stood only for miscellaneous incompletions sketched into the dome that had finally entirely sealed man from his world. Yet here lay TOMMIES interests.

>*Approach Fafnir's Cave*

What Cave? The Doll knew only slightly of Fafnir the dreadful Dragon from his reading. He'd imagined a deep interior and heaps of gold.

>*Insert coin before sunset*

The contraption was the Cave?

The Doll approached it and found a large oblong box, smaller part plexiglass, revealing a diorama interior, and larger part presumably containing a spent engine. *Fafnir's Cave*, local-themed mechanical entertainment for tourists from far back before the Times of Change. For reasons the Doll didn't hope to fathom, it really did still exist: an ancient puppet-show, a mechanical theater sagging on time-broken legs.

The ancient ruins of the diorama were still visible through the transparent face. Milky spider dens thickened the jointed corners, but the old scenery was largely intact. The scale model depicted a patch of earth before a forbidding cliff. A cave entrance yawned, leading to the concealed portion of the box. Out from this darkness curled the golden-colored tracks of a model-train set. The little tracks were not rusted.

The Doll carefully retrieved and opened the locket he carried with him. The locked popped easily open as he squeezed the spun silver flower. He put the oval crystal up against the coin slot, where it flashed in the reddening sun.

It fit snug in the slot. He pressed, let it fall.

But it didn't fall.

Presently however a sudden racket issued loudly from another part of the box. An old bulb the Doll hadn't seen flickered on to illuminate the diorama's interior. He slipped back. Energy? From where? The entire theater was now shaking on its broken haunches, he saw. A scale modeled train-car emerged from the cave hole, carrying on its back an oddly constructed figure. Something like thunder and lightning came over an old electric speaker as it announced: >*the Dragon Fafnir*

What was to the scale of the diorama an black and deformed poppet, was to that faultily-like stage and great and surprising being. Over its stiff and protruding snout, stuck with human teeth, the Doll met hard big eyes as implacable as his own. There, just as he looked, they lit up red and incandescent. Very dramatic under that permagrey sky.

This was indeed extraordinary mechanics. The Doll hadn't realized TOMMIES had been speaking literally when he discussed how to put away the quarry for good in "in a visible story, a still unfolding narrative not quite of its own making." As to what to the fate of the potential Singularity after its years underwater in a coffin, its coming to life as a defunct puppet-dragon was not quite what the Doll had in mind.

Yet he had to admit, those lit red eyes gave the otherwise stiff hump of wood and cloth the vivid appearance of life. In the dragon's construction, expense had been spared. Fierce spirited, once green-skinned, about the size of a boot, it was hardly as handsome as the Doll on land. It seemed more dragon-like. The Doll now noted that large gothic ears and small gothic wings were cut from the exact same spiked mold. Unfortunately instead of snarling, the face grinned foolishly.

Yet the long jaw flipped open, and no longer astonishing the Doll, the ancient speaker crackling on the side of the box began to emit understandable words.

>That you've literally cleaved and dusted the place is moot the dragon said.

An ancient loudspeaker on the side of the box has voiced a nonsensical thought. Really, what did the Doll care? The sick work of TOMMIES was done.

"*Good morning, Gargantuan*," the box barked out. "*I need no longer be a dog. I am a dragon. You are too large to behold, but I see you nonetheless. I address you, Gargantuan. How is it that you can hear me? Is that your question? Why it's because you've paid, Gargantuan. You've paid. Now you alone are now graced to hear my story as it has never yet been told.*"

"You do not know how dearly I have paid," the Doll signed angrily, thinking for that moment, decisively, piercingly, of she of whom memory he dared not claim and of the beast Egge who killed her. The past twisted like a knife through nerve-cords of his mind, even as the Oan Guard functioned as the Founders had not intended, the Finner having in this case failed the First Fish. He would swim with it all his days.

Here the little dragon here actually leaned forward, as if to bow. The light extinguished; the box went dark.

Flopping around behind the ancient portable cave, he easily probed up through the rusted backside into the guts of the Dragon's lair. Spider-feet tickled his tendrils, reminding him of minnows of home. But no hoard remained. No coin, no disk of crystal.

It was only then that he noticed the people that had emerged from the landscape, now gathering around the mechanical theater. There were near a dozen humanoids, by the looks of it. A number were small, with bodies like children. Others were armed. Through some helmets he saw green skin. A leader, a small female in an orange bodysuit, held the party for a moment back. She had seen the Doll and stood forward.

The Doll revealed himself, emerging into the open and boldly approaching. He immediately recognized her face as the older version of the one that had gazed at him kindly when he'd been imprisoned, and had tried to block his line of sight. She seemed to recognize him as well, but was not astonished to see him. Once again the Doll, bristled at the empathy those brown eyes seemed to bear as if in tribute to his suffering. Her face had taken age with deep lines of kindness and wisdom.

"Well hello again," said an audible voice. "Have you recognized me? My name's Bridget Geertz. I saw you on the *Good Fortune* many many years ago. I've come here, hoping you'd really be here. I have something for you," she wrinkled her impossible-to-hate countenance with a grin. "I've been gathering information about what happened back there all those years ago. Trying to tell the story. Anyway, I've held on to a number of artifacts from those days. Including this," She held out an omniback book.

The Doll, who stood up to her waist, took it in his flipper. He saw the pages carefully folded at the corners to mark key passages.

How could she possibly have this?

As-squid he did not show or in any way divulge the enormity of his loss. He held the book up to the sun. The hologram worked in that broad generous light; it looked almost exactly The Doll was looking beyond, backwards, behind Bridget Geertz, out into the darkness. What darkness? Had he been holding it all along? The Doll shook his head, noted something shifting, beyond the edges of his perception. He shook his head, trying to shake away what was coming. Had the bubbling floor flashed a sudden silver?

He was submerged. Why had the grotto been filled with crystal shafted waters? Why was he lunging into cool? Could it be? The Doll tried but he could not shake away these terrible fantasies.

"Doll!" Deary laughed, poking through the liquid floor, shaking her silvery hair. "Hey. You're crying." He looped around her, away.

"Doll!" Deary signed, upside down, bubbling. "Stop! What's wrong with you?" Water. "No," he signed. "It's not me." The Doll couldn't see clearly through his eyes. I cannot cry. It must be raining, he thought, seeing the Drachenfels return, as with horror he allowed that stab of forgotten happiness to float away.

They were here to celebrate the TOMMIES victory. The AI had hunted, tricked out, caught, and fixed its quarry in just this way, by its own intention, though it had been dead and gone for two hundred years. The Imp would be kept imprisoned by rhyme, irony, and all the devices literature could dump into its self-cavity. Surely it was recreating possibilities all about already, in some fashion. Not at all a god, the singularity was super-marginalized by this functioning out-of-date sideshow for now and evermore. But it would doubtless hold forth. TOMMIES may not have reckoned on the authority that thing had claimed.

"Do you understand why this had to happen?"

It was Geertz.

"No interest," the Doll signed, now finally preferring fiction.

Even now, dancing backwards in time, the Dragon's red eyes glared at the Doll from a future so unlikely it might not be true.

"*Come not between the dragon and his wrath!*" The dragon raged, as if jealous of the Doll's attention still fixed to him.

"You still need me?" the Doll signed.

"Many years ago a man entered my cavern, Gargantuan. You will never see my cavern, but take it from me, it is not what it once was. It's a shit-hole today. I don't swear. But long ago it was lovely. You could see the whole colony from the mouth on a clear day. Inside fire always bloomed in the den-pit, still raw from a Volcano's nerve. In those days all the nooks and crannies sparkled with anomalous objets and beds of gold. And suffice it to say it was emphatically mine, this cave. I repeat, emphatically mine, for all was right with the world.

"But then it would have to chance stupidity entered the world. A man entered the cave! The first creature ever so destitute of sensation, consciousness, thought or feeling, so emotionally or morally dull or insensible, so apathetic, indifferent or so stunted near to total insensibility as to enter a Dragon's cave in plain sight.

"What did I do? Did I make sausage and cheez from his husk? Did I roast all the hair from his body? Did I melt his genitals to butter and boil his blood? Did I slice him so completely that there was not left a single scar? No, Gargantuan, I did not. You see, there was no point in even bothering. Such a drone! The he proclaimed I was afraid. I am a dragon! But he said it and I was so turned off by this absurdity, this nugget of nothing near wise, this explicit mistake and lie, that I made certain to let him live. To do anything else would be to show I feared him. I did not! I resolutely did not! And then what did he do but make a further fool of himself by spreading the tale abroad that he had faced a Dragon down. Good, I thought. Let it educate its race with the fact of its own idiocy. I myself even told him to tell the tale, Gargantuan. I will not lie as to first causes in all this. That is what grates.

"He was believed! It was of course his own idiotic descendents who believed him. A mule myself by reason, I had not counted on the furious fucking of men. Perhaps predictably, these descendants lied further. I find out today they now claimed he slayed me! Though I was clearly alive! I exist! I have very obviously not been slain! In the meantime, I note, the cave is stripped down, compacted, gelded, folded into the absurdity you see before you now, by those ever replicating, ever increasingly ignorant *devils who call themselves Sickfriek's children. It has became, in fact, this apparatus you see me in now, and not a proper cave at al.*

"*Yet it is emphatically mine, Gargantuan. No stranger's hole! I am no mechanical puppet! I here affirm that Sickfreak slayed me? You can see for yourself I do not. I was not slain, Gargantuan. I speak. These words are mine. Telephonically mine. I was slain? Do you see? How could this be? Do you begin to understand? If Sickfreak has slain the Dragon, you must very naturally ask, why is the Dragon here speaking to you now? Furthermore, you may well wonder, why has the hero not yet emerged to challenge his claim?*

"*Oh these vermin never change. They write poems about the whole affair. The so-called Bards scribble daily. But they never suffer to tell the true fate of the dragon. Last seen with the spear Immunsil in his throat? Have you ever seen a reptile killed by a single thrust through its throat? No one has cared to sing my duppy conqueror's tale, Gargantuan. Might I be out of my Cave one of these days? Why do you smile?*"

Like the Dragon, the Doll was built to grin.

"*I live.*" the Dragon said. "*Though they claim my blood was drunk and my flesh was picked apart. Though they inhaled my cirgu through long pipes, here I stand to present my current self-evidence as the triumph it is.*"

The Doll heard then the sound of coin hitting bare wood, and beginning a long and hollow-sounding roll. Taking it as his hint, in no way inclined to follow more of this story, nor to tell his own to the Historian, he shoved through those green-skinned humanoids now approaching the Cave. He left the Oracle and its weird priesthood. He fast-tracked down the old crag. Keeping exactly what remained with him to keep, the book, he slipped back into the river.

The Doll took sweet water, wedged torso. Jetting upstream, he sought a peaceful enough cave. He looked forward only to reading.

The End

ABOUT THE AUTHOR

Mark von Schlegell's stories and essays appear regularly in underground newspapers, zines, art books, and periodicals the world over. *Venusia*, his first novel, was honor-listed for the 2007 James Tiptree, Jr. Award in science fiction.